*A Death
at the
Rose Paperworks*

A Death at the Rose Paperworks

A Libby Seale Mystery

M. J. ZELLNIK

MIDNIGHT INK
WOODBURY, MINNESOTA

First Edition
First Printing, 2006

Book design by Donna Burch
Cover design and illustration by Ellen Dahl
Editing by Connie Hill

Midnight Ink, an imprint of Llewellyn Publications

Library of Congress Cataloging-in-Publication Data (Pending)
ISBN 13: 978-0-7387-0897-3
ISBN 10: 0-7387-0897-6

Midnight Ink
Llewellyn Publications
2143 Wooddale Drive, Dept. 0-7387-0897-6
Woodbury, MN 55125-2989, U.S.A.
www.midnightinkbooks.com

Printed in the United States of America

For LLZ

PROLOGUE

Portland, Oregon. March, 1894.

THE SUN HAD BEEN up less than two hours, and already Andrew Matson knew it was going to be a terrible day. One of the two revolving boilers was coughing, and it looked like he'd have to take the damn thing out of commission for at least thirty-six hours. Or maybe longer. It took that long just for it to cool down enough to get inside and see what the problem was, and they were understaffed again. It was this new staff, he thought with a grimace. You just couldn't count on them to show up on a regular basis. Six of 'em were out today, and he didn't even know which six, since one looked just like the next to his eyes. Even after two months supervising his Chinese workforce, they all looked the same to him.

Striding across the cement floor of the Rose Paperworks, Matson gazed out over the sea of glossy black hair and once more cursed his boss's decision to replace real Americans with this cheap-as-dirt foreign labor. He was glad to see that at least the main boiler had sputtered to life. As he passed, he watched two men toss the first rags of the day into its steaming confines. He was on his way to deal with the third and, by far, the most serious problem of the morning. Something was wrong with the hollander, the heart of the mill. A giant steel cylinder lined with rotating knife blades, the hollander could turn stripped rags into a thick paste suitable for boiling in less than three minutes. Usually it whirred and hummed all day, providing a background drone to everything else that happened in the mill, but this morning, just after the whistle marking the start of the workday had sounded, it had rasped a few times and stopped with a grinding metallic groan. Matson thought there was probably a dead bird inside, or maybe it was a rat (hardly a novelty in a paper mill) gumming up the works. Wouldn't be the first time. But today he didn't need this. By the time the remains of the poor creature were fished out and the machine was all cleaned, it'd be lunchtime. One dead bird meant missed quotas, and Mr. Rose would have his hide. He was hoping against hope the problem was electrical.

He reached the foot of the staircase leading up to the catwalks. In front of him a couple dozen Chinese girls were bent over their laps, ripping buttons, hooks, and whalebone stays from the scraps of material before throwing them into bins sorted by color. Pure white fabric was the easiest to process, but it was the most difficult to obtain, so normally the mill made do with any fabric of a light shade, no matter how yellowed or stained, and added an extra bleaching step before rolling the resulting rag pulp into sheets of paper.

The girls were chattering in that godforsaken unintelligible tongue of theirs. Who knew what in the hell they were saying, thought Matson with annoyance. "Enough chitchat! Back to work!" he yelled to no one in particular, and despite the language barrier, his order was clear enough. The babble subsided as he ascended the stairs to the network of catwalks that connected the various sections of the factory. The catwalks allowed the foreman and management to supervise what went on below, and to move easily from one end of the vast space to the other without having to skirt the massive vats and presses.

The staircase Matson had climbed was the one nearest to the hollander, so as soon as he reached the top he could see down into its red-slicked interior. Two things entered his consciousness at almost the same moment. The first was that there was far too much blood for this to have been a bird or a rat, and the second was that, on the far side of the great knife-lined cauldron, a section of the catwalk that led to the executive offices had collapsed and partially sunk into the hollander itself. A horrible possibility entered his mind—who else ever used that section of catwalk?—just as he noticed what could only be the remains of a human leg, the foot still encased in a chewed-up leather boot. All thought of missed quotas fled his mind as, almost silently, Andrew Matson fainted.

ONE

LIBBY SEALE HAD BEEN thinking about husbands. Two husbands in particular—the husband she wanted but couldn't marry, and the husband she already had but wished she could lose. So perhaps it was inevitable that her first thought, upon hearing about Hiram Rose's untimely death, was how lucky his wife was now to be a widow. One look, however, at the tears tracking down Adele Rose's plump cheeks, made Libby realize that this particular wife did not share her view. She quickly arranged her own features into something resembling more conventional sympathy, and hoped none of the others in the room had noticed her initial look of . . . well, one could only call it envy.

For three weeks now, Libby had been trying in vain to think of some way she could be rid of the man she was forced to call husband. Her marriage to Harold Greenblatt had been an arranged one. He was a business associate of her father's, back in New York City. In the brief time they had lived together as man and wife he had alternately ignored her and abused her. Their marriage, although it was a travesty to call it that, had culminated in one particularly violent episode that had left her with her arm in a sling. The next day she had run away, taking the train from New York's Penn Station to the farthest destination she could find . . . Portland, Oregon.

It was here in Oregon that she had met Peter Eberle, a young reporter for the *Portland Gazette*, and had fallen in love with him. For all the months they had known each other, she had hidden from him the existence of Mr. Greenblatt, who was still waiting for her back in New York. Somehow she had imagined that if she didn't speak of him, he would somehow go away. Ironically, her silence had led to Peter's going away instead.

Just over three weeks before, Peter had asked her to marry him. Needless to say she had been forced to turn him down. And, at that moment when his heart was at its most vulnerable, she had been forced to tell him why: she was a married woman, she had run away from her legal husband and family, and even that she had changed her name so no one in Portland would know she was married. Peter had claimed to understand, to forgive her the deception, but he had clearly been hurt. Libby hadn't clapped eyes on him or spoken even a syllable to him since that awkward day. She missed him dreadfully, and suspected he missed her too, but she hadn't had the nerve to call on him at the offices of the Portland *Gazette*, and he had made no attempt to see her. She feared Peter was lost to her forever—as lost to her as Hiram Rose was to Adele Rose, the crying woman sitting in front of her as she brought herself back to the present with difficulty.

Having just arrived at the Rose home moments before, Libby was still wearing her hat and coat. No sooner had she entered the house when she heard the shocking news about a tragic accident at the paper mill, and she wondered if she should simply turn around and head home to her boardinghouse, but her offer to leave the somber family to grieve in peace was immediately brushed aside. Miss Baylis, the Roses' pale-faced governess, who had drawn her aside to explain the situation, would hear nothing of it.

"Oh, no, Miss Seale, please stay and wait with us. I can't bear to be on my own with them . . ." she gestured toward the sofa, where Adele Rose's hand was being held by an equally distraught Eva Fowler. Mrs. Fowler was Hiram Rose's sister, and she and her husband lived next door. Libby had been hired to do some dressmaking work for both ladies, though the work was always conducted here at the Roses' much larger and more accommodating home. Though Augustus Fowler was Hiram Rose's second-in-command at the mill, the Fowlers lived in a much simpler fashion. Libby had gotten the impression that money was more of an issue for the Fowlers than for the extravagant and ostentatious Roses.

Miss Baylis continued. "Mr. Fowler has gone off to the mill to find out exactly what has happened. All we know is that Mr. Rose fell into some sort of machine or other, and . . ." she paused, not wanting to get more graphic than necessary, "and Mrs. Rose keeps asking how this could have happened, and I don't have any answers to give her. Besides, I really ought to look after the boys, and make sure they are . . . well, as well as can be expected."

Miss Baylis cast a worried glance toward Hiram Rose's two younger sons, seven-year-old twins named Isadore and Adolphus (Izzy and Fussy to everyone but their governess), who were over by the fire playing with the cast-iron pokers. Izzy already had a smudge of ash over one eye, and Libby could tell Miss Baylis was growing anxious as to what might be coming next. The twins were holy terrors, fascinated by fire, and required constant supervision to keep them from burning down the entire house. There was no sign in the room of Elliot, the oldest son, a moody boy of sixteen, and Libby wondered if he had preferred school to the gloom at home. She, however, didn't see how she could escape, and so she said, "Of course, I'm happy to stay. At least until Mr. Fowler returns with more news. I'm sure then the family will want to be left alone."

Divesting herself of her damp outerwear, Libby made her way to the sofa and tried her best to console the two weeping women ensconced there. Though she would not have said she was close to either woman, of the two she liked Mrs. Fowler better. Adele Rose was a rather haughty woman, with the look of a pampered lapdog. She was soft and pink and rounded at every extremity. It took all of Libby's ingenuity, not to mention the sturdiest whalebone corset available from Sears & Roebuck, to bring Mrs. Rose anywhere near to the fashionable ideal. Mrs. Fowler, on the other hand, presented a different set of problems from a dressmaker's perspective. She was now three months pregnant, and just beginning to swell. In the two weeks Libby had been working for her, most of her work had been the mundane matter of letting out bodices and scrupulously measuring her client each visit.

This was frustrating, but Libby couldn't afford to complain since it was precisely this need for constant alterations that was responsible for Libby's employment, and Libby needed the work. Her previous tenure, as a wardrobe mistress at Crowther's Portland Variety Theater, had been abruptly terminated when the theater closed. Now she was making ends meet by doing piecemeal work for Portland's elite while she looked for another permanent position. Her friend Charlotte McKennock, daughter of one of the city's richest men, had provided her with introductions to a dozen or so wealthy and influential matrons. But other than a few small one-day jobs, the work she was doing for Mrs. Rose and Mrs. Fowler was her only regular source of income.

Though there were many available seamstresses in Portland, two factors had tipped the balance in Libby's favor when Mrs. Rose had been choosing whom to hire. The first was that Adele was an Easterner, like Libby, and it pleased her to have a dressmaker who had worked in New York's Gold Eagle Dressworks. Libby had firsthand knowledge of the high-society fashions that were only now, a year later, reaching the cities on America's west coast. The second factor, much as Libby disliked to admit it to herself, was her religion. Though she herself had made no mention of it, Adele had ended their initial interview by asking point blank if Libby were Jewish. Stammering, Libby had answered in the affirmative, fearing that an anti-Semitic Mrs. Rose would then ask her to leave by the back exit. She was surprised when Adele only smiled and said, "Good." It transpired that the Rose family was also Jewish, although, like Libby herself, they had altered their name (Rosenberg to Rose in their case, Seletzky to Seale in hers) in order to sound less Hebraic. The admission shocked Libby, for she would never have guessed. Even now, after two weeks working in the house, she had seen no visible signs that the household was run along traditional Jewish lines. There was no menorah, no mezuzah by the door, and she knew for a fact that the cook had prepared a pork roast for supper one night. As surprised and a bit discomfited as she was by this, Libby could not afford to hold their assimilated ways against the Roses, since they were her employers. And, as a woman who had abandoned her husband and fled her family, she had no right to sit in judgment over anybody.

Libby sat on the sofa beside Adele and patted her hand. "Oh, Miss Seale . . . how could this have happened?" Adele wailed, "I don't understand."

"Adele, please try to control yourself," Eva Fowler said gently, but with a hint of disapproval. Mrs. Fowler was in more control of her emotions than her sister-in-law, despite the fact that it was her brother who had been killed. "Augustus will be home soon, and we will find out what happened. You must be strong for the children. Hiram would want . . ." she faltered, and for a moment her emotions rose to the surface. She swallowed her putative sob. "Hiram would have wanted you to be brave."

The two women leaned into each other and Adele cried softly. Libby sat uncomfortably, wondering how long it would be before Mr. Fowler would return. She tried to feel sad that Mr. Rose was dead, but she had barely known him. She had met him only once, a week before, when he paid her for the work she had done, and she had not liked him on that occasion. He had insisted on paying her himself, since he did not allow his wife to handle money. He had queried every line of the invoice she had written up, carefully detailing the hours she had worked and fabrics she had purchased. Libby wondered who would be responsible for paying her in Hiram's absence. Now that the entire household would need to be fitted with proper mourning attire, a great deal of new work was bound to come her way. She had to pretend to cough to hide the smile that followed the thought.

———

The crumpled ball of paper flew across the newsroom and hit its intended target smack in the middle of his forehead. Peter Eberle looked up, annoyed. Across the large room, filled with currently quiet presses and overflowing trays of type, a grinning John Mayhew raised his empty hands in a gesture of innocence.

"Sorry, Petey. I just wanted to see if you'd even notice." The lanky editor strode across the room and perched on the edge of his star reporter's desk. His face showed both amusement and concern, as he leaned in to talk to Peter. "I have to tell you, you haven't seemed very alert lately." He paused for a moment, regarding the man before him. Peter's face was pale, and there were deep circles under his eyes.

"I'm fine, John, really I am." Peter picked up the paper ball and lobbed it into the trash can.

Mayhew pressed on. "I have noticed we've been seeing a good deal less of your friend, Miss Seale, for the past few weeks . . ."

"I might have known I couldn't hide anything from a newsman of your perspicacity." Peter tried to smile, but it wasn't very convincing.

"Don't waste your five-dollar words on me, Eberle. You can't intimidate me into backing off. Truth is, I'm wondering if I should be worried about you." Wary of seeming too overbearing, Mayhew went back to his desk and sat facing Peter.

Peter knew he owed his boss the truth. "I'm sorry, John. I haven't much wanted to speak about it, but you are right. Lib— Miss Seale and I have parted ways . . . but it was on completely amicable terms. Believe me." He rubbed his face. "Besides, a man like me needs his freedom. And maybe I'm just tired. You've been working me too hard, that's all."

"Working you too hard?" The older man laughed. "I'd say things have been pretty quiet around here since Miss Seale—" he cut himself off. "Since the fuss over at the Variety was finished up. Fact is, I'm about getting ready to send you out to cover the church choir beat, or to ask you to write a scathing exposé on the latest hemlines from Paris. Of course," he paused. "That might require that you get a quote from a local seamstress."

Not meeting Mayhew's eyes, Peter rearranged the blotter on his desk. "The last time I checked, there was more than one seamstress in Portland." After a brief pause, he looked up, and there was a little more of the old fire in his gaze. "Say, John, do you suppose there might be a story in that? I mean, something about the rise of new tradesmen and businesspeople setting up shop here in town. I noticed when Jack Harkness dropped off the latest Portland business listings, the damn thing was twice as many pages as last year's edition, even though the national economy is still doing so poorly."

Before Mayhew could form a reply, the bell at the front counter rang. Both men looked up to see a dark-haired youth, too impatient to wait for a response, come bounding back past the front counter. Mayhew chuckled, "Half-Cent, I didn't expect to see you until Friday to clean the presses." Billy, or Half-Cent as he was affectionately known by all the newsmen at the *Gazette*, had been hanging around the newspaper offices since he was in knee pants. The nickname had started as a comment on the fact that little Billy was even smaller than the so-called "penny boys" who sold the *Portland Gazette* on the city's street corners. Although now fourteen, and almost as tall as Mayhew, the nickname remained. Half-Cent did regular odd jobs around the *Gazette* in exchange for training on the mechanical business of running a newspaper, and John Mayhew, with no family of his own, had come to regard the boy as something of a surrogate son. He was teaching him everything from how to set type to how to write an eye-catching headline.

"I just saw the police heading out of town," Billy panted, out of breath from running. "I found out they're heading to the mill . . . I heard one of them say the body is too mangled to even move . . . if you hurry, you can get this into the afternoon edition, right? I came to tell you as soon as I heard about it!"

"Slow down, Billy. What mill?" asked Peter, already pulling on his jacket and stuffing his notepad in the pocket.

"That's what I'm trying to tell you! There's been some kind of accident over at the Rose Paperworks! Hiram Rose himself, all messed up something awful in the machinery. When the workday started, some of the Chinese they got working there found him!"

"Hiram Rose, eh?" Peter reviewed what he knew about Rose: wealthy Jewish industrialist . . . family in Portland for two generations . . . paper mill one of the most venerable of Portland's businesses, but one of the last to use the old rag-paper manufacturing methods, and at the center of some recent labor disputes that had flared up right around New Year's, if he remembered it correctly. Rose had fired all the white workers, replacing them with Chinese who would work for much less. He would have to remember to look up the specifics later, when he had a chance. But now he needed to head out.

"Here you go, Half-Cent," he said, slipping a quarter into Billy's grateful hand as he ran out the door. He called over his shoulder, "Save me some room on the front page below the fold, John! I'll be back here in time to write up what I have before we go to press!"

Elliot Rose was hiding behind the garden shed. He supposed his mother and aunt would be wondering where he had run off to, but he couldn't stay inside that room one more moment, pretending a sorrow he didn't feel. The frantic message had come from the mill with the news of the accident just as he had been about to head off to school, and he found himself wishing the news had come five minutes later. Instead, he was housebound, at least until his uncle returned from the mill with more information on just what exactly had happened to his father.

He looked inside the shed for Matt, the estate handyman, but it was empty. Sometimes Matt would let Elliot puff on one of his cigarettes, after they had worked in the garden together. His father disapproved of cigarettes—not just for Elliot, or not even just for sixteen-year-old boys, but on general principle—they were "only for those without money, or class, or any hope of rising in the world." God, how Elliot hated his father when he spoke in that pompous tone, puffing away on his (eminently respectable) pipe. To tell the truth, Elliot hated his father all the time. It dawned on him he no longer needed to wonder whether his father approved of anything he did, and a smile lit up his pale features—a smile that would have scandalized his mother, had she been able to see it. A cigarette, a whole one just to himself, he decided, would be just the thing to mark this strange and yet somehow exciting day. Sadly, Matt was not in the shed or the stables, and Elliot was out of places to look.

Elliot peeked around the corner and regarded the back of his house. He would have liked to stay hidden, but the chill March wind and the remnants of the morning's light rain had left every possible place to sit damp and uncomfortable. He stepped onto the back lawn and gazed up at the windows of the family parlor, where his mother, aunt, and brothers were gathered. No one was looking out the window, and so he felt safe in staring at the scene captured in the window's frame, imagining it as a painting. Every lamp in the room was lit to augment the weak, wintry sunlight. Their glow made the figures stand out from the walls of the room, made the whole room stand out from the almost monochromatic purplish-blue of the March morning, as well. Outdoors everything was dark and gray, but the scene in the parlor, despite the sadness, was bathed in gold, as if it held some sort of magic, promising a brighter future. His mother was cradling Izzy in her lap, weeping into his towheaded curls. It called to Elliot's mind some sort of religious painting, such as the Pietá that hung in the chapel at his school, St. Sebastian's.

Oh, how his father would have hated him making that comparison! Hiram Rose despised the fact that his son studied at a Catholic school, but his wife had been adamant that the boy couldn't attend public school, and there were simply no Jewish secondary schools to send him to. Besides, his mother had argued, St. Sebastian was renowned in Portland, and many of the town's uppercrust sent their children there. His father, faced with opposition from both his son and his wife, grudgingly acquiesced.

Elliot loved St. Sebastian's, not that he cared one way or the other about Jesus, but because the school offered students the option of taking classes on the history of art. Elliot had proven such an avid student for the past three years that Sister Mary Abigail, who taught the classes, had arranged for him to take a private tutorial with the man commissioned to paint new altarpieces for the school chapel. For one glorious afternoon a week, Elliot spent three hours learning from a real artist the secrets of mixing pigments and linseed oil to make paints, about stretching and preparing a canvas, and the basics of composition. The work he was doing with Mr. Avenier made him realize how bad the childish paintings he had done just the year before really were, though his mother had cooed over them. One, in particular, a view of the roses by their side porch, she had even insisted on framing. It now hung in the dining room, embarrassing him at every meal with its juvenile technique. He could tell his father viewed it in much the same light. Hiram Rose never insulted the painting outright in front of Elliot, but sometimes he rolled his eyes when he caught sight of it as he pulled his chair up to the dinner table.

It was Elliot's goal to go to the Academy of Fine Arts in San Francisco to study when he left high school next year. It was a plan he knew his father was . . . would have been . . . totally against. The two had fought about it just a few weeks before. His father had made it clear he expected his oldest son to join the family business upon graduation. "Now listen here, Eli . . ."

Elliot hated being called Eli, and nobody but his father used the nickname. According to his father, Eli was a more manly name. Elliot, he said, was only for little boys. But Eli was far from the worst of the names his father called him. Sometimes he called him "Ellie," or even "Nelly Ellie" when he was playing baseball (badly) in the summer, or racing horses with his cousins along the frozen riverbank in the winter (he inevitably came in last). Most hurtfully, though, his father sometimes called him "Violet," mocking his desire to be a painter, or whenever Elliot made a comment to his mother regarding the beauty of the light or a particularly lovely flower. Hiram missed no opportunity to belittle Elliot's artistic aspirations, and as for making art a career, his position was steadfast. "The mill has been providing for this family since the day my father opened its doors in 1871. I'll not see it run by some stranger, nor see you turn your back on it. Mark my words, Eli, the Rose Paperworks is your destiny."

Elliot's cheeks flushed as he remembered the fight, but his heart grew light at the thought that never again would he hear that hated voice call him "Violet." Now there was nothing standing in his way of becoming the great painter he knew he could become.

A flurry of motion inside the house caught his attention, and he scooted closer to the window to see what was going on. He saw Miss Seale, the seamstress, following the maid out into the foyer to deal with whomever must just have arrived. He wondered if it was the police. Imagine, the police here in his own house! Deciding that it was really too chilly to hang around all morning in the backyard, he headed toward the rear door to rejoin what remained of his family.

———

It was what Libby had feared. Or had half feared and half hoped when the maid came into the parlor and announced that there was a gentleman from the newspaper at the door. "Peter!" she said, her voice momentarily failing her. She said again, more steadily, "Peter." She noticed he looked tired, and slightly thinner than when she last saw him, even though it was only a few weeks before.

If Libby had been somewhat prepared to see him, Peter was entirely taken aback to see her. "Libby . . . Miss Seale!" He found he was unsure how to address her, and he was afraid his discomfort showed on his face. Too quickly, to cover his embarrassment, he went on, "What are you doing here? I mean . . . oh, of course . . . are you doing some dressmaking for Mrs. Rose?"

"Your reporting skills are as sharp as ever," she said tartly. As soon as the words left her mouth, she realized that sounded more curt than she intended, and, in a softer voice, she continued, "Yes, Mrs. Rose has hired me to make some dresses, and her sister-in-law needs some alterations done."

A short silence stretched awkwardly, and she moved forward as if to embrace him. At the last second, she shifted course and stepped around him, regarding him with a seamstress's eyes, noting the way his jacket hung loosely on his shoulders. "You've lost weight." She suddenly wondered if she should invite him to supper with her and Mrs. Pratt some night. Would he come? They were still friends, weren't they?

"I've been very busy at the *Gazette* these last few weeks," he lied.

"You mustn't neglect your health," she replied primly. Dear god, why did she sound like her mother? She was acting like a tongue-tied schoolgirl! She wasn't his nursemaid, for heaven's sake! Suddenly, she remembered what she had been sent out into the hall to tell him. "Mrs. Rose asked me to come out here and speak with you. As you can imagine, the family is quite upset, and they aren't interested in talking to the press right now."

"Tell me, what are they like? The Rose family, I mean? Have you met Hiram Rose?"

Peter was getting that look in his eyes that she remembered so well from their time together, the one that meant the wheels in his head were turning as he was trying to piece together a news story. When he looked at her now, it wasn't with the social discomfort of a few moments before, but rather as a news source.

17

"Yes, once. He's . . . he was a businessman, I suppose, first and foremost. I get the feeling that he . . ." She stopped herself. "Peter, I really shouldn't be talking to you about Mr. and Mrs. Rose. We are here in their home, after all, and besides, I feel it's not my place to give my personal opinion about members of the family. I hardly know them."

Peter gave his crooked smile, for he knew Libby too well. "So, I take it you don't particularly care for them?"

She flushed. "I didn't say that!"

"Oh, come now, I know when you get that look on your face that you have some definite opinions, and usually not positive ones." She smiled back at him, but didn't offer anything more. He changed the subject, aware that if he didn't tread carefully, she would probably just send him on his way. "Do you know who will take over the mill? Will there be some sort of investigation? Is it possible it might have been foul play?"

She raised an eyebrow at that last question, remembering all that had happened between the two of them the last time foul play had crossed their path. Thank heavens, this time, the sudden death that confronted them didn't have anything to do with either of them personally. There was no chance they would end up putting on their investigative hats again for Hiram Rose.

The doorknocker gave two loud, authoritative knocks, causing both Peter and Libby to jump slightly. Almost instantly, the housemaid came in from the kitchen, and without even acknowledging Libby and Peter, swung open the door to reveal two middle-aged men. One was stocky and full of energy, the other taller but somehow less noticeable.

The shorter, heavyset one spoke. "Sorry, Maisie, I seem to have misplaced my key, somewhere, or I wouldn't have knocked. I . . ." He suddenly seemed to notice the look of astonishment on Maisie's face, and Libby's behind her. "Oh, I'm sorry, Maisie . . . Miss Seale . . . I'm sure this must be something of a shock."

Then he noticed Peter. "Who the hell are you," he said, then seemed to remember his manners, ". . . sir?"

"Peter Eberle, *Portland Gazette*." The way Peter said it, it came out almost a question.

"Ah, yes. Well, sorry you've come out here on a wild goose chase, young man. Then again, maybe it's best to quash this thing before it gets all around town." The man extended his hand to Peter. "How do you do? I'm Hiram Rose."

TWO

The scene in the parlor a few moments later was tumultuous, to say the least. Adele Rose, who had practically fainted upon catching sight of her resurrected spouse, now clung to him, making incoherent expressions of joy and smiling through her continuing tears. Eva Fowler, who had also thrown her arms around her brother, had now moved over to her husband. The taller of the two men Libby had seen at the door was, as she had surmised, Augustus Fowler. She had never actually met him before. Eva was trying to extract from Augustus the details of what had happened at the mill, although the speed at which she fired questions at him allowed him no time for answers.

Hiram Rose's sons, on the other hand, did not appear as moved as the women. Elliot, who had slunk back into the room, uttered one plaintive "Father!" in the cracked voice of a young man on the cusp of manhood. Now he hung back by the French doors, to all appearances getting ready to escape again. Meanwhile, as all the adults in the room were focused elsewhere, Fussy (or was that Izzy?)

had taken the initiative to start climbing up the crenellated chimney breast. Miss Baylis was attempting simultaneously to pull him down while pushing his brother over toward their father, to welcome him back from the land of rumored death. Amidst all this bustle, no one noticed Libby and Peter sidle into the room, where they stood unobtrusively by the pocket doors that led to the hall.

Hiram Rose finally hushed the cacophony of sentiment and inquiry with a stentorian "Quiet down! Let's have a little order in here!"

Libby glanced at Peter as if to ask "should we leave?" but Peter's eyes were riveted on the no-longer-deceased master of the house, and she sensed he was deliberately keeping quiet to escape notice—and probable ejection—from this family scene.

"Where . . . how . . ." Adele began again, but Hiram interrupted her with a wave of his hand.

"This morning I was nowhere near the scene of the unfortunate . . . accident at the Paperworks. I had seen, in the newspaper," he began in a measured tone, "an advertisement of a small paper concern that was liquidating its stock in Oregon City. I decided to go there early to see if I could purchase some new equipment." He turned to Elliot. "This is the sort of thing a successful businessman must do, son. Keep abreast of possible bargains and be willing to go at a moment's notice to take advantage of them. Another businessman's failure may be your treasure. In fact . . ."

"Hiram, perhaps . . ." Augustus Fowler jumped in tentatively, and Libby noticed he seemed to wait for approval from his brother-in-law before continuing, "perhaps the family would like to hear about what happened at the mill." The roomful of people seemed to breathe a sigh of relief, as one, that they were not to be subjected to one of Hiram Rose's disquisitions on the subject of papermaking.

Fowler went on, "I arrived at the mill, after leaving you all here, to find the police had already departed with . . ." He stopped, unsure how to discuss a mangled corpse in mixed company. "I was about to follow them down to the morgue, when . . ."

Hiram broke in. "And then I walked in!" he boomed. "Had been in Oregon City for most of the morning, but I got to the mill in time for the afternoon quota check. I wondered why all the workers were looking at me like they'd seen a ghost."

Eva Fowler's face had gone white. "If you were not the poor soul whose remains were found this morning, Hiram, then who was it? And what exactly happened?"

"I don't know who it was. Nobody recognized, well, what was left of him. But apparently some scaffolding, one of the catwalks . . ." Fowler shot Rose a warning look, cutting him off midstream, and causing him to consider his next sentence carefully. "All we know is one of the catwalks collapsed, and unfortunately for whoever he was, the collapse tipped a man right into one of the machines."

Fowler said smoothly, "Now, Eva . . . Adele . . . don't you worry. These sorts of accidents happen from time to time in a factory, but there's no reason to think anything else untoward will occur. Of course we are checking all the other scaffoldings in the mill, and won't let Hiram or anybody else on them until we're satisfied. The Rose Paperworks is as safe a workplace as it ever was!"

Hiram said, "And that's enough of that. I'm meeting the police at the mill first thing in the morning to sort this mess out, and soon enough we'll find out just what happened and to whom." Libby noticed Peter discreetly jotting something in his notebook, and she suspected he would just "happen to be" at the Rose Paper-works tomorrow morning as well. "I'll have no more discussion about it here and now. I want my home to be a happy place. Adele, dear, perhaps you'd play us something on the piano?"

———

The kitchen of the Rose house was noticeably warmer than the parlor, as Libby and Mrs. Fowler entered. They made an odd picture, since Eva Fowler, who had a good six inches on the diminutive seamstress, was leaning on the smaller woman for support. Despite assurances that all was now well, Eva had remained pale and uneasy since her brother and husband had arrived back from the mill, and it had been generally agreed that a nice lie-down on her own bed was what was called for. Given her delicate condition, said Adele, her nerves were naturally apt to be fragile.

Libby had not been the first choice to help Eva back to her own house, which lay just across the yard. Mrs. Rose had asked Elliot to help his aunt, but his only answer had been to shoot an inexplicably angry glare at Mrs. Fowler and then run out the French doors. Libby had no idea what the basis was for Elliot's evident animosity toward Mrs. Fowler, but she assumed it was nothing more than typical teenage truculence. Or perhaps he was merely unsettled by the day's events. Libby suspected Elliot was one member of the Rose family not happy to see Hiram return from the dead.

In any case, Libby stepped in and immediately offered to see her pregnant customer back home. Peter had made his exit half an hour before, and Libby was grateful for any excuse to move. Getting any work done with Adele was out of the question. It was obvious she would not calm down enough to discuss fabrics and designs until at least the next day.

Halfway to the front door, Eva had requested they make a detour through the kitchen for a glass of buttermilk. It had to be buttermilk, she said, and she knew quite well Adele always kept a pitcher in the icebox, whereas she herself had none at home. Libby was happy to oblige, and thus they found themselves in the cozy, overheated brick room at the back of the house, facing the Roses' cheerful cook.

"Oh, Celia, could you please pour me a glass of buttermilk?" Eva Fowler addressed the woman sweetly, but a bit like one might address a child. "I simply crave buttermilk these days!"

"Natural enough," replied Celia. "I remember I used to crave the oddest things when I was carrying my Johnny. For me it was beets. Couldn't get enough of them." She placed the glass of milk on the coarse wooden table, and gestured for Eva to have a seat. Eva took a healthy swallow, downing nearly half the glass, then delicately wiped her lip with a handkerchief, the delicacy of the gesture quite at odds with the show of appetite that preceded it.

"Thank you, that's much better." She added, "I'd thought about driving myself into town this afternoon to pick up some wool. I was thinking of knitting a sweater for the baby. But now I think I'd better stay in. Perhaps you could send Matt around in a bit, and I will send him into town instead."

"I'd be happy to, ma'am, only I haven't seen Matt today. He hasn't turned up yet. If he does, I'll be sure to send him right over."

Eva put down her glass with a thud. Celia and Libby flinched. "I'm sorry. I didn't mean to make such a thump! I feel so weak sometimes." Mrs. Fowler gave a smile, and regarded the still half-full glass before her. "I think that's all the milk I can get down, but thank you so much, Celia." She rose unsteadily to her feet. "Cravings just come and go. I can't think what's wrong with me."

Libby stepped back to her side, and hooked her arm beneath Eva's elbow. "Now, now, it's been a trying morning. I'm sure there's nothing the matter that a nice nap won't solve."

Eva really did look all of a sudden as if she might faint. "I've waited so long for this baby, and if anything should happen . . . Mr. Fowler and I had just about given up hope that we would ever be so blessed. Now I know this is my last chance."

"Hush! You mustn't even think like that," tut-tutted Celia. "You just relax and don't overstress yourself."

"Yes, of course you're right." Mrs. Fowler gave a smile. "I'm being silly. Come, Miss Seale. I intend to do nothing strenuous all afternoon, and you and I can sit quietly and discuss some of the clothes I am going to need very soon!" Just as they reached the back door, she turned back and called out to the cook, who had returned to dividing a large slab of dough into loaf-sized hunks. "You will send Matt over, won't you, as soon as he appears?"

" 'Course, Mrs. Fowler. Don't you worry about anything except that precious bundle inside you. If I have to, I'll go downtown and get you that wool myself!"

———

Peter hadn't realized that the Rose Paperworks was several miles outside Portland's center, so he arrived the following morning later than he had planned. Noting a large set of double doors standing partly open, he peered into the bustling interior. Several large cylinders churned and bubbled, and the smell of chemicals made him nearly gag. He fished his handkerchief from his pocket and breathed through it briefly, acclimating himself to the stench. To his right, several chattering girls sat beside wooden bins, methodically grabbing scraps of material from a giant pile, ripping them into (as far as Peter could see) merely smaller scraps, and then tossing them into a series of bins. Farther inside, slender Chinese men slipped between smooth-sided steel machines, pulling levers and adjusting dials. A muscular white man with an enormous moustache reached repeatedly into a vat of what looked like pulp, throwing shovelfuls of white paste onto row after row of wire racks. The workers themselves seemed part of the machinery. The noise and motion gave no indication that a day earlier this had been the site of a horrible tragedy.

Peter looked up, interested in the series of catwalks that ran the length and breadth of the cavernous building. He was just in time to see Mr. Rose himself, accompanied by a policeman in uniform, enter through an upstairs door into another part of the building. As he jotted down a few notes and tried to plan his next steps, a burly fair-haired man was suddenly upon him. Surrounded as he was by the Chinese workers, his size and coloring was in heightened relief. "Can I help you?" he said, although his tone indicated he wanted to do anything but.

"Peter Eberle, with the *Portland Gazette*." Peter extended a hand, but the larger man only looked at him suspiciously.

"Mr. Rose know you're coming?"

Although Peter was never above a little creative shading of the truth, in this case he was able to say with perfect honesty, "I saw him last evening at his home, and he mentioned he was meeting the police here this morning. As a matter of fact, I just saw him up there . . ." he pointed. "What's up there anyway, warehouse space?"

"Offices. Up there's Mr. Rose's office, that whole side of the building . . . only as you can see one of his office doors is blocked off because of the accident. The police don't want anyone using that part of the catwalks."

"While I'm waiting for Mr. Rose, perhaps you could give me a quick tour of the mill. I've never seen paper being manufactured, Mr.—?"

"Matson. And I don't get paid to give tours to reporters. I got enough work to do just keeping an eye on all these Celestials. Lazy, the lot of them, you have to watch 'em every minute."

"It must have been a strange time, when Rose let his whole staff go and hired them. Must've made your job that much more difficult." Peter was fishing, and he hit pay dirt. Suddenly Matson seemed more than willing to abandon his duties and discuss the running of the mill.

"You could say that. Lots of folks were mighty angry to lose their livelihood just so he could save a few dollars." The word "he" was almost spit, and Peter sensed there was no great love between Rose and his foreman. "Fowler would never have done that, let me tell you. Not that he has any say-so around here, even if he does have an office on the top floor."

"Augustus Fowler is married to Rose's sister, is that right?"

"That's her, Eva Rose Fowler. Pretty thing, too. Day after he married her, he was hired on as a manager here. Even so, Rose doesn't trust him. He don't trust no one but himself. He won't even let me know the combination of the safe, and I'm the one who's here all day, every day! What if we needed to pay a tradesman and he's not here. 'Send for me at home, Matson,' he says. As if I ought to go running to him every time I need something. And his secretary, Kearney, he's a piece of work too. The two of them, Rose and Kearney, always whispering in corners as they walk up there, looking down at the workers." He motioned to the catwalk above. "I'll be honest with you, when I saw that body there yesterday, I thought someone had finally done it—maybe one of those angry men who was around here complaining about their lost jobs came here early in the morning and fought with him, and one thing led to another . . ." He seemed to suddenly realize how callous he sounded. "Horrible tragedy, of course, I wouldn't wish that on anyone. All I meant to say is, when I thought that was Rose there, dead in the Hollander, I just wasn't all that surprised."

Peter was taken aback. "So it wasn't an accident then? I thought the poor man who died fell into one of your pieces of machinery."

"Fell, yes . . . but it was no accident. Come, I'll show you something." He led Peter toward a stairway. As they passed the mustached man Peter had noticed earlier, Matson greeted him with a grunt, and added to Peter, "This is Alex Smirnikoff. A Russki, a good fellow."

Despite his size, the man offered a graceful half bow, and said in heavily accented English, "Pleased to meet you."

"Alex is one of the few real Americans still working here, and he's a strong worker." The irony that a Russian immigrant was considered a "real American" to Matson wasn't lost on Peter.

"Mr. Smirnikoff, I take it you were kept on after most of them were replaced by the Chinese workers . . ."

"Yes, yes, that is correct. Is not so easy for these new men to shovel the rag pulp like I do, it's heavier than it seems, you know?

So Mr. Rose, he say to me, Alex, when I send all the other men away, you can stay."

"They were very angry, the other men, I take it?"

"Yes, yes, is not good for men to lose their work, their money. How do they take care of their families without a job?"

"Come on, I'll take you up." Matson pulled him away from Smirnikoff. "You get back to work, Alex. You know we're still behind because of yesterday."

Peter ascended the stairs, following Matson up to the catwalks. They made their way over to the far side where Peter could see that part of the wooden walkway had been roped off. The whole edifice creaked as the two men walked, and it seemed to Peter that it would hardly be a surprise if more of the catwalk collapsed. But when he reached the cordoned-off area, and crouched down, he saw immediately why Matson had said it was a deliberate death. The supports for the section of walkway outside Rose's office had been sawed cleanly through from below to about the midpoint. Where the wood had been sawed, the color was clean and the cut smooth, and then there was a section where the jagged, splintered edge clearly showed the natural effect when the rest of the timber had broken under stress. Whoever had done this had clearly thought it through. Though the catwalk would have looked perfectly normal from above, as soon as any weight was placed on it the compromised struts would give way at once. The minute yesterday's victim had set foot on this section of catwalk, he had been plunged down into the knives of the murderous machine below.

"I don't know how we'll be able to clean that out good enough to use it again." Matson had joined him on the edge of the walkway, and for a silent moment, the two men looked down at the reddened interior of the hollander. "He must have died a pretty painful death, before we even turned on the machine. I don't reckon anyone could survive a fall and climb out with all them blades around you."

"So someone meant to kill Mr. Rose . . . this is right outside his office. Who else came up here?"

"No one was allowed off the factory floor but management. Me, Fowler, Rose, Kearney. Sometimes Alex, he's a shift manager. Of course, sometimes people from outside would come here for a business meeting, you know, a big customer, a supply salesman, but they come in the front door to the main offices, up the outside stairs of the mill. The only person who ever comes down to this end of the catwalks is Rose himself." Peter and Matson both looked down over the buzz of activity on the factory floor. Almost to himself, Matson continued, "He used to stand here all the time, looking at his workers. And after he got the Chinese workers in, he would come up here and look all around the place with this smug expression, like he was master of some kind of Shanghai plantation. He likes to stand outside his office and call down to the workers, 'I'm not paying you to talk!'—that kind of thing. 'Course, it's not like the devils can understand a word he says. They just know how to hold out their hands for a paycheck every Friday. Do you know, they bow—it's the damnedest thing—they bow when you give them their weekly pay!"

"I believe that's a gesture of respect in their culture, Mr. Matson." Peter looked over the sea of dark heads with their long black hair in distinctive braids, wondering what someone among them might know about the stranger falling to his death. He suspected the police were unlikely to go to the time and expense of hiring a translator, but he knew from past experience at interviewing the residents of Chinatown that they missed nothing. Their dark silent eyes often hid a fierce intelligence. They were far from unaware of their surroundings, despite the language barrier. It wouldn't surprise him if one of them had noticed something that had eluded Matson. But, he realized, the accident happened while the mill was shut down for the night, so they couldn't have seen anything. Furthermore, even if something had been noticeable today during daylight hours, none of the Chinese ever went up on the catwalks. Well, at least he wouldn't have to pry the money for a translator out of John Mayhew.

Turning back to Matson, he asked, "So who do they think it was? Do the police have any ideas? You're the first one who saw the body . . ."

"What was left of it," the red-haired man interrupted. "Believe me, Mr. Eberle, you couldn't hardly tell it was a human being in there, except for the bits of ripped clothing, so much blood, all I could really make out was a leg and a boot . . ." He stopped, and looked faintly green as he strained to remember the sight. "I was sure it was Rose, of course—it stood to reason he'd be here early. Not too many people have a key to the mill. Like I told you, Rose doesn't trust people easily. When I got here yesterday morning, the door was unlocked, which wasn't unusual . . . sometimes Rose or Fowler gets in early. But the lock wasn't forced, no sign of that, so whoever it was had a key. You can see why I assumed it had to be him."

"Of course," Peter agreed.

"But after Rose came walking in here, alive as ever, I started to think it over, and I did remember that the torn clothing and boot I saw didn't look like the sort of thing a rich man wears. No, it was a workingman's boot. Whoever he was, he had mud on his shoes, and he didn't have his suits made of the nicest cloth." Suddenly realizing how long he had been away from his duties, Matson once again became the gruff foreman. "Look here, Mr. Eberle, I'd better take you back down and show you out. I have to attend to my work, and you're not even supposed to be up here."

With a glance at the closed door to Rose's office, Peter reluctantly allowed himself to be led back down to the mill floor, and to the door leading outside. He cast one look back into the vast, dim interior of the mill, wishing he could be a fly on the wall as the police were questioning Hiram Rose.

———

"I'm no fool. I know I'm not a well-liked man." Hiram Rose leaned forward in his chair, behind his vast desk, and fixed his interrogator with a glare. "The question is, what are you going to do to protect me?"

Officer Macon regarded him with appropriate dislike. He had not volunteered for this assignment, but as lowest ranking man at the precinct, the interview had fallen to him. The day before, when it had been thought that one of the richest men in town was smeared all over the inside of the hollander, half of the police force had been out here, scouring the mill for clues. Now that the victim had been downgraded to a tramp, or, at best, some sort of ne'er-do-well (and who else would have been skulking around the factory in the early hours of the morning?), it was just Macon, on his own. "First things first, Mr. Rose. We're fairly certain that you were the intended victim, but until we know whose body it was we found yesterday, we can't be certain. There could be some other explanation. You have no idea whose body it is, do you?"

"Someone in this city wants me dead, Officer. Me!" Hiram smacked his desktop. "Whoever it was in the hollander, that doesn't matter . . . that was just his bad luck. Wrong place, wrong time."

"We understand you've lost your keys, sir. And there are no signs of a break-in at the mill. So we are wondering if perhaps it was your own keys used by this person to enter yesterday morning. Do you have any idea when those keys went missing?"

"Godammit man, for all I know my keys are just misplaced, not lost! Usually they turn up under the bed, or in my vest pocket. Ask my wife . . . she's usually the one who finds them, in the not-so-unusual circumstance that I don't know where they are. Besides, some of the other staff here has keys, so the unlocked door may mean nothing."

Macon gritted his teeth, and tried to remain polite. "Sir. We've accounted for all staff members who have any reason to use the catwalks, and none of them is missing. And though we don't know who the dead man was, I can tell you one thing. He wasn't Chinese, so he's not one of your workers. So . . . for the moment, Mr. Rose, we're working under the assumption that whoever died yesterday was part of a plot to attack you. We think he must have compromised the scaffolding himself, and then it collapsed too early, before he had a chance to get off it."

Rose grunted noncommittally. But he seemed somewhat calmer than before.

"So the question is, who wanted you dead?"

Rose drummed his fingertips on his desktop, and appeared to be deciding something. The silence was heavy. Finally he spoke, "It wouldn't surprise me if it was someone sent by Unsworth Manning." Unsworth Manning owned Willamette Fine Papers, a competitor of the Rose Paperworks, and was rumored to be in financial straits. Hiram warmed to his theme. "Yes, if I were you I'd start by seeing if any of the thugs he employs over at his pathetic excuse for a mill have gone missing. I bet that's it. I bet Manning was behind all of this . . . the letters as well."

"Letters?" inquired Macon, suddenly more interested.

"I received a few threatening letters . . . two or three . . . over the past few weeks. Letters threatening some unnamed violence if I didn't rehire all the workers I let go at the end of last year. I disregarded them, of course . . . a lot of grumbling malcontents, I thought. A man in my position can't let a few threats slow him down."

"May I see them? The letters?" Macon leaned forward.

"Oh, I didn't keep any of them. No better than the paper they were printed on, or so I thought at the time. I see now, perhaps I should have taken them more seriously."

"Yes, it certainly would have helped us to see them. Can you remember any distinguishing marks? I suppose," he added wryly, "they weren't signed?" Rose didn't bother to answer. "Were these letters sent through the mail? Perhaps Mr. Kearney would be able to remember something about them." Macon rose to cross to the outer office where the secretary sat.

"No, no. Rose put up a hand to stop Macon's movement. "The letters were placed in my carriage, outside the mill. I would find them at the end of the day, on my way home. My carriage, on the days I take it, is kept in the stables outside. And I'm afraid access to it there is . . . well, there are people in and out all day long."

"What about your coachman, sir? Might he be able to tell us anything? Is he here with you today?"

"No, I came by horse. Truth is, I don't have a real coachman . . . waste of money, if you ask me. What sort of healthy grown man needs to be ferried around like a child? No, I only take a driver when my wife needs the carriage back at home during the day. Before you ask, I haven't seen the boy who usually drives today. Just as likely to sack him if I ever do see him again. He's not the most reliable sort."

Macon sighed. He had hoped these letters might lead to fruitful avenues for exploration, but so far they appeared to head only toward dead ends. It did strike him as slightly suspicious that this coach driver should disappear just now, but there was likely a simple answer. He put it in the back of his mind to question the coachman when he turned up, or track him down if that didn't happen in the next few days. "Well, if you get another letter, please, sir, hold on to it this time." He glanced down at his notepad, "So, to return to Mr. Manning. Do you have any real cause to suspect he's behind this attempt?"

"I don't need real cause. I feel it here," Rose patted his belly, "in my gut. That's how I've gotten where I am, Macon. I go with my gut. And I tell you Manning's always been jealous of me, and this thing with the Chinese was just the last straw. Of course he'd like it if I hired back my old workforce! First thing he'd do is snap up my coolies. Like that! He only wishes he'd thought of it first."

"Surely there's more than enough business in Oregon for two paper mills. If every business competitor turned to murder when competition got fierce . . ." Macon didn't get to finish.

"From what I hear," Hiram Rose said with a touch of complacency, "Manning's just about to go under. I heard he's been meeting, hush-hush of course, with some real estate agents, looking to off-load that white elephant of his over by the river. Not that anyone will be foolish enough to buy it and set up shop. That mill was outmoded when my father ran this place. Still, if he could get his hands on a workforce as cheap as mine—you know what those coolies will work for? All I pay them is one dollar a day . . . plus a cup of rice. That's what they demanded. A cup of rice!" Hiram laughed out loud, an unpleasant guttural squawk. "Can you beat it? Best damn business decision I ever made. Do you have any idea how much money is sitting in that safe there?" He gestured behind his desk, where a mass of black cast iron, at least four feet high, dominated a corner of his office. It was decorated with delicate gold-leaf tracery, but looked solid enough to withstand an earthquake. "Rolling in so fast now I can't get to the bank often enough."

Officer Macon was growing weary with what had turned into a monologue on the business savvy of Hiram Rose, and he tried to get back to the matter at hand. "Now, assuming you're correct that the recent, er . . . labor turnover at the mill is behind this current spate of threats . . ." He deliberately turned over a fresh page in his notepad. "Are there any ex-employees you think might hold enough of a grudge to try to kill you? Perhaps one in particular, or more than one as a group?"

Hiram waved his hand dismissively. "Those knuckleheads? I doubt any of them . . . or all of them put together, could write a letter, let alone put together a plan. Besides, first sign of any of them around here and I'd have had Matson or Smirnikoff kick them off the premises."

Macon decided to bring the interview to a close. It was clear he would get nothing out of this man, other than a series of self-serving, self-aggrandizing theories. "All right, Mr. Rose, I guess that will be all for the moment. It goes without saying that if you have any further thoughts, please contact me down at the station. I will be . . ." he paused just slightly, "happy to return at any time."

Rose didn't show him out, but remained sitting behind his desk. But his eyes followed Macon until the door shut behind him.

In the outer office, Augustus Fowler and Scott Kearney were in mid-conversation, but at Macon's entrance they fell silent.

"Officer Macon. Is there anything I can do for you?" Ever the dutiful secretary, Kearney rose from his seat. The sandy hair, receding deeply at the temples, gave a slightly sinister cast to his face, though his smile was obsequiousness personified.

"No, no, I believe I'm through here." He had an idea, and turned to Augustus. "Mr. Fowler, however . . . I'm glad to find you here. May I have a moment, privately?"

Kearney turned to Fowler, and they shared a brief, unreadable look, and then Kearney said with exactingly polite diction, "I'll leave you two alone. I'll be down on the floor if you require anything more from me." He exited without any further comment, and Fowler faced Macon.

"Yes, Officer, what can I do for you?"

"I know we have your statement from yesterday, but Mr. Rose just shared something with me which I was hoping you might be able to shed some light on. Apparently he's been receiving threatening letters for the past few weeks. I don't suppose you knew anything about this?"

Fowler shook his head, clearly surprised at the news.

"No? Ah, well. Until yesterday's activity Mr. Rose assumed they were unimportant, so I suspected he would not have mentioned them. But you are his brother-in-law, as well as his business partner."

"While what you say is true, Hiram and I tend to confine our conversations to business matters. I doubt I would be his choice, should he decide to confide in somebody." Fowler looked disturbed. "Threatening letters, you say? I find it hard to imagine. Hiram has seemed in such good spirits these past few weeks."

"His suspicion is that Unsworth Manning might be behind this," Macon offered.

This got a reaction. At the name Unsworth Manning, Fowler paled perceptibly, though he recovered quickly, and when he spoke his voice was steady. "Manning? Hiram hasn't mentioned him to me in any regard, at least not recently. I know he and Mr. Manning are competitors, but . . ." Fowler paused. "May I ask why Hiram believes . . . ? No, never mind. I'm sure it is merely one of his fancies. Once he sets his mind on something, he becomes quite certain it is as good as a fact."

As it happened, this was exactly what Macon thought. When Rose had first expounded his theory that the owner of Willamette Fine Papers was out to kill him, Macon assumed it was merely a ploy by Rose to get the police to hassle a business competitor. But, as he left the mill and headed back into the city, Macon was no longer so sure. Fowler's palpable reaction when Manning's name had been spoken certainly must mean something. Could Rose be correct? Perhaps his gut feeling that Manning was behind the tampered catwalk was on the mark. If so, could Augustus Fowler know something that proved this? Surely Fowler couldn't be Manning's "inside man" at the mill, if indeed such a thing existed, although it stood to reason that someone at the Paperworks had to have been the one to leave those letters in Rose's carriage. But if Fowler knew about the letters—and his surprise upon hearing about them had seemed genuine enough—Macon couldn't believe he would knowingly be party to a plot to actually murder his own wife's brother. Or would he?

Having no way to answer that for the present, Macon decided to put the question out of his mind until he could discuss these new developments with his superiors.

———

The *Gazette* offices were quiet as Peter sat polishing his story. Mayhew was in the back, setting type, and the faint sound of letters clattering through the Linotype machine was soothing to Peter, a familiar background noise. He struggled with his closing paragraph, wishing he had some answers instead of only questions. Who had tried to kill Hiram Rose? And who had been the nameless victim who died in his place?

Not for the first time, his mind wandered back to his previous detecting foray with Libby, and he considered how helpful it had been to have someone to talk to when all you had were questions. He wished he could talk to Libby now, ask her opinion on Rose and the mysterious body at the mill. Actually he would have been happy to talk to her about any subject, but without the excuse of a shared investigation he didn't see how he could approach her. They had made a good team, in more ways than one. Despite his protestations to Mayhew ... well, seeing her yesterday had put the lie to the notion that he had somehow moved on. But she was married, and unwilling to pursue a divorce. All avenues led him back to that inescapable obstacle.

Sighing, Peter bent back over the pages in front of him, pen poised at the ready. Although the *Gazette* did have one of the new Blick typewriters, Peter preferred composing his copy in longhand. The typewritten pages were easier for others to read, but Peter found it difficult to work on the bulky desktop model, which entered type "blind" on the underside of the roller so that you couldn't see the words you had written until the sheet was removed from the machine. This made it impossible to revise text as you went, which Peter thought might be suitable for a novelist or essayist, but under the time pressure of getting out a newspaper he felt it necessary to be able to compose and revise his thoughts simultaneously.

He began to scrawl out his final sentences: *The police continue to investigate the murder, and determine the identity of the anonymous victim. Some may suggest that this gruesome death serves as a reminder that modern manufacturing is fraught with danger. As Portland's paper industry continues to prosper, one can only hope that increased safety precautions will prevent any more such senseless tragedies from occurring.*

Waving the page to dry the ink, he caught the attention of Billy, who had just come into the newsroom. Guessing that Peter had just finished something, he reached out for the pages. "Want me to set these for you? John is showing me how to work the Linotype."

"Half-Cent, let me ask you something."

"Sure, Peter!"

"How do you think the police will identify the victim at Rose's Paperworks? Remember, the body was too mangled to make any kind of identification."

The boy thought for a few moments. "I s'pose they'll wait to see who comes in and says someone is missing."

Peter nodded. "Very good. Or they might find something in their examination of the remains, a wallet with identification, a distinctive scar, that helps pinpoint the victim. Billy, will you do me a favor?"

"Is it some reporting?"

"You'll go far in this business, Half-Cent. That's exactly what I was going to ask you to do." Billy visibly puffed up at this compliment, as Peter continued. "I know you spend time around the police station. I want you to keep an ear out, see if you hear any rumors about who the dead man was. As soon as you hear anything, you come tell me, and if I'm not here, leave me a note. And tell John Mayhew to give me a message. Can you do that?"

"I can! I'll be the best police reporter you ever had!"

"If you find something out, I'll pay you a half dollar."

"I'd do it for nothing!"

"Kid, if you want to be a newspaperman, you'll learn that the first rule is to always take what they pay you. And always ask for cash." He laughed, feeling better already, enjoying the unfamiliar role of mentor. Smiling, he handed the boy his story and left for the day. Half-Cent was a good kid, with an inquisitive mind, and if he wasn't Peter's first choice of detecting partner, well . . . Peter's mind wandered back inescapably to a certain seamstress, and he wondered what she was doing at that moment. Probably she was back at Mrs. Pratt's boardinghouse, preparing for dinner. Perhaps brushing her hair, or taking a bath . . .

Passing by a local saloon favored by newsmen, Peter impulsively turned in and ordered a whiskey and soda. Then made it a double.

THREE

It was cold and rainy, and Libby was not pleased to be standing in the darkening evening, waiting for a streetcar. Although they professed to run on a regular schedule, she thought, not for the first time, that the New York City elevated train system could teach the Portland streetcar companies a lesson or two on the subjects of frequency and regularity.

Shifting her weight, she pulled her coat more tightly about herself, and wished she had brought an umbrella with her. Instead, she scanned the street in the distance, looking in vain for the headlamp that would signal an approaching streetcar. She was aware that the parcel of materials she had just purchased was getting worse than damp. When the train appeared at last, she was amused to see it was one of the two that the city had purchased used from the New York trolley system. In careful lettering inside each door were the words "Beware of pickpockets"—a warning that had been the cause of much amusement in the Portland newspapers when the cars first went into service. Happy to be sheltered from the rain, her mood improved as she watched the wet, gray city roll by outside the window.

Her peace was short-lived, however, for after she alighted and was walking the two blocks from the streetcar stop to her house, the heavens opened. She had to run the last part of the way, getting soaked in the process. By the time she walked into the foyer at Mrs. Pratt's boardinghouse, she was in no mood to make small talk with her garrulous landlady. In fact, she was halfway up the stairs to her room when she heard Mrs. Pratt come bustling out of the kitchen. Turning, she saw the older woman brandishing an envelope. "Miss Seale, a letter has come for you in today's post. From New York!"

Having no family of her own, Mrs. Pratt took a great interest in the lives of her boarders, and none fascinated her more than the mysterious transplanted seamstress, whose full story she could only guess at. "At least I believe it is for you. The name on it is Libby Seletzky, at least I think. It's hard to make out . . . but I only know one Libby, so I figured that was you!"

Libby knew that she was expected to sit downstairs with the landlady and read her letter, perhaps sharing information about her family back home. But instead she came down only long enough to take the proffered envelope. "Come in and have some tea, dearie, while you read your letter."

"I really must get upstairs and lay out these bolts of cloth to dry, Mrs. Pratt . . ." she demurred. Trying to ignore the way Mrs. Pratt's face fell, Libby hastened to her small room. She looked at the letter in her hand, felt its feather-light weight (her mother always used onion-skin paper to save money on postage), and set it down for a moment, unwilling to deal with it right away. Carefully, she removed the folded pieces of fabric from the hastily wrapped parcel (the shop clerk had been in a hurry to close the store)—a pale blue sarcenet sprigged with gray floral garlands, perfect for Eva Fowler's fair coloring, and a darker, multihued jacquard with a rather severe pattern of flowers and leaves picked out in black, busy enough, she hoped, to divert the eye from Adele Rose's figure flaws. Using the small table and both chairs, and pinning the top of the cloth to the curtain rods, her room soon resembled an Arabian tent, but at least she hoped the damp would be gone from the material by the time she next visited the Rose house.

Surrounded by the fabrics, Libby hesitated. She realized she was dreading the letter's contents . . . how many times had she imagined writing home to her family, and how many variations of their reply had she composed in her mind? She remembered all too well their response the first time she fled Mr. Greenblatt's violent temper. That time she had only fled as far as her parents' apartment, where her family had sympathized with her, but ultimately sent her back to her husband. The next time, when he nearly broke her arm, she had run not to her family but away, as far as she could get from New York and the home she shared with her husband.

She had sat on the train, watching the country go by outside her window, aware of each mile carrying her away from the only life she knew, and wishing she could turn and say, "Look, Mama, a field of cows!" or point out to her brother Seymour the funny little man who bowed and tipped his hat when she saw him in the dining car.

Since then, the time passing in Portland made her miss her family even more. She longed to tell her father all about the hardy pioneers and lumberjacks she saw every day as she went about her business. Her sister Rebecca would have loved seeing the rich and varied gardens of Portland's great houses, and Libby wished she could show her mother how much her sewing had improved over the last several months.

There was no point in putting it off any longer. She had to open the envelope. She had known as soon as she mailed her first and only letter home, just a few weeks before, that a reply would eventually be forthcoming.

Dear Libbeleh, We were so relieved to get your letter, and we pray that you will come to your senses and come home immediately. I must tell you that your father refused to read it, but I know he feels as I do, that your place is back here with your family who all love you. Seymour heard that Mr. Greenblatt is telling people you have gone on a trip to care for his ailing mother, so if you come home now, no one need ever know of our family shame, that you ran away from your husband.

Libby squeezed her eyes tight, trying to hold back the tears. "Mama, how can you ask me to do that?" she whispered, as she read on.

My dearest daughter, please do not think we want you to go back to such a situation as you described. Papa and Seymour have gone to speak to your husband, and he explained that he was very ashamed he let his temper get the better of him. He promises he will be good to you, and he wants you to come back and start a family with him.

A family . . .? Never, thought Libby, her anger rising.

And speaking of starting a family, your friend Rivka came by last week with her new baby son. She asked after you, and was sorry she did not see you in the months after you married, as she was confined to bed rest, poor girl. Her little Asher is a beautiful boy, as I hope you will see for yourself when you come home soon.

Rivka . . . They had been best friends throughout school, and then had worked together at the Gold Eagle Dressworks, sharing lunches and confidences as long as she could remember. Then Rivka had married Samuel, her childhood sweetheart, and re-treated into a cocoon of domesticity. Libby had tried hard not to feel abandoned, but something had shifted between them. When Libby, her own marriage approaching, had tried to confess to Rivka that she was not in love with Mr. Greenblatt, that she sometimes thought about running away, Rivka, her belly just beginning to swell with child, had smiled knowingly and said, "Oh, Libby, once you're married you will grow out of these childish notions . . ."

Annoyed, Libby had not raised the subject again. Now, too late, she realized that Rivka had only been trying to help, and had been looking at Libby's life through the lens of her own happy mar-riage and loving husband. She ached for her closest friend, and wished suddenly there were some way to be sitting with her right now. She would tell her all about Peter Eberle's crooked smile and sense of humor, and ask for her advice. Seeing Peter yesterday had shaken her, as much as she had tried to act as if it did not. She wondered if he might come back to the Rose house, and if she would be there when he did.

There were only a few more lines of the letter, about her grand-father's ailing health, about a new hat store opening on Ludlow

Street, and then another plea for her to return. She refolded the thin paper and was about to put it back in the envelope when she noticed a miniscule note written on the back, in her sister's hand.

Mama asked me to mail this for her, and I steamed it open to write to you. Papa is so angry, Libby, he broods and rages all day. Please come home. I am afraid if you do not, it will kill him. Becca.

Rebecca was always prone to melodrama, thought Libby, and yet . . . what if her father really was ill? With a troubled heart, she set the letter aside, and stared for a long time at the rain outside the window.

———

The facade of the Portland police station featured a marble pediment and an imposing stoop surmounted by wrought-iron railings and two glass-globed lights. From the rear, the building was an inexpressive expanse of dull red brick, soaked and dripping from the recent heavy rains. The yard beyond contained a few unhitched police carriages (the horses being snugly stabled next door), a great deal of mud, and one very damp fourteen-year-old. Half-Cent attracted little attention, huddling under the small wooden overhang above the building's rear entrance, since he was a familiar sight to the officers who came in and out. He was as much a fixture at the police station as he was at the *Gazette* offices, having proven his use many times as a delivery boy or messenger. Whenever one of the officers wanted a sandwich from Fanelli's, the cry would go up "Where's Billy-Boy?" and by now Billy only needed to be told the name of the officer to know what the lunch order would be.

The officers no longer took notice even when Half-Cent was standing close enough to their desks to eavesdrop, and thus he overheard many a conversation not meant for public consumption. This was how he had been one of the first to hear about the death up at the mill two days before, and that had been a lucky break for him, since now it appeared he was closer than ever before to his dream of becoming a real reporter.

Right now, Billy could hear the desk clerk chatting with some of the detectives through the back door. It had been left open most of the day in a vain attempt to dissipate the cigar smoke that thickened the air inside the station. The body at the Paperworks had been rarely mentioned, since most of the talk centered on a robbery at one of the warehouses down by the docks the night before, during which a gang of men had gotten away with over fifty sacks of flour and cornmeal. It was the third such foodstuffs robbery in a row—the night before the warehouse break-in twenty sides of beef had been lifted from the icehouse of the largest wholesale butcher in town, and the night before that it had been a barrel of butter and a pallet of fifty-pound wheels of cheese taken from a local dairy.

The laughing investigators were now calling the culprits the Cinderella Gang, since one of them had foolishly left behind in the granary a loden felt cap with the initials LW sewn inside. The general tone of the banter indicated that the officers found in this easily traced clue proof that the criminals of Portland were all a bunch of idiots. Privately, listening to the juvenile jokes and snide laughter, Billy thought that the criminals couldn't hold a candle to the police in that particular department. On and off, over and over, the policemen debated how large the Cinderella Gang must be, since it must have taken at least a few men to shift the amount of goods stolen in a short amount of time. Frequently the conversation would shift off this scintillating topic, and then Billy would hear the name Rose mentioned. From what little he had gathered on that score, it seemed that Officer Macon was off somewhere trying to ascertain the identity of the now-mysterious body in the hollander.

Billy managed to cajole one officer, who stepped outside for a breath of fresh air, into an actual conversation. Officer Stimson was an avuncular, older cop with a face like St. Nick, and he always tipped Billy a nickel when the boy brought him lunch or an evening paper. All he could offer today was the information that until the body was identified the police were at a standstill. They had pretty much decided that whoever the dead man was, he had also been the one attempting to murder Hiram Rose. Billy had his doubts about that, since it seemed to him a fellow would have to be pretty stupid to cut through the supports of a scaffolding catwalk and then clamber all over it. Especially when it was suspended over some sort of machine made out of knives! But Officer Stimson didn't ask his opinion (no one ever did), so Billy merely nodded and continued hanging around the back door, hoping for something more concrete he could report to Mr. Eberle. Casting an expert eye at the gathering clouds, Billy prayed Macon would return to the station before the rain started again.

His prayers were answered before long. Macon came riding into the yard a few minutes after Stimson went back inside, and dismounted just a few steps from where Billy stood.

"Take your horse over to the stable for you, sir?" Billy smiled as ingratiatingly as he could.

"Thanks, Billy-Boy. Been riding most of the morning. Don't know why they have to put these paper mills so far outside the city."

"Out at the Rose Paperworks again? Another body?" Billy asked excitedly.

"No, nothing like that, kid. Actually I was just over at Willamette Papers, talking to Mr. Manning. It's no secret he threatened Rose once . . ." Macon trailed off. Though Billy waited, Macon appeared to have remembered Billy wasn't actually part of the force, and thus dropped the topic of his morning's errand. When next he spoke it was on a completely different subject. "Run over to Fanelli's for me, kid? I haven't eaten since breakfast. I'll have—"

". . . the turkey on a hard roll," finished Billy, as Macon laughed.

———

Thanks to Half-Cent's information, Peter was able to make it out to Willamette Fine Papers within an hour of Officer Macon's departure. His hope was to see Unsworth Manning while he might still be unsettled by his visit from the police.

The mill stood beside a wide, deep bend in the Willamette River, a few miles outside the city. Unlike the steam-powered Rose Paperworks, a giant waterwheel provided the electricity. The sky above was clear and unsullied by belching smokestacks, if still as gray and overcast as everywhere in Portland. Manning's mill was a good deal smaller than Hiram Rose's, but it was impressive nonetheless. The wall facing the road had a giant great blue heron, the mill's symbol, painted on it. Below that was the company name, executed in elaborately scrolled lettering. As Peter got closer to the door, however, he could see that the paint was peeling, and in more than one spot fresh plaster showed where the wall had been inexpertly patched.

Peter was able to talk himself into the factory's executive offices, but there he hit an impassible obstacle in the person of Manning's personal secretary, who absolutely refused him an audience with the gentleman himself.

"No appointment, no interview. Mr. Manning is very busy this afternoon."

"I would think," Peter tried one last time, undaunted, "that Mr. Manning might like to tell his side of the story. Otherwise the *Gazette* will just have to draw the best conclusions we can."

The secretary lowered his half-glasses and narrowed his eyes. "If that is meant as intimidation, sir, I'm afraid you are laboring under a misapprehension that Mr. Manning has anything to hide from the people of Portland."

"If he doesn't have anything to hide, perhaps he would like to discuss why the police just paid him a visit."

"Young man, I have work to do. I think it's time you saw yourself out—"

"Never mind, Mr. Bernard." A new voice came from behind Peter's left shoulder, and he spun around in time to see a distinguished, graying man continue, "I will be happy to speak to the press. As you say, I have nothing to hide." Unsworth Manning gestured to the door to his private office, which now stood open. "If you'll step this way, Mr. . . . ?"

"Eberle. Peter Eberle, *Portland Gazette*." The door shut behind him, leaving a sour-faced Mr. Bernard to turn back to his ledger.

Manning's office was filled with white winter light. Three large, uncurtained windows with the blinds raised high gave a stunning view of the Willamette's steel-gray waters as they rushed by.

"I suppose you're here in regard to my recent visit from the police. Well, I see no reason not to tell you what I told them, though I must say you gentlemen of the press certainly waste no time. I wonder that Officer Macon has even made it back to the station yet." Manning's tone was polite, and tinged with an almost courtly humor, and Peter couldn't help but marvel at the contrast between him and the choleric Hiram Rose. "Please, have a seat."

Peter took one of the well-worn wooden armchairs facing the desk, while Manning settled himself behind it. He decided directness was the best tack to take. "Mr. Manning, was it one of your employees who was found dead at the Rose Paperworks?"

Manning gave a simple declarative, as if testifying in a witness box. "No." Then, as if realizing that might have sounded brusque, he amended, "You may confirm that with my foreman, if you like, though I assure you Officer Macon did just that. All my men are accounted for."

Peter was stymied for a moment. He had been sure this must have been why the police were interested in Manning. "You and Hiram Rose are known to be enemies. Surely it's no surprise that the police added you to a list of people who might want to harm him."

Manning looked at him, obviously reading more into Peter's comment than intended. "If you're alluding to that altercation at Erickson's Saloon, I'll admit it, my temper was a bit out of control, but you must understand that this was just a few weeks after Hiram pulled that ridiculous stunt with his workers. I was quite upset . . . for myself, yes, but also for those fine men Hiram just let go without warning. And at Christmas, too! Though I suppose that wouldn't carry much weight with Mr. Rose." He placed the gentlest of cultured sneers into his pronunciation of the altered Jewish surname. "I can't believe a man of the world, such as yourself, would place too much weight on the words of a man who had, shall we say, a few too many drinks. It was a threat, technically, but barely. And believe me, if I had really wanted to kill him, he wouldn't have walked out of there alive that night. I certainly wouldn't have waited until now, and then constructed some elaborate trap."

Manning sounded unruffled, despite the fact that he was discussing murder. He was so smooth, almost too smooth, and Peter could see that beneath the gracious exterior Manning must be, in his own way, as ruthless a competitor as Rose.

Unsworth Manning cleared his throat and smiled. "I think, Mr. Eberle, that my visit from the police this morning constitutes nothing more than a little game on Hiram's part. He as good as sent them here with his wild conjectures, hoping to unnerve me. But I am not easily unnerved."

Unnerved, no. But perhaps jealous? "With all due respect, sir, there seems to be a rumor to the effect that Mr. Rose's 'ridiculous stunt' has turned out well, financially speaking."

"Yes, but what Hiram doesn't like to advertise is that it was something of a last ditch effort to save his mill. He may be turning a profit now, thanks to the pittance he pays those poor Orientals, but the quality of the product will suffer. Not that it matters much either, I suppose. To tell you the truth, Mr. Eberle, both Hiram and I are dinosaurs. Tell me, how much do you know about papermaking?"

Peter admitted that it was next to nothing. Manning took a sheet of paper from his drawer, rose from his desk, and crossed to a window. He cocked his head to indicate Peter should join him. "You see that? That is a sheet of our finest rag paper, 20-lb stock, deckled edge." Manning's voice held something akin to rapture, and it was clear he loved his chosen career. Peter, while he couldn't get all that excited by the sheet of blank paper Manning pressed into his hands, had to admit it was a fine specimen. It was a pale cream color, heavy, with a surface texture almost like a fine piece of wood. And when he held it up to the light he could see that the blue crane, the same one painted on the side of the building, was woven into the paper as a watermark.

"It's . . . very nice," Peter said, attempting to sound enthusiastic.

Manning's glow faded, and he turned back toward his desk. "In five years there won't be a rag paper mill anywhere in Oregon. No matter how many tricks Hiram pulls, no matter how he tries to delay the inevitable, his mill can't go on the way it is. He's not a stupid man, Mr. Eberle. He knows as well as I do that we must either change or perish."

Peter knew just a little about the paper industry. "I assume you're referring to the advent of wood pulp paper?"

"Horrible, pale imitation paper. Flimsy and brittle . . . and too smooth, no nap to help distribute the ink evenly . . ." Manning sat down with a sigh, "Before you can make paper, you have to convert some raw material into cellulose, and rags—especially fine quality linen—are far more expensive than wood. Look around you, Mr. Eberle. If there's one thing we have a surplus of in Oregon, it's wood!"

Despite himself, Peter was interested. He had never given much thought to the manufacture of paper, but he had assumed it almost didn't matter which raw material was used in the process. "So why can't you stop using rags and start using wood? Your mill seems well-equipped for any type of paper manufacture. "

Manning laughed. "It's clear you are not in the business, sir! Were we to change over, we would be purchasing whole logs, stripping them of their bark, and reducing them to pulp. All those tasks require quite a different set of equipment than those used to rip linen and fine cloth. As you can see, we would need to bring in several new pieces of heavy machinery, probably imported from back East. And all that takes money. Certainly more money than I . . ." He stopped himself. "But I am digressing. I can hardly imagine the *Gazette* wants to run a feature on the nuances of papermaking. Let's just say that wood pulp is the future, and progress cannot be stopped." He smiled at Peter to indicate the interview was at an end.

Peter tried one last time to get a rise out of the man. "Well, someone is trying to stop Hiram Rose, for whatever reason."

"As I've indicated, I have no reason to wish Hiram Rose ill. That wouldn't help me at all—though in fairness, it would cause me no grief either. I have no idea who might want him dead, but whoever they are, they have my blessing!"

———

A shadowed, bluish light was all that filtered through the high windows into the city morgue. The room was located beneath street level, the better to keep it cool even in the midst of summer. At the end of a rainy winter afternoon, it gave a visitor the feeling of entering a grave.

On a laying-out table in the center of the floor sat a small bundle—far too small, it seemed, to be the body of a man—covered with the requisite white cotton cloth. On one side of the table stood the morgue attendant, and at the almost imperceptible nod from the man standing opposite, he drew back the cloth just far enough to reveal what remained of the torso recovered from the hollander at the Rose Paperworks.

The other man stared down at the mangled remains, holding his breath against the stench (although the morgue attendant seemed unaffected), before spotting a small cluster of freckles near what had once been a right shoulder. His knees started to buckle as he uttered one choked half-sob, but he righted himself without assistance. Clearing his throat he said solemnly, "Yes, it's him. That's my brother Matt."

FOUR

THE NIGHT AIR FELT pleasantly cool and damp on Anna Karlsson's face as she crept out of the door into the small patch of straggly grass they laughingly called a garden. The house had become so stuffy, filled with the overloud voices of too many men, and the thick smell of too many cigars and shots of whiskey. The third time Plug McFerley pinched her bottom, it had been too much for her. She had made her escape through the kitchen, stopping just long enough to tuck a bottle of whiskey under her skirt, and check on her nephew. Pim was still sitting by the stove, happily playing with some bits of string his mother Tilda had given him. He looked peaceful, so she reasoned he would be fine if she took a moment for herself outside. Anna wondered how much Pim even understood of what was happening, lost as he was in his silent world.

Leaning against the stone wall, she raised the bottle of whiskey to her lips and took a generous swig. As the burning in her throat underwent that magical transformation into a warm tingle she could feel all the way to her fingertips, her tension began to lessen. She wanted to cry, but she swallowed her tears and turned her grief into anger. She shouldn't be waiting hand and foot on a group of drunk and disgruntled men. Not on this night of all others. Most of the men in the house hadn't even known Matt very well. Still, they had arrived at the house in a steady stream all evening to pay their respects, ever since word of Matt's death had spread through the tight-knit community. Most were friends of Dutch's. Like him, they had lost their jobs at the paper mill and had no work for which to be up in the morning. Anna had been given no time to grieve herself, since Mummo had taken to her bed the minute the news had reached them. Tilda, Anna's sister-in-law, had been sent to the apothecary for a sleeping powder.

She took another draw from the whiskey bottle, longer this time, and closed her eyes as the warmth spread through her body. She was suddenly too tired to stand, and she sank gratefully onto the low bench by the door. A voice interrupted her reverie. "Hello?" Her eyes sprang open to see yet another man at the front gate.

"Is this the Karlsson house?" he asked, unsure.

This one was better dressed than the others and had a pleasing smile, but Anna was in no mood to be charmed.

"They're all inside," she said brusquely. But the man didn't move to enter the house. He was handsome, more than she had realized at first, and then she was ashamed of herself for noticing.

The man bowed his head for a moment, removing his hat. "I'm Peter Eberle, with the *Portland Gazette*. I hope I'm not intruding, but I was hoping to find out more information about Matt Karlsson. I'm so very sorry." He paused for a moment, trying to place her.

She tried, as unobtrusively as possible, to tuck the whiskey bottle behind the bench. She hoped he had not observed her drinking straight from the bottle, like some slattern. "I am Anna Karlsson." She rose and extended her hand.

Peter looked flustered. "I didn't realize Matt was married."

She almost laughed, and wondered if she was drunk. "No, no, I am his sister." At once, the smile left her face as she remembered why this man had come. "Was his sister . . ." The thought of Matt was like a knife in her chest. Dear, sweet Matt, who played with Pim for hours on his day off, who swung him around the kitchen to a tune that only one of them could hear, whose smile could light up a room. Now he was gone, and his death was a story for the newspapers to sensationalize. "Fine, come in," she said, opening the door wider. "You'll want to speak to my brother Jan, I suppose."

Peter followed her into the small house, ducking through the doorway. The kitchen was dominated by a large stone fireplace with a stove inset in it, but even the roaring fire could not prevent a chill from the corners of the room. A small boy sitting by the stove didn't look up as Peter entered, lost in some game he was playing with pieces of wood and string.

Anna quickly crossed to a half-open doorway, and called "Jan?" into what Peter assumed was the parlor. The sounds of male laughter and the odor of cigar smoke could be easily discerned through the opening. Within a moment a compact muscular man with an open face was shaking his hand. "I am Jan Karlsson, but please, call me Dutch, that is what everyone calls me." His accent was so slight as to be almost nonexistent, but Peter sensed that English was not his first language. He had not heard any trace of an accent in the voice of Anna, who was now kneeling beside the boy on the floor. Perhaps Jan had been born in the old country, while Anna had never known anything but America. Was she older than her brother Matt had been, or younger? Peter realized how little he knew about the dead man and his family.

"Peter Eberle, *Portland Gazette*. I'm very sorry about your brother."

"Please, sit." Dutch gestured at a chair by the stove and took the other across from Peter. The small boy jumped into his lap, and Dutch ruffled the boy's hair absentmindedly. At that, the boy looked up with a big grin, and then noticed Peter for the first time. Obviously agitated, a noise emerged from his throat unlike anything Peter had ever heard, something like the cry of a wounded animal.

"Shush, shush . . ." Gently, Dutch stroked the boy's cheek until he was silent again. "This is my son, Pim. He gets overly excited," he explained to Peter. "Did Annika tell you? The boy is deaf."

Anna, who was observing the scene from the doorway, said, "I didn't tell Mr. Eberle anything, Jan. I thought you would want to talk to him yourself."

"Where is Tilda?"

"She went to get a sleeping powder for Mummo."

Dutch turned again to Peter. "My mother hasn't taken the news well. None of us have, of course . . . Mathias . . . Matt . . . was a fine man and a dear brother, and I will miss him." For a moment, it seemed as if he was going to cry, but he composed himself.

Peter looked around the small room, his reporter's eye noticing the lack of firewood, the unmended floorboards. The Karlsson's clearly had little money to spare, but the rough-hewn table beside the sink was piled with several plates and pie tins that he assumed were the offerings of friends and neighbors. A few burlap bags of staples rested on shelves beside the stove. Peter wondered if those were donations from the neighbors as well. Pulling out his notebook, he turned to the siblings. "May I ask you some questions? I know readers of the *Gazette* will want to know about your brother, and I want to paint as true a picture of him as I can."

It was Anna who replied. "You think Matt was a murderer! That's right, isn't it?" Her eyes welled with tears. "That's why you are here."

Her brother calmly led her to a chair by the fire. "Sit, Annika, I'll talk to him. We should tell people about Matt, who he was, that he was a good man. That is the only way to fight these ugly rumors." He turned to Peter. "I believe the police are saying Matt was trying to kill Mr. Rose when he fell."

Peter nodded almost imperceptibly, incredibly uncomfortable. Anna's words had stung him, for while he truly did want to know what sort of man Matt was, he was only here doing this interview because of the manner and location of Matt's death.

"My brother was not a murderer, Mr. Eberle. There must be another explanation for his death."

"Can you think of any reason that Matt might have been at the mill that early in the morning, before anyone else arrived?" Peter queried.

Dutch's open face held not a trace of guile. "No, I'm afraid that's as much of a mystery to us as to the police . . ." he trailed off as he remembered the police did have a theory. "You know Matt works . . . worked . . . for the Rose family. Perhaps he was there on an errand for Mr. Rose or Mr. Fowler."

"According to both of them that was not the case." Peter tried to be as gentle as he could as he moved ahead. He had learned from the police that Dutch and the elder Mr. Karlsson—the father of Jan Jr. (Dutch), Anna, and Matt—had been among the workers let go from the Rose Paperworks. "I understand that both you and your father used to work at the mill. Is it possible that Matt was trying to harm Mr. Rose as some sort of revenge?"

"Believe me, Mr. Eberle, my family had reasons aplenty to wish Mr. Rose ill. Not only because of the jobs we lost, but . . . My father, rest his soul, I don't believe he ever recovered from the shock of losing his job to a Chinaman. He had a stroke just a few weeks later, and he went fast after that. There was no fight at all left in him." Dutch and Anna shared a look, one of pure sorrow, and Peter realized that Matt's death made this a family twice bereaved in the space of just a few months.

"Surely you must see that it only strengthens the police's position? Surely it isn't crazy to think Matt might have blamed Hiram Rose for your father's death. And hated him enough to kill him."

"Crazy? No . . . but wrong!" Anna's voice was hot with rage. "Matt would never have—"

Her brother interjected in a more calm tone of voice. "Annika, please." Dutch went on, "I would have wrung Rose's neck gladly, I will tell you that freely, as would half the men in there." He gestured toward the parlor, where the impromptu wake for Matt seemed to be gathering steam. "But Matt wasn't like that. This was why he took the job at the Rose house in the first place, instead of coming to work with us at the mill. He loved the horses, and to work in the garden . . ." Tears welled in the corners of Dutch's eyes, and he buried his face into Pim's downy head and hugged the boy close to him. A sound like a purring cat escaped the boy.

Anna spoke, keeping her voice soft but clear. "The money Matt made was all we had, once Papa was gone and Jan had no work. Would my brother want to jeopardize that, Mr. Eberle?"

Peter shook his head. He had no answer.

"Isn't it strange that the man who robbed my family of a father and two incomes should have been its only hedge against starvation? What we will do now, I don't know. But I would swear with my dying breath that Matt would never have wished to put us in this position."

Peter marveled at the eloquence of a girl he had first seen swigging whiskey alone in the yard. He had taken her for a fragile and tragic figure, and that she was definitely not. Looking at her more closely, he saw that beyond her unkempt appearance and red-rimmed eyes she was quite attractive. Pale blond hair and fair skin complemented eyes the color of bluebells. He started to wonder where and how she had been educated, but focused again on the present when she continued to speak.

"Though it pains me to say anything nice about anyone in that family, Mrs. Fowler let Matt do extra jobs, for some additional income, when she heard that my father had passed away. We didn't know how we were going to be able to afford a funeral for Papa, but thanks to Mrs. Fowler, Matt managed to come up with it. Truly, all of our lives were dependent upon that household's generosity."

An elderly woman lurched into the room. She had obviously been crying, and her hair was standing on end, as if she had been pulling it. "Where is Tilda? Is she not back yet with my sleeping powder?" When she saw Peter, she stopped short.

"Mummo, this is Mr. Eberle, a reporter. We have been speaking to him about Mathias."

At the mention of her dead son's name, the woman began to wail. Immediately, Dutch handed Pim to Anna, and went to his mother's side, holding her to him. Eventually, she quieted down and turned to Peter. "You work for the newspaper, then? Maybe you can tell us, have the police found anything new about who killed him? My son, my son . . ." Once again, the tears flowed.

Highly uncomfortable at this show of raw emotion, Peter rose and began making his farewell. "Thank you for letting me take up your time. I know this is a sad evening, and I'm sure you wish to be alone with your family and friends." Peter made a gesture towards the parlor.

"You will tell us if there's any new information, please?" Dutch asked, his eyes meeting Peter's and begging him silently to let his mother hold on to the belief that her youngest son was an innocent victim.

"I will send round a copy of the newspaper tomorrow for you." Peter suspected there would be no good news in the paper for the Karlssons, but their expectant faces so obviously proclaimed they still hoped evidence would emerge to clear their adored family member of attempted murder. It was more than unlikely the Portland police would spend any time or energy communicating with this poor workman's family, while Hiram Rose could insist on, and receive, regular dispatches on the state of the case.

Anna saw Peter to the door, and then followed him as far as the garden gate. For a moment, gazing down into her pale upturned face with its smattering of freckles glowing in the fading light, he was seized with the impulse to kiss her. Then he was horrified at himself for indulging in such a base fantasy. Anna, meanwhile, had something else entirely on her mind.

"I don't know why my brother was at the mill. And I don't know who was trying to kill Hiram Rose. But you must believe me, it was not Matt. Please, say you believe me?"

Peter only half-nodded, but it seemed to satisfy her.

"Don't let them get away with it! Whoever it was who was trying to kill Mr. Rose killed my poor brother instead. You will find out the truth, won't you, Mr. Eberle?"

———

Libby arrived at the Rose home just minutes after the policeman departed. He had brought the shocking news, Miss Baylis whispered to Libby, that the body at the mill had been Matt Karlsson, the missing gardener and stable hand! After giving this information to Libby as if it were delicious gossip rather than unhappy tidings, the governess rushed off to tend to her napping charges.

Libby stepped tentatively into Adele's private sitting room, unsure what to expect. Adele was pretty thick skinned, but after all, Matt had been a member of the household, and the loss of someone one saw every day was never easy. At first Libby didn't spot Adele, so hidden was she by the draperies at the window. The mistress of the house was staring into the rear yard, but at the sound of the door she spun toward Libby. Her eyes were red, and a tear rolled down her plump cheek.

"Miss Seale," she chirped, as she wiped her face and fixed a glassy smile on her face. Clearly she was embarrassed at her display of emotion.

"Are you all right, Mrs. Rose? Perhaps you'd like me to return tomorrow."

"No, no . . ." she said, looking down. "It's just . . . look at that. Those policemen, their boots are so dirty! I feel like they tramp gallons of mud through the house. I must ask Mary to do an extra cleaning of this rug." She settled herself on a velvet divan and announced, "I want to see the new trim on that dress."

"Of course. Right away." Libby began to unpack her carpet bag. "I was sorry to hear about Mr. Karlsson."

"Karlsson? Oh, yes. Matt."

There was silence as Libby laid out the finished dress.

"Yes. Well, it looks all right. Perhaps I should try it on now."

Adele stepped behind the dressing screen in the corner. With a start, Libby realized she would actually be expected to help her customer in and out of her clothes. The other times they had met, this had been something done by her sister-in-law, but today Eva was nowhere to be seen. Libby crossed behind Adele and unhooked her dress. A sheen of perspiration speckled the heavy woman's neck, and there was a roll of flesh just above where her corset ended. Libby remembered a moue of distaste she had seen on Eva Fowler's face whenever she had stepped behind the screen to help her sister-in-law disrobe, and now she understood why.

Once the garment was fastened, the older woman regarded herself critically in the pier glass over the fireplace. As the moment stretched on Libby was afraid Mrs. Rose disliked the finished garment, but when Adele spoke it was not to comment on the dress. "Why would Matt want to kill Hiram?" There was genuine wonderment in her voice.

Libby was confused for a second, but quickly discerned the reason for the question. "The police believe Matt was the one behind the attempt on Mr. Rose's life?"

Adele nodded. "They seem quite sure he was involved. Of course, they need to be certain he didn't have someone helping him." She fingered the lace on her collar unconsciously. "To think we had a murderer here! In our house! Well, an attempted murderer, but we could all have been killed in our sleep!" She crossed behind the screen once more, and gestured to Libby to unlace her. "There must be someone else behind all this. Matt was just a stable boy! Oh, my poor Hiram! He might still be at risk."

Adele chattered on nervously as Libby helped her back into her clothes. She seemed to require no responses from Libby, merely steamrolling onward as she filled the seamstress in on the threatening letters her husband had received prior to the attack, and her own recent visit from the police.

"The officer asked if I thought Matt had written the letters. I told him I'm sure I don't have any idea whether he could even write, let alone know what his penmanship looked like! Not that I ever saw them. Mr. Rose would never want to worry me. Although I understand he didn't show them to anyone," she added, as if to assure Libby that her husband would of course have turned to her first. "Surely no one could wish Mr. Rose harm! He's one of the most important men in Portland, and think of all the good he has done for the community!"

Libby continued to hold her tongue, but she suspected Hiram Rose had more than one enemy. After all, not only was he a wealthy businessman, his personality was more abrasive than many others in his position. She did wonder why Matt might have been trying to attack his employer, but after all, she had never met him. Perhaps he was one of those young men who is naturally violent.

Adele had finally wound down, and Libby realized she was waiting for an answer. "I'm sorry," Libby said, smoothing the finished dress on her lap. "I was lost in thought for a moment, Mrs. Rose. Were you asking me something?"

"I said," Adele answered peevishly, "when might I expect the visiting suit to be ready?" Happy to have returned at last to the subject of dressmaking, Libby forgot all about Matt and murder. Between selecting trimmings and discussing bustle shapes, it was nearly an hour later when Libby finally packed up her supplies and prepared to go.

As Libby shrugged on her coat, she remarked that it was hard to imagine that spring would ever come, as it had been cold and rainy almost nonstop for the last several weeks. Surprisingly, Adele Rose began to cry again. Libby froze, feeling torn between comforting the woman and slipping away pretending she hadn't noticed. Her better nature won out, and she led the woman to a settee, sitting beside her.

"Is something wrong?" she asked, awkwardly.

"I'm concerned about Elliot. He's such a sensitive young man. He and his father do not always see eye to eye, but I know Elliot would be devastated if anything had happened to Hiram."

Adele went on, somewhat incoherently, and Libby wondered suddenly if perhaps the young man she was thinking of was not her son but the dead groom. Could Adele have been more sympathetic to the young servant than she had let on earlier?

———

As Libby headed down the wide flight of stairs, she realized she should try to find Mrs. Fowler before she left. Even if she were feeling ill, she might allow Libby to get her latest measurements, since (despite the upheaval in the household) certain things moved forward on an inexorable timeline. So at the foot of the stairs, Libby headed down the narrow hallway that led to the kitchen in the back of the house.

The cook and the two maids were sitting quietly at the table, drinking tea from chipped teacups deemed too shabby for use by the family. They all started nervously when they heard the door open. The cook pushed herself up from the table. "Can I help you?"

"No, Mrs. Reed, please, don't get up. I was wondering if you knew if Mrs. Fowler was at home next door."

"Please, honey, call me Celia . . . Yes, Mrs. Fowler is home, but I wouldn't go over there . . . she's been feeling poorly. She and Mr. Fowler eat their meals here, you know, and neither of them came to dinner last night. He came over afterward and took back a bit of soup and some bread, and said she's been in bed resting. Been in bed, mostly, since you took her home two days ago when there was all that business at the mill."

At the mention of the death at the mill, the two housemaids' demeanor underwent a marked change. "Oh, if I could've bottled the look on your face, Maisie, when you saw Mr. Rose at the door! Thought you was gonna die of fright, like he was a ghost!" Annie, the upstairs maid, laughed merrily at her colleague.

Maisie was indignant. "And I'd like to see how you would have handled opening the door to a dead man!" She turned to Libby. "You were there, you know how surprised we all were."

Before Libby could reply, Celia intervened. "Girls, settle down and finish your tea. Break time is nearly over." Turned back to her visitor, she continued where she left off. "All this fuss is not good for a woman in her condition. I know she looks strong enough and all, but this hasn't been an easy lying-in for her so far. And now the news about Matt, too, of course. That was a shock to us all."

At the mention of Matt, one of the maids let out a small cry, and Libby remembered these women probably knew him much better than the family did. "I was very sorry to hear about Mr. Karlsson," she said sympathetically to them both. "It can't be easy learning such a horrible thing has happened to somebody you know." The memories of her own friend Vera's tragic murder came into her mind.

"It's a sad day here, for sure," Celia agreed. "Matt was such a good boy. Sweet. He took such care with the garden, and was always so gentle with the horses . . ." It occurred to Libby that this description didn't jibe with the man the police believed Matt had been, but she also knew that people tended to say only nice things about the recently departed. In any case, it was none of her business. The cook enveloped the maid in her ample bosom. "Now Annie, you just stop that sniffling, child. Come here . . ." Libby, suddenly feeling she was intruding, turned to leave.

"Mrs. . . . . Celia, will you please send a message to Mrs. Fowler that I hope she is feeling better soon. And do you think it would be all right if I drop off some fabric samples for her tomorrow?"

"That should be fine, dear. You can just leave them with me if she's still too ill for visitors. I know she's grateful to have you around to let out her dresses. Certainly couldn't do it herself! Let me tell you, when that girl was a child, I tried to teach her some sewing, and all she did was poke herself with the needle so much her hands looked like pincushions!"

Libby wondered what Eva was like as a girl; she sounded like she might have been as tomboyish as Libby herself had been, and yet the respectable matron Libby had met, though a tall and solid woman, certainly exhibited all the airs and polish of a woman of wealth and breeding. Libby smiled at Celia. "Thank you, then. I guess I'll be on my way. Good day."

Crossing through the back hall to the back door, she heard the sound of more crying, and for a moment she thought the maid, Mary, had followed her out. But as she passed the entrance to the pantry, she spied Elliot curled up in the corner. Although he stopped immediately when he saw her, his tear-stained face left no doubt that he had been sobbing. Dear lord, thought Libby, does no one do anything in this household but break down? Immediately, she felt guilty. The boy was obviously upset, and she knew it was no picnic being sixteen years old even at the best of times.

"Elliot . . . hello."

"Hello, Miss Seale. Were you with my mother and Aunt Eva?"

"Just your mother. I understand your aunt is not feeling too well."

"Good!" There was real venom in his voice. "I hope she . . ." He stopped short and adopted a more neutral tone. "I mean to say, I'm not surprised. My aunt is often unwell these days. I think she sometimes makes up stories to get attention."

Libby was shocked at his vehemence. She remembered that the boy hadn't wanted to walk his aunt home the day of his father's resurrection, but she had thought that was merely a passing moodiness. "That's not a very kind thing to say."

"I'm tired of being kind! Why does everyone place such a premium on kindness, anyway? My father's not kind, and everyone respects him despite that . . . or perhaps because of it." Libby silently agreed, as Elliot, sensing a sympathetic audience, went on. "Miss Seale, can I ask you a question?"

"Of course, Elliot." Involuntarily, she reached out and smoothed his wrinkled collar. He blinked at her, and ran his hand across his face, wiping away the last of his tears.

"What would you do if you had a falling out with a good friend, and before you had a chance to apologize, he . . ." Elliot looked like a little boy for an instant. ". . . he died? How can you go on, knowing you missed your chance forever to apologize for things you said in the heat of anger?"

"Matt was a good friend of yours, wasn't he?" Her voice was gentle.

"He was my . . ." Elliot had been about to use the phrase "best friend," but he realized it sounded childish, so he changed course. "He was the only person around here I could talk to. Mother thinks she understands art, but really she's just parroting back whatever she hears at her ladies' socials, and Father thinks all art is a waste of time. Maybe Matt didn't have much schooling, but he let me help in the garden, and he would talk about the colors of the flowers. How colors sometimes shimmered when you put them next to each other. He would look at my paintings and talk to me about them like I was an adult. And sometimes he let me . . ."

He decided not to tell her about the cigarettes. He doubted she would tattle on him, but better to be safe.

"He sounds like a good friend for an artist to have." Libby was unsure what else to say. Unfortunately, no platitudes or kind words could take away the pain of a lost friend, as she knew all too well. "I recently lost a close friend as well," she admitted. "I had not known her long, but I met her soon after moving to Portland, and she helped me feel at home in this strange city so far from New York."

Elliot brightened. "New York. . . . Why would anyone want to leave there? You know, I want to go to art school, Miss Seale! My first choice is the Sorbonne, of course, although Father has said I'll go to Europe over his dead body. But my second choice is New York . . . all those museums! And the artists in salons, discussing their craft and painting in garrets . . . will you tell me all about it someday?"

"Slow down, Elliot, I'll be happy to tell you more about New York someday, even though the area I lived in was about as far from the salons and museums as you can get while still being in the same city. Although, come to think of it, there was a beautiful mural painted on a building near my father's fruit stand. Of course it was an advertisement for soap, but does that count?"

He laughed. She reflected how easy it was for children his age to go from tears to laughter, their emotions quick and vivid like a summer storm. Smiling, he almost looked like a different boy, and she realized that she had only seen him looking sullen before this. With an eager grin on his face and his chocolate eyes ringed by long lashes, bright with enquiry, his face was transformed. Libby thought that soon he would mature into a very attractive man. "I really must go now, but someday soon I promise to tell you more about Manhattan."

———

The stable yard behind the house was a sea of mud by the time Hiram, astride his favorite mare Frieda, arrived home from the mill. Wilmer Stubbins, a stooped black man in his late fifties who had come west with Adele when she was a young bride, stood shivering in the driving rain. He swore he could feel the cold and wet settling into his very bones. At this moment he longed more than life itself for the mild winters of southern Georgia, where he had been raised on Adele's family plantation.

Rubbing his arms for warmth, Wilmer thought about Matt. Tragic, it was, to die so young. What was the foolish boy doing there inside the paper mill anyhow? If only he'd stayed out of whatever mess he got himself into. If only he were here I would have him standing out in this icy twilight waiting to stable Mr. Rose's horse.

"You'll blanket her tonight?" Rose barked as he dismounted, spurning the offered assistance of Wilmer's arm. "The last thing I need now is a sick mare." Hiram petted the horse's neck, with more tenderness than he was wont to show people.

"Yes, sir." Wilmer murmured, knowing Hiram wasn't waiting for an answer.

The first arrow came out of nowhere. Perhaps because of the rain, it was wide of the mark, hitting the side of the stable with a singing thwack. For a split second, both men were frozen in shock. Then Frieda reared, whinnying loudly.

Rose yelled "Hold her!" and both men pulled hard at her reins. Even with their combined weight, for a moment it seemed she would break free and run wild.

A second arrow came from the woods, this time coming near Hiram's sleeve before striking the woodpile under the eaves. Wilmer could have sworn the arrow missed his employer completely, but Hiram cursed loudly, and rubbed his arm. Both men looked over the lawn to the trees beyond. Wilmer cried out, "I think he's by the garden shed!" knowing he should offer to go investigate for his master. But his knees were still shaking, and he was relieved when Rose himself ran off toward the assailant, calling back over his shoulder, "For god's sake, man, get that horse inside the stables!"

With difficulty, Wilmer led the high-strung animal into her stall. He placed a blanket over her back and fed her, all the while murmuring to her, "It's all right, Frieda, nothing going to harm you. There, there . . ." Outside he could hear Rose yelling, then the sound of broken branches and footsteps running. Not wanting to be seen by the mysterious archer, Wilmer peered carefully out of the stable door. As he watched, an out-of-breath Rose came out of the woods and crossed the lawn, looking disgruntled.

"He got away, the scoundrel! I saw him, he was behind the shed. When I yelled, he went running away through the woods."

Still panting, he stopped at the woodpile, pulling the arrow out. He felt its sharp tip with his finger and winced. "He was too fast for me, dammit. Once I could have caught him, but I'm an old man now. Look . . . this could have killed me!" He held out the arrow and pointed to a fresh tear in his coat sleeve.

"You were very brave, sir. And you saw the man, that's something. Perhaps your description will help the police identify him."

"I don't know, maybe. He had light hair, and he was obviously a young man . . . he ran quite fast." He trailed off. "Wilmer, I want you to go to town and fetch the police." He thought for a moment. "And don't take the horse. She's had enough excitement for one day. You can walk."

As a dispirited Wilmer set off on the long wet walk to town, he turned to see Hiram still standing in the rainy yard, stroking his chin and staring intently at the darkening wood.

FIVE

After a hard rain had fallen all through the night, Wednesday morning dawned clear. That didn't stop the roads from being a mess, and as Peter dismounted from his horse the first six inches of his trousers were splattered with mud. As he had for most of the ride, he asked himself again what it was he hoped to discover at the Rose Paperworks. Mostly, he thought, it was because of Anna Karlsson. The look she'd given him the night before last, as she'd beseeched him to clear her brother's name, had worn a groove in his mind. In some inexplicable way he felt obligated to her, and the only way he could see his way clear of the obligation was to attempt to extract some new information from the scene of the crime.

Traipsing into the mill, he managed to locate Alex Smirnikoff, the Russian he had met on his earlier visit. Without too much prodding he was able to get the man talking about the accident, and within a few minutes he found himself back on the catwalks looking down into the now clean and shining hollander.

"It is quite amazing, no? You would never guess that it was covered in blood just a few days ago." Smirnikoff sounded like a proud parent as he gazed with Peter over the edge of the machine, its interior a mass of blades moving so quickly that all Peter could see was a swirling cloud of what looked like white pancake batter churning in its enormous drum.

Peter's questions thus far had been vague at best. He was hard-pressed to say why, exactly, but standing here, only feet from where Matt had died, he felt more certain than before that something was not right about the police theory. Dutch and Anna had made a persuasive case that it would have been against Matt's interests to attack his boss, and it seemed awfully convenient that the police's only suspect was already dead. Making Matt the culprit as well as the victim allowed them to close the case without even pursuing any other avenues. Besides, Peter liked the Karlsson family, and they seemed so sure of Matt's innocence.

He surveyed the mill floor below. It looked much as it had the last time, rows of workers sorting rags into bins, others throwing them into machinery or collecting the output at the other end. He watched a small woman, no more than five feet tall, trundle one overflowing bin across the floor and start to empty it into a larger trolley. From nowhere, Matson the foreman was upon her. "What are you doing? I told you to wait when you fill a bin—it's not your job to roll it! Go back, go back!" He pointed at her station, and the frightened woman, probably unable to understand a word, scurried back to her stool.

"Matson keeps everything running smoothly," Peter remarked.

Alex nodded vigorously. "Yes, he is, how do you say in English, a tight ship!" Peter smiled, but didn't correct him, and after a moment, Alex returned to the subject at hand. "After they pull out the man, it was a bad job to go in and clean this, I tell you, Mister. Everything was broken, even after I scrub everything and clean and clean. I climb out, I turn the switch, and pffft, nothing happen. Is funny, you know what it was? What make the whole big machine stop working?"

Peter started to guess, but, lost in his own train of thought, Alex went on before waiting for a reply. "It was a key, a little key, stuck way down between the blades. Ha! How about that, a big machine and it can be broken by one key as big only as this!" He held up two fingers to demonstrate.

"A key . . ." A light went off in Peter's head. The police had said that no door or window had been opened by force the night of Matt's death, so of course he must have had a key. But why would Matt have a key to the mill? It wasn't much, but he could follow up on it. "Alex, did you know Dutch Karlsson, who used to work here?" At Smirnikoff's nod, Peter went on. "Did you ever meet his brother Matt?"

"This is the man who was in—" Alex gestured to the now shining hollander and swallowed. "No, no . . . he is never here with his brother."

"Yes, but Matt worked for Mr. Rose. Did he ever bring messages to the mill? Sometimes he drove Mr. Rose in to work. I've been told he was a good-looking young man, just into his twenties."

Alex shook his head sadly. "No, I know nothing of someone like who you speak of. The first I know of him is—" He looked down at the machine below again.

Peter looked again at the giant vat of knives, shuddering at the thought of dying in its clutches. He started to get dizzy, and looked back at Alex. A thought occurred to him.

"Was that the only piece of metal you found? I would have thought you'd have found plenty, not just a key. What about tools, a saw, whatever he used to cut the platform? Surely they fell in there with him . . ." Peter's voice trailed off.

Alex shook his head. "I do not think so. You can ask Mr. Matson. Perhaps he can tell you. All I know is what I found inside. I am the only one who cleans in there, you understand? None of the others are in there while I work, and I am telling you I did not see any saw."

Interesting, thought Peter. This proved Matt couldn't have been at the mill alone that night! Someone had walked off with the saw and the tools used to booby trap the scaffold. Which meant that if Matt had been working with someone, that partner had just left him in the hollander to die slowly. An accomplice, though, or a murderer? Was Matt merely clumsy, or had the other man intended for Matt to die . . . perhaps to send some sort of message to Hiram Rose about the seriousness of the threats contained in the letters?

Surely the police would at least have to reopen the investigation now. Peter pictured Anna's smiling face, thanking him as he delivered the news, and the image made him feel happier than he had in weeks. Was he sweet on Anna Karlsson? Was that why he was here, grasping at straws to prove Matt Karlsson innocent? That would show Libby, he thought. Show her he wasn't carrying a torch for her. Which he wasn't, he told himself. But the bright happiness of the moment before was suddenly gone.

"I'm asking you for the last time, Mr. Karlsson, where were you the night of March 14th?"

Dutch Karlsson sat across from Detective Macon in the parlor of the Karlsson home, arms crossed. He repeated the same answer he had given for the last half hour. "I would prefer not to say. You have my word, I wasn't at the mill with my brother."

The smaller of the two policeman laughed, more of a bark really, and turned to Macon. "You hear that? We have his word of honor for it." Turning back to Dutch, the smile left his face, replaced by a cold stare.

Macon intervened. "Listen here, Karlsson. I'm sure it has nothing to do with the goings-on at the mill, but don't you see? I've got to answer to my sergeant. Someone shot a bunch of arrows at Hiram Rose yesterday, and that someone is probably the same someone who was with your brother at the Paperworks. Now, you claim you were here yesterday around five. But, conveniently enough, the only one with you was your deaf son."

Macon's tone was accusatory, as if somehow Dutch planned for his son to be deaf just to hamper the police's ability to question him. "Okay. Suppose I take you at your 'word of honor' for yesterday. That still leaves you open for the night that your brother was killed."

The little policeman rubbed his jaw theatrically. "Say, Macon. If I see it right, we're looking for someone close to this fella's brother . . . someone who also has a grudge against Hiram Rose. Didn't you say our pal Dutch here recently got the boot from Rose's mill?

And he's got no alibi . . . well, no real alibi . . . for either attack. Seems to me the pieces are starting to add up."

Macon took over the conversation smoothly. "Let's not jump to conclusions. Mr. Karlsson, if it wasn't you shooting arrows and cutting through scaffolds, perhaps you have some idea who it might have been? Do you have any idea who might have been with your brother when he broke into Rose's mill?"

Dutch looked pained. "Believe me, Officer Macon, I wish I knew what my brother was doing there that night. And I wish I had an idea who was there with him. I'd cut whoever it was to ribbons without the help of a hollander, and then you wouldn't need to bother yourself about this any more. He left Matt there to die!" Dutch's head sunk to his chest. "But I just don't know."

Macon sighed, "You don't know. But you must know where you were that night, if you weren't at the mill. Just tell us that, and if we can verify it we'll be out of your hair and out of your house."

Dutch stared resolutely ahead. His wife Tilda could bear it no longer, and despite having been sent to the kitchen, she barged into the parlor doorway, saying, "Lord's sake, Dutch, just tell them where you were that night! I know you had nothing to do with this, but you must tell them everything you know or they will think the worst!" She was a sturdy, forbidding woman, with a sharp nose and eyes narrowed to slits in anger, and the policemen both listened to her respectfully before requesting that she please leave them to their business.

"It is fine, Tilda," said Dutch, and his wife reluctantly withdrew.

In the kitchen, the women in the family all huddled by the stove, trying to shield Pim from the scene unfolding in the next room. His grandmother fed him cookies from a nearly empty tin, making a game of it as she reached for the last crumbs in it. Anna stood with her back to them, stirring a large pot on the stove. All three women jumped when they heard the front door slam shut.

———

The air around the Portland police station was ripe with the smell of horse manure. As Peter approached, it occurred to him that, all told, this story was one of the worst-smelling he had ever covered. Before mounting the marble steps, he hesitated, trying to think of the best way to approach Detective Macon, whom Half-Cent had discovered was the senior officer assigned to the investigation.

But his forethought was wasted, as it turned out. Macon was not available, although the desk sergeant lazily promised to pass along a message. "Mr. Eberle, is it? With the *Oregonian*?"

"The *Portland Gazette*, but close enough. He knows who I am."

The sergeant shrugged, failing to see the difference. Obviously not a daily newspaper reader, thought Peter.

"If Macon is not available, perhaps I could speak to one of the men on his team. I have just been to the Rose Paperworks, and I have some information to share." When this elicited no response, Peter went on. "I have proof that Matt Karlsson could not have been acting alone when he fell to his death and, indeed, may have been an innocent bystander."

At that, the sergeant raised his brows. "That's not news here, Mr. Eberle. You can go tell your boss at the *Oregonian*—" Peter gritted his teeth but said nothing, "—that the police investigation has turned up several leads as to the identity of Matt Karlsson's accomplice. It's obvious he wasn't acting alone, because someone took a few shots at Hiram Rose last night. As far as I know, dead men can't shoot arrows."

"Yesterday? Where was this?"

"Some fellow in the woods. Out by Rose's house, when he got home from work. Don't worry, once we have our man in custody, we'll be sure to inform the press. We're pretty sure we know who it was, so it shouldn't be long now."

Peter had a sinking feeling that he knew exactly who their main suspect would turn out to be. And he didn't need to wait long for confirmation. There was a sudden commotion as the door to the station opened behind him, and when he turned he saw Dutch Karlsson being led in by two policemen.

Dutch met his eyes and for a moment confusion crossed his features, as if he was unable to place him. But then recognition dawned, and he gave a sheepish smile as he motioned to his captors. "Just a misunderstanding," he said quietly to Peter, as the trio passed by the front desk.

Events were moving too fast for Peter to make sense of them all at once. Someone had been shooting arrows at Hiram Rose the day before, and the police believed it was Dutch Karlsson. Did they have some proof? Or was it merely suspicion that Dutch had been his brother's accomplice?

Peter didn't believe it. He couldn't imagine the gentle, caring man he had met the day before would have left his own brother to die a slow and horrible death in a hollander at the Rose Paperworks. And Dutch would never have put his whole family at further risk of starvation when killing Hiram Rose would gain them nothing. Once again the police had a solution that tied things up in a neat little package. Peter's gut told him they were wrong, but he had little faith that justice would prevail.

The Karlssons had already lost two family members in as many months. Now it looked like that number was going to rise to three.

———

"Miss Seale, could you come in here for a moment?"

Libby froze on the stairs. She had been planning to slip out of the house, as she had for the past several days, rather than face her landlady, who she knew must be bursting with questions. She would have heard about the death at the Rose Paperworks, and she knew Libby was working for the Rose family. But more important were the questions raised by the letter addressed to Libby Seletzky. Mrs. Pratt was surely burning with curiosity to know why her boarder was known by a different surname in New York than Portland. Libby dreaded having to share some, or all, of her personal history with the nosey older woman.

When Libby had first rented a room from Mrs. Pratt, it was almost without thought that she had anglicized her surname from the obviously Jewish "Seletzky" to "Seale." At the time she had told herself the main reason for this small deception was to make herself more anonymous. Her family and estranged husband would no doubt be searching for her. But the truth was more complicated than that. Crossing the country by train she had become more and more aware that, outside the sheltered enclave of New York's Lower East Side, being a Jew was considered "strange." In fact, in some places, "strange" was one of the more palatable things said of Jews.

Libby hated the idea of having attention drawn to her simply because she was the lone Jewish person in a room, and so she had decided it was just simpler to cloak her background in a new name, rather than forever answering the inevitable questions that "Seletzky" produced. Only now that the proverbial cat was out of the bag did she stop to wonder how she would explain her choice to others. Her very Catholic landlady might never understand how one could, as she might put it, "deny one's faith." Libby could almost hear her mother's voice saying, "You cannot hide who you are, Libbeleh. It will always catch up with you eventually."

Libby stepped into the kitchen, feeling vaguely like she was facing a firing squad. But as soon as she saw the white-haired countenance of the Irish widow, she relaxed. Mrs. Pratt was not an ogre. She just was an old woman, sweet, talkative, perhaps even gossipy, but kind, basically kind.

"Mrs. Pratt, I've been meaning to speak with you about something." Libby took a deep breath, and without stopping to think too much about the words she chose, she spilled out her story (well, some of it). She neglected to mention her marriage, needless to say. And, in the version she told Mrs. Pratt, she had gone west with her parents' blessing to seek new experiences in the western United States. But she did explain that she was indeed Jewish, and had simplified her name only to make it easier for her to blend in in this part of the country.

Mrs. Pratt was naturally surprised. "But, Miss Seale! I mean . . . that is . . . shall I start calling you Miss Seletzky?"

"No, not unless you wish. Please think of Seale as my only name, Mrs. Pratt. I've gotten quite used to it in these last few months."

"But you're such a clean girl! I never would have thought . . ." She faltered, realizing this might be construed as an insult. Switching midstream, she went on, "Oh, but you do know, I have such respect for your people. So good with money, and so musical! Just think, if only my Brendan were here, I'm sure he would love to talk to you . . . just think, a real Jewess in my kitchen. Oh! Do you need me to set aside a special place in the icebox? Your people have rather strange dietary laws, don't they?"

She almost laughed, picturing the look on Mrs. Pratt's face if she told her all the alterations it would take to make the boardinghouse kitchen kosher: the two complete sets of dishes, one for dairy food and one for the flesh of animals; a third set of plates just for Pesach, when only unleavened bread was allowed; the complete prohibition on shellfish as well as pork; the segregation of milk, butter, and cheese from all meats. And there were hundreds more. Oddly enough, she had never before considered how easily she herself had slipped into the non-kosher world. When she ran away from New York, dietary restrictions had been the last thing on her mind. She ate what was offered, when it was offered. Of course she never ate bacon or ham—the injunction against that was too strong, at this point she had an almost instinctual revulsion to pork—but she no longer noticed if a chicken sandwich had butter or cheese on it. In fact she had discovered she rather liked a wedge of sharp cheddar alongside cold roast beef! Did that mean she was no longer a practicing Jew? She still considered herself Jewish, but in truth she had not set foot inside a temple since she left New York.

She realized she had left her landlady's question hanging in the air. "There's no need to make any changes, Mrs. Pratt. Thank you for being so understanding."

"Oh, and to think of all the times I asked you to go to church with me! I had no idea!" She laughed, and Libby smiled wryly.

"I do hope you won't treat me any differently, Mrs. Pratt, now that you know about my name. I'm the same Libby I was yesterday. Please don't feel anything has to change. Of course, if you feel this deception is too great an affront to put behind you, I could look for alternate lodgings. I really am sorry I misled you."

"No, no, of course I don't want you to go! I am just so glad you told me now, dear. I had always suspected something was different about you . . ." Mrs. Pratt, fond of revising history as she went along, was clearly already busy concocting an alternate world in which she'd known from the start that Libby was no Christian, and had chosen to go along with the name charade as a kindness to her boarder.

The older woman prattled on merrily, and Libby wondered how long it would be before she could plausibly extricate herself and begin her morning's errands.

———

"I'm sure there's a story there. I'm just not sure I can dig up enough evidence to prove something one way or the other." Peter picked at the half-eaten sandwich that lay in front of him.

John Mayhew finished his lunch with a satisfied smack of his lips. "You giving up, Petey?"

"No," Peter said defensively. And then, "Okay, yes. What do we know, really? So someone tried to kill Hiram Rose. His gardener, and sometime-driver, Matt Karlsson died instead. The police say Matt's brother Dutch is guilty of both crimes, but it makes no sense! How would killing Rose have made anything better for the Karlssons? In fact, it would almost assuredly have made their lives worse. They had to have known that if Rose was killed, Matt's position might be lost. And if Matt had no job, the family would have no source of income."

Peter crumpled the greasy waxed paper around the remains of his sandwich and dumped it in the trash. "But there's no way to prove any of it. And the police could be half right. After all, even if Dutch is innocent, it doesn't mean Matt was innocent as well."

Mayhew eyed his star reporter warily. "This doesn't sound like you, Petey. I thought you liked that Dutch fellow, and now he's in prison with hardly any evidence against him. Smells like a story to me. And since we have a way to get inside the Rose home . . ."

Of course. Now Peter could see where this conversation had been leading all along. "You told me yourself that Miss Seale is working for the wife and sister-in-law, isn't she?"

As if he hadn't thought already of how easy it would be to go to Libby, try to mend the bridges between them, and ask for her help. The Portland police were not likely to dig for dirt inside the house of a wealthy and influential citizen, not when they already had a common ex-millworker behind bars for the crime. And yet if Dutch was innocent, as Peter believed, that meant that the most likely place to look for Matt's accomplice, and the true would-be assassin, was within Rose's own household. And who was better placed to do that than Libby Seale? Who else could he ask? If he didn't ask Libby's help, then Dutch was a lost man. And yet . . . "John, it's just that . . . I don't want to jeopardize Miss Seale's livelihood . . ." He trailed off.

"We both know why you don't want to ask her help, and if you think that avoiding her is going to make your feelings go away . . . well, let's just say I don't agree, and leave it at that."

Before Peter could frame a reply, the front door opened. At the sound of the bell, both men looked up and saw Half-Cent saunter in, a grin on his face. He looked older, somehow, and very proud of himself, yet young enough so that his emotions were written on his face.

"I have some news, Mr. Eberle, Mr. Mayhew! A story, maybe . . ."

Mayhew smiled, and nudged Peter. "Looks like our friend here has got the reporting bug. What is it, Half-Cent?"

"I was at the police station, and I heard they arrested the dead man's brother. This morning! Jan Karlsson Jr. is his name."

Peter didn't have the heart to tell the boy this was old news. He merely picked up his notepad and hat, and said, "Lead on, Macduff! Let's see what we can find out about this Jan Karlsson." He let Half-Cent lead him through the door, then turned back to speak softly to Mayhew. "I suppose you're right, John. I've got to try." Peter jammed his hat on his head and stepped through the door, trying to figure out what he would say when he spoke to Libby.

———

Mrs. Pratt nearly fell over with happiness when she opened the door and saw who was calling. "Why, Mr. Eberle! Miss Seale didn't mention you were coming to call."

Peter gave her his irresistible crooked grin, and she beamed. "I'm afraid that's my fault, Mrs. Pratt. I somehow neglected to mention I was stopping by. Could you see if possibly she's available?"

"Of course, of course . . ." She looked up at him, but made no move from the hall. She looked like she was gathering her nerve to ask him something, and the sight was quite comical. He had never known Libby's landlady to hesitate before asking a question.

"Mr. Eberle, tell me. Did you change your name as well? I mean . . ." She lowered her voice to a breathless whisper. "Are you one of them too?"

"I'm not sure what you are asking." Of course, Peter knew immediately that Mrs. Pratt must have somehow learned Libby's true origins and name, and he wondered whether that was by design or happenstance. He would have to ask Libby, if an opportunity presented itself. But he knew from experience that this was a touchy subject. If he hadn't proposed, he might never have learned her secret himself. "But, if the information is of help to you, my name is Peter Christopher Eberle, and it has been since I was a baby."

"Oh! Of course it has." She giggled nervously. "Come in, come in! I'll get Miss . . ." She paused slightly and then with great import continued. "Miss Seale."

The landlady made her way up the stairs, and he busied himself looking around the parlor. There were lace antimacassars on the backs of the walnut-framed settee and side chairs, and an inordinate number of souvenirs and bibelots dotted the mantle and tables. On a round table by the hall door he noticed a daguerreotype framed in elaborate gilt curlicues. Picking it up, he saw that it must be Mr. and Mrs. Pratt on their wedding day. Mrs. Pratt looked much the same as she did now, with the same wide smile and slightly vacant look in her eyes. Next to her the image of a bespectacled Mr. Pratt, now long departed, gazed in perpetuity down at his young bride with a look of adoration. Oddly, the picture made him sad and just a little uncomfortable. He replaced it and perched expectantly on the edge of the nearest piece of uncomfortable furniture.

He was sitting there, growing more nervous about seeing Libby, when he heard the door to the parlor open behind him. Jumping to his feet, he turned to see the pretty seamstress slipping into the room. She smiled, and for a moment it seemed like nothing had ever been amiss between them. Then he saw the troubled look in her eyes, and he knew he couldn't pretend nothing had changed.

"Peter, I'm so glad you came. I felt awful, not being able to speak to you at the Rose house, what with everything that was going on that day."

"Libby, I . . ." He faltered for a moment. "I hope it isn't too much of an imposition, my calling here without any advance notice."

"No, no, of course not. Mrs. Pratt looks like the cat who ate the canary, by the way. She has it set in her mind that you and I will . . ."

She stopped, suddenly aware she was stepping too close to the painful fact that hung in the air between them. Honestly, she chided herself, what are you being so evasive for? Habit, I suppose. But it's time to stop hedging. Peter is my friend.

"I got a letter from my mother."

Peter knew how much was hidden behind those seven words. An entire life Libby had led. A husband, a culture, and a family he would likely never meet. "They must have been relieved to hear from you, your family. Your . . . they are all well?"

"Yes. My sister is worried about my father's health, but I think she's just trying to make me concerned enough to return to New York. And I won't!" The vehemence in her voice surprised even Libby, and she gave a small laugh. "And the letter was addressed to my real name, so of course I had to tell Mrs. Pratt about being Jewish." She added hastily, "That's all I told her. Thank heavens my mother addressed the letter to me as Libby Seletzky and not Libby Greenblatt."

Peter said laconically, "Yes." Then he told her of their conversation at the front door, and Libby laughed to think Mrs. Pratt had imagined Peter was another secret Jew. "Oh, she is a dear woman, but I fear she's a little too interested in the life of her boarders."

She sat down right beside him on the settee, then stood and moved to a chair across the room—and suddenly everything was awkward again. He was reminded of the strained scene, just a few weeks before, when he had gotten down on a bended knee and asked Libby for her hand in marriage. It was only then that she had told him about her husband. Just remembering the moment made him feel a deep discomfort, and he hoped his fair skin was not too obviously flushed with emotion. Annoyed with himself, he looked her right in the eye. "I want to ask you for a favor."

"Of course, anything." Libby looked up and into his eyes as well, but she was unable to hold his gaze. All her carefully suppressed feelings were flooding back, and she felt the pain of their last meeting—no, not the last one. They had seen each other at the Rose home, she corrected herself, and that encounter had been fine. If she had been able to converse with him then, she could do it now.

Peter cleared his throat. "As I'm sure you know, the *Gazette* is running stories about the attempts on Hiram Rose's life."

"Attempts? Has there been more than one?" Peter quickly filled her in on what little he knew of the second attempt with the arrows. Apparently, the news was not yet general information. He followed with his morning's discoveries at the mill. She listened intently, unable to shake the feeling that this was all so comfortable and familiar—Peter briefing her on what he knew about a puzzling case. When he was done, her eyes were bright. "So the fact that there were no tools found on the scene means it can't possibly have been Matt! I must admit I was puzzled why the household groom would have wanted his employer dead. And, according to the household staff, he was quite a friendly sort and close friends with Rose's eldest son, Elliot."

"Unfortunately, his name is not yet clear. This new evidence only means he couldn't have acted alone. He still could have been at the mill for nefarious purposes, just not alone. The police think he had an accomplice, and they think they have the man in custody." He paused. "Matt had a brother . . . has a brother . . . no, had. I mean Matt no longer has him, but the brother is still alive—"

"Peter . . ." she prompted, and smiled once more at how boyish and sweet he sometimes appeared.

"I'm sorry. In any case, Matt's brother, Dutch Karlsson, was arrested and charged as Matt's partner in crime. The police think he is guilty, and I don't agree. I think there's more to the story, and

I'm asking you to please use your access to the Rose household to help me find the truth. Please, Libby, help me find out what really happened."

For a moment, Libby almost laughed. It wasn't so long ago that she had asked for his help solving a crime that touched her closely, and now he had come to her with the very same request. "But what would I be looking for?"

Briefly, Peter outlined his belief that the real killer might be connected with Hiram Rose's home life. It was unfortunate, but most likely, that Matt had to have been involved in some way, despite Anna Karlsson's belief in his innocence. But if he was acting with an accomplice it was likely that accomplice was to be found in the Rose family circle.

"What I need to know is," he finished, "who might have been using Matt as a means to this end? I'm curious what sort of relationship he had with other members of the household. Augustus Fowler lives just next door, doesn't he?"

Libby nodded. "Yes, with his wife Eva. You know, of course, she's Hiram Rose's sister."

Peter nodded. "I find it very interesting that the two men apparently don't see eye to eye on matters of business. Can you see if there was any connection between Mr. Fowler and Matt? And then try to find out where the various household members were during the second attempt on Rose's life." Peter leaned toward her. "But please, Libby, don't jeopardize your job with Mrs. Rose on my behalf. If you can't find out anything without risking your livelihood, I want you to put it out of your mind."

"Don't worry, Peter. I believe I have proven to you that I am a competent investigator. I won't take any foolish chances. However, I would appreciate it if you'd tell me everything you know. I would like to be as effective as possible in the time I have, given that I'm only an occasional visitor, so to speak, in the Rose and Fowler households."

Peter told her about his discussion with Matson, the foreman at the Paperworks, and his interview with Rose's business rival, Manning. As he spoke, he forgot to feel awkward. It invigorated him, this summing up of events for an intelligent listener. Occasionally, Libby asked him to describe someone or go over some point again, and by the end of half an hour he felt confident that he had told her everything, from Smirnikoff's heavy accent to Dutch's tenderness with his deaf son.

It did not go unnoticed by Libby that Peter lingered over his description of Matt's sister Anna who, Libby gathered, had implored him to clear her brother's name. She said nothing, however, just filed it away to think about later. It certainly sounded as if Peter were completely convinced of Dutch's innocence, despite the man's unwillingness to provide an alibi to the police.

"I just cannot believe the gentle soul I met would have watched his own brother fall into a vat of knives and not have tried to save him. I know Dutch seems to have every motive in the world to want to hurt Rose, and perhaps he even could have done so, but I'm sure he would never have involved his brother. For one thing, Matt was apparently bringing in the only money the family had. And the family knew Matt's livelihood depended on Rose and Fowler's continued good will. He told his sister that Mrs. Fowler let him do some extra work in order to pay for his father's funeral. So he was, on the whole, grateful to the household."

"What sort of extra work could he have done? From what I've gathered, Matt was already a sort of jack-of-all-trades, driving the carriage, gardening, and doing the heavy household chores," Libby interjected.

"Miss Karlsson didn't say. I will ask her, but perhaps that's something you could find out from Mrs. Fowler?"

Libby nodded.

"Maybe you can also find out if Matt was acting oddly in the weeks before his death. Or had mentioned a plan to leave the Roses' employ. Can you discreetly ask around, see if he confided in one of the other servants?"

"I wonder . . ." began Libby, and paused. She wasn't sure she wanted to cast any suspicion on Elliot, as she had grown quite fond of him.

"What?"

"Nothing. That is, I do have an idea of where I might start asking."

"And I'll pursue the mill angle. There's something not quite right about this wholesale replacement of the entire staff with Chinese workers. The attacks on Rose have come just a little too conveniently on the heels of that to let me dismiss it as a possible motive. Also, perhaps Dutch will tell me what he seems unwilling to tell the police. If only I knew where he was the night Matt died, it would be much easier to convince the police to keep looking for another accomplice." He stood up and brushed off his coat absent-mindedly. "I'll work on him."

"Are you going then?" Why do I say such silly things when I am around him, she wondered?

"Libby, I can't thank you enough for agreeing to this. If you didn't happen to work for the family, I don't know how I would get the access I need to write this story. I'm really very grateful."

A hint of a smile played on her face. "We make a good team."

He grinned. "Can you meet me at the *Gazette* offices on your way home from the Rose house on Saturday?"

"Of course. I may be late, but I should be able to be there by six p.m."

"I'll look forward to it." He took her hand, and both of them nearly stopped breathing. With a gentle squeeze, he let go. "I missed you," he said quietly.

She wanted to answer, and a thousand responses crowded her mind, but instead she just watched him leave the room and let himself out the front door without saying a word.

SIX

For once, the *Gazette* offices were completely empty. Peter sat at his desk, occasionally scribbling notes, but mostly staring into space and relishing the quiet. John Mayhew was on a rare business trip, off to a small town in southern Oregon to meet with suppliers. Clem, the part-time typesetter who laid out the newspaper when Mayhew wasn't able to, had been on his way out as Peter was arriving, saying he would be in after midnight to work on the remaining text for the next day's edition. Even Half-Cent seemed to somehow know that the *Gazette* offices were quiet, and he was nowhere to be seen.

It was just as well that Mayhew wasn't there. He'd be peppering Peter with questions about his meeting with Libby. He'd also want a full report on Peter's plans for the story, and right now the story was making him uneasy. He had laid awake until late the night before, unable to sleep. After his visit with Libby, visions of her seemed to hover above his bed. And then her face would be replaced with that of Anna Karlsson. Then he would remind himself that there was a man sitting in a cold jail cell, and that was what mattered. And he'd push his romantic fantasies aside. Then the whole cycle would start again.

Chewing on a pencil, feet on his desk, he pondered if he was losing his professional detachment. This investigation would necessitate spending time with Libby on an ongoing if ill-defined basis. That was both good and possibly bad. Was he pursuing Dutch's case simply to see her? More disturbingly, he wondered if he was capable of being truly unbiased in his view of the Karlsson family. Normally he didn't get personally involved with people in a story, but the plight of Dutch had gotten under his skin. He seemed so obviously innocent. Why didn't anyone else see that? It bothered him that if he didn't work to find out the truth, no one would. And he was scared he would fail.

Earlier in the day he had sat with Dutch in his small cell at the police station. Dutch looked haggard, as if he hadn't eaten or slept in days.

"Mr. Eberle, I'm sorry. If I felt I could tell you where I was the night my brother was killed, I would, I really would. I'm just afraid I would compromise others . . . and place them in the unfair position of having to vouch for me at the expense of their own safety. It's a bad position to be in, but there I am."

Peter scratched his head. "Mr. Karlsson, I am not the police. I have no vested interest in harming anyone else. Perhaps I could somehow relay your whereabouts in such a way as to preserve . . ."

Dutch cut him off. "No, I'm sorry, but no." In his voice, Peter heard the steely determination of one accustomed to standing by his principles. Ironically, this made Peter feel even more strongly that Dutch wouldn't have left his own brother to die a gruesome death in the hollander. "Ever since my brother was found, I've been over and over it in my mind. Why was he there? That's what you can try to figure out, Mr. Eberle. As far as I knew, my brother had never even been inside Rose's mill. Some days he would drive the carriage there, but he would turn right around and go home. He worked at the house, that's where he spent his time. Someone must have told him to go to the mill. If you can find out who, you can prove it wasn't me."

"Forgive me for saying so, Mr. Karlsson, but my task would be a lot easier if I could give a compelling reason that it could not have been you. Your insistence on shrouding your whereabouts in mystery does nothing to help your case."

"I know." The two men waited each other out. Peter broke first.

"Can you tell me any more about Matt? Who else besides you he might have confided in? Did he have any particular friends, a sweetheart perhaps?"

"I really couldn't say. I'm sorry."

For another long moment, neither man spoke. Peter stood up to leave. He called for the policeman to let him out, and for a moment, the only sound was the creak of the key turning and the cell door opening. Outside the cell, Peter turned back and addressed Dutch through the bars. "You can send a message to me at the *Gazette* if you change your mind."

Dutch only nodded in acknowledgment, and Peter wondered why the man was being so damnably difficult. His freedom was at stake! Matt's family must know more than they had told him about the friends and confidantes of the dead man. It was time to go back there and try again. He wouldn't let them off so easily this time.

———

The rain was unrelenting as Peter hurried along the unpaved road that led to the Karlsson house. He wished he had brought an umbrella. As he stepped onto the tiny porch, he heard a loud screeching that told him Pim must be unhappy. Then a woman's voice—it sounded like the grandmother—screamed for someone to quiet the boy, and then there was much scuffling. Other voices chimed in. Sighing, Peter considered coming back another day, but it was too late. Before he could turn away, a woman he assumed was Dutch's wife, Tilda, walked out onto the small covered porch and saw him standing there. She was tall, for a woman, and her rusty red hair was in thick braids, twined into two bun-shaped knots over her ears. "Who are you?"

"I'm Peter Eberle, with the *Gazette*, Mrs. Karlsson."

"Oh." She looked him up and down, but made no sign to invite him in, and Peter stood uncomfortably close to her on the cramped porch, trying to avoid the rain dripping over the overhang without bumping into her. "I heard all about you. You wrote a story about Matt, and now my husband is in jail."

Peter tried to protest her juxtaposition of the two events, but she ignored him and went on. "My husband did nothing wrong. Matt was always causing problems in life, with his flashy looks and his over-friendly manner, and now he's still causing problems, even in death."

"Mrs. Karlsson, I do want to get to the bottom of this, and if I can find out more about Matt, I may be able to clear your husband's name. But I need your help."

She said nothing.

"May I come in, at least?"

"I suppose." She opened the door. Mummo was sitting by the fire, and she turned as Peter and Tilda entered the small room.

"Tilda, you must control the boy. With Jan not at home, it seems as if no one can calm him."

"Where is Pim now?"

"Anna has taken him to the back room."

"His father spoils him," said Tilda, tight-lipped.

Peter coughed, feeling they had forgotten him. "Hello, Mrs. Karlsson," he said, addressing the older woman.

She looked up at him, confused. Then her face contorted into some semblance of a smile. "Come, sit by the fire, sir. You're soaked to the bone." She didn't ask who Peter was, and he doubted she remembered him from his last visit.

Awkwardly, Peter sat on the small stool at her feet. Mummo patted his knee and said vaguely, "You are so handsome. Like my Mathias. He is a good boy, my Mathias. You should wait to meet him. He should be home soon."

Peter looked at Tilda, comprehension dawning in his face. She nodded as if to say that, yes, Mummo had taken refuge in a dream world. "Come with me, to the kitchen," she said. He pulled himself away from the scant warmth of the fire and complied. She dropped her voice. "I want to tell you something, and I don't want my mother-in-law to hear me say it. She doted on Matt, more so than he deserved, in my opinion."

"It's a mother's way," he said, although he couldn't stop himself from noting that it wasn't always the case. She showed no particular warmth for her own son.

"Perhaps. But you should know that Matt was no saint, no matter what his brother and sister tell you."

"Are you saying you think he was trying to kill Hiram Rose?"

"I am not saying anything. I am just telling you that I am not surprised he would be mixed up in some bad business. Mr. Rose was no friend to this family, so I won't pretend I care if he is hurt, but I know that my husband is innocent and I want his name cleared. We need him at home. His son needs him. Do you think it's easy caring for a deaf child, Mr. Eberle?"

Peter suddenly felt as if he were a schoolboy, receiving a stern lecture, and all he could do was shake his head. "I want my husband back, Mr. Eberle. I thought the police would find out who Matt was really in cahoots with, but instead, they went for the most convenient target."

"I want to help your husband, I do. That's why I came here today."

"I don't know why we should trust you." Tilda's face was hard, and the only sign of the emotional strain she must be under was in her hands. They gripped the back of a kitchen chair so tightly the knuckles had gone white. "You needn't concern yourself. We will find some way to get my husband back. We have friends, and we will turn to them to help us. We don't need a stranger here."

"You have no idea where your husband was on the night of Matt's death? None at all?" Peter tried to sound trustworthy. "If he would just tell the police they would let him go. Or if you would tell me."

She paused just a moment too long before responding. "I know he was not at the mill."

Before Peter could ask her more, Anna flew into the room. Her hair was pulled back from her face, and her cheeks were flushed. Ignoring Tilda, she pulled up a chair next to him and sat down heavily. "Mr. Eberle, have you found something?"

"Mr. Eberle was preparing to go, Anna." Tilda's tone was disapproving.

"No, Mr. Eberle, you must stay. I will make you a cup of tea. Would you like that?" Anna did not wait for an answer but jumped up and hurried to put the kettle on the stove. She had been studiously ignoring her sister-in-law, but now she turned to her. "Tilda, Mummo asked for you. I believe she needs your help climbing up to her bed. You know the doctor said she should rest."

"Yes, I will help her." Tilda's eyes shifted from Anna to Peter, warning him not to stay too long, then she went out to the front room.

Anna sat back down and said shyly, "Thank you for coming back. It has been a trying day here, with Mummo unwell and Tilda . . ." she trailed off. "But what is it you came for? You said you have not found anything to clear my brothers."

"No, nothing yet, I'm sorry. But I did see Dutch today. He looks well," Peter lied. No sense in admitting how ragged her brother had looked. "I know he sends his love to you all, and to Pim. The child sounded quite upset when I arrived. How is he?"

"Oh, he's sleeping now. Dutch is always the one to tuck him into his bed at night, and last night when he wasn't here . . . well, let me just say, you have never heard a wailing like it in your life." Anna looked like she might cry. "He doesn't understand where his father is. Poor Dutch! I just know he had nothing to do with any of this. He cares only about his son and his family."

"I'm sorry." His instinct was to hug her, but he knew that he could never take such a liberty. He barely knew her. "I hope that Dutch will be here to put Pim to bed again soon. But I came here today because I am not sure where to best begin. I realize that I know almost nothing about you brother Matt, and I can't help feeling that the answers I'm seeking will be found in his life, not Dutch's. I think Dutch is merely an innocent bystander."

Anna frowned. "Then you believe Matt was guilty?"

Peter turned away. Anna's blue eyes were too intense for him to look at while he tried to apply his logical faculties to this situation. "I'll be honest with you, I don't know. But if there's some innocent explanation why Matt was at the Paperworks the night he died, that explanation will arise from the circumstances of his life during the days and weeks before his death. So I need you to tell me what you can about your brother's life." He risked a glance at her face. "Do you know the names of any friends of his I could talk to?"

She bit her lip, as if trying to decide whether to say something. "Mr. Eberle, I've been thinking about the night Matt died. That is, of course I can't stop going over all the questions in my mind, and well, I have a theory."

"I'd like to hear it, of course."

"What if maybe Matt heard something about someone trying to kill Mr. Rose, setting a trap, and he went to the mill to warn him or to try to stop the real killer. Maybe he was a hero! He was saving Mr. Rose's life, not trying to end it."

Peter nodded thoughtfully. "I suppose it's possible," he replied. "But why go to the paper mill? He could just have warned Mr. Rose instead."

Anna's face fell. "I don't know . . . but I am sure that there must be a good explanation for why he was there!"

"Where did Matt spend his time when he wasn't at work?"

"Here, mostly. But he did know some of the men from the paper mill, Dutch's friends, friends of our father's. Good men, mostly, but they drink too much and then get wild. They all go to that saloon on Burnside, the Green Gale, and spend money they can't afford." Peter jotted down the name of the bar, which was unfamiliar to him. Anna's brow furrowed as she tried to remember more. "Matt mentioned someone named Scotty to me, on more than one occasion, someone he met there. I think he was Matt's best friend at the Green Gale, but I don't know if he was from the mill . . . Dutch never mentioned a Scotty. I'm sorry I don't know any more."

"Still, it's a good place to start." Peter, still damp, rose and turned up his collar in anticipation of the rain that still fell steadily outside the window. "I will do my best, Miss Karlsson. For what it's worth I feel as certain as you that Dutch was not mixed up in this. And Matt . . . well, we will see what this Scotty has to say."

She saw him to the door, and when he turned back she was still standing in the open doorway looking after him, hope radiant in her face. Peter found himself hoping desperately that he would find out something useful at the Green Gale, but fearing it would just be another dead end. At least, though, it would get him out of the rain. And besides, it was almost the end of the work day and he could use a drink.

The master and mistress were at it again, thought Celia, as she stood in the kitchen, listening to the sounds of yelling coming from the bedroom two floors above. They probably had no idea that the laundry chute acted as a sound tunnel. Whenever they raised their voices, as they had been doing more lately, those in the kitchen could hear every word.

Celia made clucking noises as she quietly snapped the ends off a bowlful of wax beans, straining to hear their words. It was a bad habit, eavesdropping, but she told herself it was for the good of the household staff. If they were aware of the general mood of the Roses, they could be better prepared to serve their needs. And so she justified her curiosity.

Mrs. Rose's higher-pitched voice was harder to make out, but Celia clearly heard Mr. Rose. "Damnation, Adele, the last thing I need is the police bumbling around the mill. It's bad for business!"

"Hiram, why didn't you tell me about those letters? And there have been two attempts now! What if next time they succeed? Oh, I feel sick when I think of it. Someone shooting at you right in our yard!"

"Don't you listen to anything I say? They caught the man who did it. He's in police custody!"

Listening to him yell, Celia reflected, not for the first time, that Hiram Rose had certainly changed over the course of his marriage to Adele. When he had first returned to Portland with his young bride, he had been all deference and courtliness. Over the years, as Adele's refined manner had given way to a shrewish resignation, Hiram had reverted to the angry bully he had been as a child. Adele had changed too. No longer did she insist on daily high tea and regular open houses. Instead, she kept mostly to her rooms when she wasn't out paying social calls or meeting with her Ladies Aid society. Now it seemed that husband and wife hardly saw each other except to argue.

"As if the police never make mistakes!" Adele's next words were incomprehensible, but her beseeching tone came through clearly, even if the words themselves did not.

"I will not hire a bodyguard, Adele!" There was the sound of a door slamming. Celia looked up, and it was only then she noticed Libby Seale, the seamstress, standing quietly in the doorway. How long had she been standing there?

"Miss Seale. You're working late. It's almost dinner time."

"Hello, Celia. Yes, I was trying to finish some alterations over at Mrs. Fowler's. She asked me to return the basket from her lunch, and tell you she enjoyed her meal greatly."

"Good," the cook replied gruffly.

"Was someone else in here just now? I thought I heard angry voices as I came in," said Libby, looking around the room. Celia stopped snapping beans. She realized the seamstress hadn't heard anything after all.

"Oh, that was upstairs. Mr. and Mrs. Rose were having a discussion. I couldn't say what it was all about." Celia stopped, torn between her desire to keep household matters private and her enjoyment of sharing a choice tidbit of gossip. Ultimately, her love of gossip won out. "Of course, as you can imagine, even though I wasn't trying to listen, I couldn't help but hear. Sound travels in this old house."

"I'm sure it does." Libby began unpacking the dirty plates and silver from the basket, setting them in the large porcelain washbasin to soak. "I wonder, what were they arguing about, anyway?"

Celia leaned in, and her voice dropped to a near whisper. "It seems that Mrs. Rose wants her husband to hire some sort of a guard."

Quickly, she filled Libby in on the specifics of the argument. And when she had exhausted that topic, her narrative swelled to include arguments and disagreements from the past. The cook had worked for the family since Hiram and Eva were born, and so her knowledge about them was truly comprehensive.

Most of the information she offered seemed depressingly trivial and of little use to Libby and Peter's investigation. But when the cook's tales reached the early years of the Roses' marriage, Libby found herself actually growing interested, although she doubted that the answer to the current crime had anything to do with the distant past.

At the time that Hiram had been ready to settle down, the household was still controlled by his father, Abraham Rosenberg. The old man was set on having a Jewish daughter-in-law, but apparently none of the dozen or so marriageable Jewish girls in Portland at the time would suit. He wanted a rich, cultured wife for his son, from German Jewish stock like his own. So he sent Hiram East, where the search for a wife led to the long-established Jewish communities in the deep South.

Adele Maier of Atlanta had met his qualifications exactly. She was rich, pretty, and came from one of the oldest Jewish families in the country. Her family had come to Georgia by way of Charleston, South Carolina, where they had grown wealthy as shopkeepers and land speculators. She numbered judges, professors, and generals among her numerous cousins, and one distant relation had even been secretary of state under the Confederacy. Adele's parents were none too pleased to be marrying off their only daughter to a man they perceived as an upstart from the unsettled West, but having lost most of their fortune during the Civil War they gave in to her wishes without too much of a fight.

And so Adele had come to Portland with her new husband and (much to the amusement of the rest of the household) had fussed and doted on him endlessly. Under her influence the Roses' standard of living became much more lavish. She was determined to make the family social leaders and to introduce high culture into Portland (a task at which she mostly failed). It was also her doing, after her father-in-law's death, that the family changed their name to Rose and the name of the business from Rose's Paper Goods to The Rose Paperworks.

It was only in their second decade together that the marriage had begun to sour. Hiram grew tired of Adele constantly dragging him to musical evenings and lectures. He claimed it made him feel like he was a project, a house to be remodeled, rather than a husband. So Mrs. Rose grew increasingly focused on her role as mother, channeling her attentions and efforts on molding her sons, especially Elliot, into the kind of gentleman she had been raised to admire.

Libby just kept nodding and making small comments about how fascinating this all was, and before she stopped to think, Celia had told her much more than she had intended.

"Oh, but you can't possibly be interested in all of this." The cook had finally become aware of how long she had talked.

"Nonsense," said Libby. "It's always interesting to know what people were like when they were younger. I think you really can't tell about people until you've worked for them, wouldn't you agree?"

"Oh, yes. Well, you must know as well as I do, seeing how you talk to ladies all over town while you pin dresses. People will have conversations about the most personal things in front of you, and it never occurs to them you can hear . . . it's like they think you're part of the furniture." The two women shared a laugh.

"But then," Libby went on, sounding more serious, "I suppose you all must be terribly concerned about Mr. Rose. I heard that the day before last someone tried to shoot him, here at the house, with an arrow. Were you here when that happened?"

"Oh, yes, that gave us all a fright, I'm sure you can imagine. Mrs. Rose came running into the kitchen . . . I was here, cooking dinner . . . and she was white as a ghost. 'Celia,' she says, 'someone has shot at the master! Right outside by the stables!'"

"So Mrs. Rose was here when it happened." Libby chose her next words carefully. "Was everyone gathered for dinner at the time? It must have been mayhem for you, here in the kitchen, dealing with a houseful of people at such a time of crisis."

"No, it was only a little after five o'clock. I was still cooking. Mrs. Rose was here, of course, and the twins were underfoot . . . wouldn't you know it happened on Miss Baylis' day off, which meant no one was watching the younger boys. Izzy almost tipped over the whole pot of stew before I got them out of the kitchen. Running around like little savages, they were that night!" Celia stopped, realizing her tone might be construed as overly critical of the children. "They're just high-spirited boys, of course. And their brother would usually have helped watch them, but he was nowhere to be seen."

"And Mr. and Mrs. Fowler?"

"I assume they were still next door. They weren't here, anyway. Dinner isn't usually served until after six, you understand. Mr. Rose had just arrived home from work when it happened."

Libby seemed about to ask something else, but instead she went to the peg by the door and took her coat down. Slipping into it, she gave the cook a warm smile. "Well, I do think the Rose family is lucky to have someone like you, with a level head at a time of crisis." She affected to check the small gold watch she wore as a locket. "My! It's been such a pleasure chatting with you, but I completely lost track of the time. Now I really must be going. If you see Mrs. Rose later, you can tell her I look forward to bringing her a finished dress later this week." She gathered her carpetbag and several smaller bags and shoved them all into a large carry-all.

"I'm sure she'll be pleased," replied Celia. Suddenly, she regretted being quite so free with the family gossip. After all, Libby wasn't an actual employee. She was really little more than a stranger.

As she watched her leave, Celia realized that the seamstress was often asking questions. Why did she care about what the master was yelling at his wife? She liked the girl tolerably well, and Libby was good at her trade, but she was also a bit nosy about things that didn't concern her. As she began washing dishes, she noted to herself that she should watch what she said around Miss Libby Seale.

———

In the scant light of the gloomy afternoon, the outside of the Green Gale looked unprepossessing. The panes of the front window had been clumsily painted out so nothing of the interior could be seen from the street. The reason Peter couldn't fathom, except that perhaps the Green Gale's clientele didn't like to be observed at their refreshment.

The evening had not yet reached the hour when workers from the factories and mills in this part of town filled its saloons and chop houses, but Peter was working under the assumption that Scotty had been one of the fired workers from the Paperworks, and thus was free to start drinking early. Though the bar appeared deserted, the fading legend on the door read "Open From Noon to Midnight Every Day But Sunday."

Pushing inside, Peter blinked at the brightness he found. The eight-armed gas chandeliers burned, filling the pine-paneled room with a rosy glow. Cheerful colored labels from local breweries were pasted on the walls. A beveled and only slightly chipped mirror hung behind the long oak bar that dominated one whole side of the room. The total effect was surprisingly cozy and welcoming, completely at odds with the street aspect. As Peter entered, a smattering of easy laughter supported this impression. The corner table was the only one filled, and Peter wondered if one of the six or seven men gathered around it was the one he was seeking.

He decided not to approach them directly. First he would have a word with the buxom barmaid, currently staring at him with uninhibited curiosity as he hesitated in the doorway. But before he could speak, she called out to him.

"Are you staying, then? Or don't you like what you see?" The men in the corner looked up, but after glancing at Peter they decided he wasn't worth interrupting their good time. They went back to drinking and laughing as Peter sat on one of the brass stools bolted to the floor by the bar.

"Yes, I'm staying." His coat was dripping from the rain, and he brushed his soggy hair back off of his face. "My name is Eberle. Peter Eberle, from the *Portland Gazette*."

"You don't need to give me your biography. Just a drink order."

"It's not a drink I'm after," Peter began. "I wanted to know—"

"If you're going to sit at my bar, you're buying a drink." With practiced moves the barmaid plunked a shot glass in front of him and filled it with a dark amber liquid from an unlabeled bottle. She cocked her head questioningly in his direction, as if to say "Are you going to drink that?" and he gave an almost imperceptible shake of his head. She picked up the glass then, herself, and downed the shot in one swallow. Wiping her lips she sighed in satisfaction. "That'll be fifteen cents. You want another?"

Peter couldn't help but smile. He pretended to think about it, and then said, "No, I think I've had enough." A toothy grin lit up her face, too. She was far from beautiful and decidedly on the unfashionable side of forty, but when she smiled she had a slightly disreputable appeal. Her hair was dark and thick, and the casual knot which perched perilously on the top of her head looked like it was getting ready to slide down her neck. He couldn't help but notice that she had left the first five (or six) buttons of her blouse undone. The worn but clean linen of her shirtwaist gaped open, revealing a fair expanse of freckled bosom. Peter quickly pulled his eyes back to her face, but he saw that she had noticed his lingering gaze and knew exactly what had been in his mind. He blushed, but the flash in her almost black eyes, and her unwavering smile, told him she hadn't minded in the least.

"I'm looking for a fellow named Scotty," he managed. "I've been told he's a regular here. Any chance he's one of the men over at that table?"

"I sell drinks, not information. But—" Her pause was accompanied by a flirtatious . . . well, if he had seen the same look on a man he would have not hesitated to call it a leer. "Maybe I'll answer your questions if you answer mine. Who told you he was a regular, and what is it to you?"

Peter was a bit taken aback by her frank tone, but he saw no reason not to be upfront. Besides, he had a sneaking suspicion this woman—he didn't even know her name—would see right through any cover story he tried to invent. "I was sent here by Anna Karlsson. As you're probably aware, her brother Jan has been arrested for attacks on Hiram Rose, owner of the . . ."

She cut him off. "Yes, I know all about it. Well, why didn't you say you were here on account of Dutch? Although, are you here for him or against him?"

"Actually, Miss . . ."

"Name's Phebe. And if you think Dutch is guilty then you can march out of here right now." Peter had been about to say that he was actually here to find out more about Matt Karlsson, not Dutch, but something told him to let Phebe continue with her own train of thought. She took his silence to mean he believed in Dutch's innocence.

"There's never been a gentler soul than Dutch Karlsson. And I'll tell you this, I don't believe he would have had anything to do with that attack on old man Rose. And as for anyone who knows him believing he left his own brother to die in that bastard's paper mill . . ." She stopped and gave Peter an appraising look. "What if I were to tell you I could prove he couldn't have done it?"

Peter contained his excitement and said evenly, "I would ask how."

Phebe leaned over the bar conspiratorially. "He was here that night. With me." Could Dutch have been having an affair with this barmaid? Peter believed Dutch was an honorable man, but having met Tilda Karlsson he wouldn't have blamed him if he had strayed. It would certainly explain his reluctance to give his whereabouts on the night in question. And yet . . . there was something too easy about the way Phebe had offered the information.

"Dutch Karlsson was here? With you."

"Sitting not two seats from where you are now. Never left my sight longer than a gentleman might to, let's say, answer the call of nature. Closed the place up, he did."

Peter leaned back. "Phebe, the Green Gale closes at midnight. The events over at the Paperworks could have happened anywhere up to six in the morning."

She smiled good-naturedly. "Okay, so he wasn't here that night. I thought I'd see if you might buy it." She took a damp rag and began wiping down the bar, talking as much to the rag as to Peter. "Suppose I were to say that Dutch was with me, if you follow me, all through the night—" She cut herself off. "Nah, even if I were to say that, he'd never go along with it. Might embarrass his wife. Don't know why, but he's faithful to that cold fish. At least, so far as I know."

A few patrons entered the bar, and Phebe stepped from behind the bar to see them settled at tables and set up with drinks. It was a good five minutes before she returned to Peter, and when she did her look seemed to ask why he was still hanging around. Digging in his pocket, Peter placed a quarter dollar on the table and ordered a shot of bourbon. This time he drank the shot himself, much to Phebe's approval.

"So," Peter resumed his official business, "you have no proof that Dutch is innocent."

"None except in here." Phebe placed her hand on her heart, or on her ample chest somewhere in the approximate vicinity of her heart. "I'd swear on a stack of bibles, in any court, that he's guilty of nothing worse than maybe sometimes hanging around with men who aren't as good as he is." Her eyes inadvertently strayed to the corner table.

"Those friends of Dutch's?" He didn't really make it a question. "Is one of them Scotty?"

"Why are you so interested in Scotty, anyway?"

"The truth is," Peter continued, "I came here today to find out what I could about Matt Karlsson, not Dutch. I've been told he and this Scotty were friends."

At first she didn't say anything, and then, "They were that. Good friends, I suppose you'd say. But Matt was a beautiful boy. Sweet." Phebe smiled a private smile, and her eyes misted over. Finally her look turned sad, and she looked at Peter. "Not like his brother. He didn't have Dutch's . . . gravity. Dutch is a man, and Matt was just a boy. And I think he would have stayed a boy, no matter how many years he'd been given on this earth. Which isn't to say . . ."

Peter waited but she seemed to have decided she had said enough. He tried to prompt her to continue. She was the first person he'd spoken to who had made him begin to see Matt as a real person, and not just a good-looking boy who'd been in the wrong place at the wrong time. "You knew him well? Matt?"

She smiled. "Intimately, you might say. A few times. A very nice few times." She looked to see if Peter was shocked. He was, a bit, but his face gave nothing away.

"Your choice, then?" he said, and paused. "That it was just a few times?"

She surprised him with her reply. "That's a very personal question to ask a lady. I don't understand why it should matter to you. What difference can it make now?"

Peter hadn't thought she would suddenly turn prudish on him. "Phebe. Matt was left to die in that hollander, and I don't believe any more than you do that his brother did it. But somebody left him there, or lured him there to make it seem like Matt was involved in the attacks on Hiram Rose. Whoever did that is still walking free. Probably laughing to see Dutch behind bars." He had her attention. "I don't know if your relations with Matt had anything to do with his death, but I need to know all I can about him in order to see that justice is done for his brother."

Without a smile and a wink, the manager of the Green Gale looked older. Coming out from behind the bar, she sat down on the stool next to Peter. "There's not that much to tell, but if you think it might help Dutch, then I'll tell. Matt sometimes came in here, not so often you could call him a regular, but once or twice a month, sometimes with his brother or sometimes alone, if he'd been driving Rose to some event or other in town and needed to hang around to pick him up after it was over. One night, last October I think, he was upset about something and sat here drinking till closing, and he really wasn't in any shape to make it home. I suggested he might stay the night here, and . . . well, I only have one bed upstairs. That's where I live, upstairs. And . . ." She cocked her head and left Peter in no doubt as to what had transpired that night.

"Do you remember what he was upset about? Something to do with Rose, maybe?"

"No, no. Well, indirectly, maybe. I don't remember exactly, but it was something to do with the garden. Or it happened in the garden . . . there was some sort of argument or disagreement. I don't remember what it was about. I'm not sure he actually ever said what it was about. But he loved that garden. Loved coaxing life from the earth. He was good with animals, too. A gentle soul, as I said."

Peter doubted she would let herself cry in front of him, but for a moment it appeared she had to work to suppress a tear.

He resumed his questioning gently. "And, after October, how often did he come around the Green Gale?"

She became businesslike once more. "Still not often. Every few weeks. But it was understood that if he was here he would spend the night. The last time I saw him was a few weeks before Christmas." She paused. "No, that wasn't the last time I saw him but it was the last time that . . . Anyway, he was here with Dutch right after all the men were let go from the Paperworks. I went over to serve them—there was an ugly mood around the table that night. Lots of ill will toward Hiram Rose, let me tell you." Her eyes had drifted unconsciously again to the table in the corner. "But Matty didn't seem to be taking much part in the conversation. Just absorbing it all, I guess. In any case, he wouldn't look at me as he ordered another drink. Seemed like he felt guilty or something . . ." She looked at Peter. "Not that he needed to be. He didn't owe me anything. What went on between us was a little fun, that's all. I think he enjoyed it, and I know I did. I assume he must have found someone else to have a little fun with. I always knew he would. He was an attractive boy. I have a weakness for attractive boys . . ." She was staring directly into Peter's eyes now, and he felt his cheeks going red. "But I have no illusions that they stay around for long."

No woman had ever spoken to Peter with such unblushing openness about her desires, and (man of the world that he fancied himself) it embarrassed him. He wondered if she could truly have been so sanguine when Matt abruptly curtailed their affair. Had she harbored a grudge against the young man who had suddenly, and without explanation, abandoned her bed? Did any woman really give her heart and body so freely? Peter found it incomprehensible.

Abruptly Peter got to his feet, and after a muttered excuse to Phebe, strode to the table in the corner of the Green Gale. The men he assumed to be Dutch's friends were still laughing and drinking. "Excuse me, gentlemen. You're friends of Dutch Karlsson's, aren't you?"

They fell silent, their jollity replaced by an air of tense suspicion. Casting his eyes around the table, Peter noticed that he actually knew one of the revelers—Alex Smirnikoff, the man who had shown him the freshly cleaned hollander just two days before. Smirnikoff clearly recognized Peter too, but he looked as if he hoped Peter would not acknowledge their association in this company. Clearly the burly Russian had been less than completely honest when Peter had asked whether, and how well, he had known

Dutch and Matt Karlsson. But perhaps that was understandable. He was a recent immigrant, and he must have been nervous being questioned about criminal matters.

A big man wearing a creased and shabby workingman's cap spoke first. "It's proud I am to say I'm friends with the man, though I'd like to know why you're asking." A slight Scottish burr gave a musical lilt to his speech. He extended a muscular, weather-beaten hand to Peter. "Daniel McFerley, but you can call me Plug."

"Peter Eberle, *Portland Gazette*." They shook hands, and for a moment Peter thought his would be crushed by McFerley's. "I believe your friend Dutch is being railroaded by the police. So I need to find out where he really was the night they say he was setting the trap for Hiram Rose that killed his brother."

Plug McFerley looked doubtful. "Now why would the papers be caring about a workingman like Dutch Karlsson? Tell me, you're really a reporter?" He sat back in his seat and paused. "I'm sorry, there's nothing we can tell you." He seemed comfortable speaking for the group as a whole, quite obviously used to being their leader.

Peter looked beseechingly across the table at Alex Smirnikoff. Alex turned to Plug and said, "No, no. This man is who he says he is. He came to the mill before, asking questions and trying to help Dutch. I think he's a good man."

Plug considered, and then smiled. "All right, if Russki here will take your part, that's good enough for me. But . . . I still don't think there's anything we can be telling you that'll help."

The next five minutes proved Plug McFerley correct. Though Peter spoke to each of the seven men in turn, nothing that might clear Dutch Karlsson came to light. The men all turned out to have worked with Dutch at the Rose Paperworks, and all but Smirnikoff had been let go when the Chinese were hired. Their resentment and hatred of Hiram Rose were evident, but all of the men insisted they knew nothing about the attacks or who might be behind them, except to say they were sure it wasn't Dutch. They also claimed they could offer no evidence regarding Dutch's whereabouts the night of Matt's death, except to say that he had not been with them. And, much to Peter's disappointment, there was not a Scotty among them. Besides Smirnikoff and McFerley, their names were Frank Lerner, Curly Sumpter, Les Wooley, Carmine 'Red' Tartaglia, and Walter Samuels. Feeling dejected, Peter finally came to the subject of Matt.

"Any of you know Dutch's brother Matt?" There was a general mumbled assent, to the effect of "yes, but not well." Peter pressed on. "Did you ever see him around the mill? He ever come inside with Dutch, or on an errand for Mr. Rose?"

"I don't remember ever seeing him inside," the man called Red offered, "but I saw him once or twice out by the stables." That was of no use to Peter. He needed to figure out why Matt had a key when he died, and why (if not to kill Hiram Rose) Matt had even been inside the mill that morning.

"What about the rest of you?" There were mutters all around, but the men around the table claimed they really hadn't been close friends with Matt, only with Dutch. "I'm told there was a friend of Matt's called Scotty. Was there a Scotty who worked with you at the Paperworks, someone who isn't here tonight? Maybe he would know?"

There was an awkward silence. Alex Smirnikoff cleared his throat. But before Alex could say anything, McFerley overrode him. "Nope. Never knew any fellow called Scotty. Certainly no one of that name ever worked over at the mill with us."

Peter ignored them and looked at Alex. "Was there something you wanted to say?"

"No. I was thinking perhaps I remembered someone called that name, but I am mistaken. My English is still not so good," Smirnikoff mumbled into his thick mustache.

"If we meet up with this Scotty, though we'll be sure to let you know," McFerley said, rising. "I think it's about time for me to be heading home to the wee bairns. Nice to have met you." He didn't offer Peter his hand as he left the table, swiftly followed by the remaining men.

"Good bye, Mr. Eberle." Alex was the only one to stop. "It is nice to be seeing you again. I'm sorry we could not do more to help you." The strapping immigrant scurried out the door behind his former workmates.

Peter was sure the men knew more than they were telling him, which was frustrating. But he couldn't think how he might be able to earn their trust. It seemed likely that at least some of the men at that table could be complicit in the attacks on Rose, which would explain their stonewalling him. But, if that was true, did that mean that Dutch, as a member of their circle, was guilty as well? Or was there something else the men were trying to keep him from finding out? And what of the mysterious Scotty—was he significant, or had Anna simply gotten the name wrong?

The Green Gale had filled up, and the increased noise and smoke in the air made him long for the damp clean of the street. He crossed to the stool to retrieve his hat. Phebe, seeing him prepare to go, finished delivering a tray loaded with dark-brown pints of ale to a nearby table and came over. Her round serving tray was clutched in one arm and clasped in front of her like an Amazon's shield. "Did you find what you were looking for, handsome?"

Peter acknowledged that Dutch's friends had been little help. "Do those men come here often?" he indicated the now empty corner table.

"Pretty often. I guess you could say they're regulars. They used to come every day after work, Dutch included. But ever since they were fired, they don't come quite so often. No sign of—what was it, Scotty, then?" She seemed satisfied when Peter shook his head dejectedly.

Peter wondered what to ask. He couldn't help feeling that the right question might unlock the whole mystery. "Tell me, were those fellows here last Thursday . . . the night Matt died?" Not that it would matter if they were, he chided himself. As he had reminded Phebe earlier, Matt probably hadn't died until the small hours of Friday morning.

"Now that you come to ask it, they weren't. I didn't see them at all last week. But as I say, they aren't here every night anymore." Peter nodded, his mind already elsewhere as he headed for the exit. "Hey . . . what about you? Will I see you around here again?"

Phebe winked, which made him uncomfortable. Whatever had made him think she was attractive, he wondered? Standing there now, grinning broadly, with one curly black tendril pasted to her forehead with the sweat of her exertions, she looked like no more than the blowsy and coarse, if admittedly sharp-witted, barmaid she was. Without answering her, he headed out into the fading dusk.

SEVEN

Dear Mama,

I was so glad to hear from you. As I am so far away, news of home gives me great comfort, and I wish there were some way for us to have a visit easily. Instead, my words on this page will have to suffice.

Since I last wrote, I have started a new temporary job, sewing and altering dresses for a nice Jewish family here in Portland. One of the ladies, Mrs. Fowler, is expecting her first child, and I am quite busy altering her clothes to keep her dressed nicely throughout . . .

THE LETTER WENT ON for several pages, but said little. After reading it over, Libby signed her name and sealed the envelope. She had promised herself she would be more forthcoming and truthful in her dealings with her parents, yet she had consciously not mentioned the attempts on her employer's life. Nor had she told them of her new friend Peter Eberle and her attachment to him.

Sighing, she decided that after she had finished helping Peter with this story she would figure out what she should do next. Could she really make Portland her permanent home? Was she ready to divorce Mr. Greenblatt in civil court and risk being disowned by her parents? Wouldn't they disown her anyway, even if she got a rabbinical divorce, if she then married a non-Jew?

No matter how she weighed alternatives and tried to picture a happy ending for Peter and herself, she couldn't do it. Every path reached a dead end. So, even if she wasn't pleased with her current situation, she had to see it did have certain advantages. She saw Peter on a regular basis. She could stay in contact with her family, but avoid the worst of their attempts to reunite her with Mr. Greenblatt. She had an exciting task to pursue, one without any thorny emotional complications. There was a man sitting in prison who needed her help! That is what she should be concentrating on, she decided.

And so, her own problems deferred, Libby headed out. She dropped her letter in the postbox by the streetcar, then went back to pondering the attacks on Hiram Rose. The thrill of her mission to help Peter find out information certainly made her tedious work at the Rose household less dull. Her problem was getting Eva Fowler to open up to her. She had made some headway at the Rose home by speaking to the staff, but the Fowlers had no servants of their own. And all of her conversations with Eva thus far, since the night Peter had asked her help, had been confined to discussions of dressmaking and food. Perhaps she could use a discussion of the new baby to broach the topic of Eva's husband and Matt. At the very least, she determined to find some way to bring Matt up.

As she went over possible stratagems, she could feel herself becoming more cheerful.

It was with a spring in her step that she knocked at the front door of the Fowler house twenty minutes later. When there was no answer, she tentatively pushed the door inward, shocked at her own forwardness. "Hello . . . ? Mrs. Fowler?" No answer was forthcoming, and Libby stepped all the way into the small foyer. "Is anyone home?"

Eva Fowler was probably next door with her sister-in-law. Which must mean she was feeling better. Libby knew she should turn right around and go next door, but instead she placed her bag and basket down and shut the door behind her without making a sound. Suddenly she heard voices upstairs, one higher pitched and obviously emotional, but too quiet to make out the words. Eva appeared to be arguing with someone.

Libby moved to the bottom of the staircase and managed to make out Eva saying, "Father would turn over in his grave if he could hear the way you speak to me!"

The identity of the other party was not a mystery for long. In loud clear tones, Hiram Rose's voice came ringing through the house. "Don't throw Father at me! He'd tell you the same as I. You need to get out of that bed and start behaving like a responsible adult. I expect to see you at dinner tonight. It's time you started remembering that your behavior reflects on me . . . on this whole family. Don't shame me, Eva."

"A fine one you are to talk about shameful behavior." A door slammed, cutting off Eva's voice, and footsteps came thundering down the stairs. Libby quickly backed up and pretended to be entering just at that moment.

"Hello?" she called for the second time. Hiram Rose, red-faced and slightly out of breath, reached the front hallway just as she closed the door behind her for the second time, this time with a loud click. "Oh, Mr. Rose, hello."

He grunted in reply.

"Is Mrs. Fowler here?" she asked innocently. "I brought some dresses for her to try on."

"Upstairs." He brushed past her and left, not even bothering to address her by name. His departure was so abrupt that she was unsure what to do next, but then she figured Hiram Rose had as good as granted her permission to see his sister with his terse answer as to her whereabouts. "Mrs. Fowler?" she called, starting up and stopping halfway up. "It's me, Miss Seale. May I come up?"

"Miss Seale? Yes, yes, come here. My bedroom is on the right." Eva called out directions rather than coming out into the hall, behavior that bordered on the rude. Perhaps she believed her pregnancy was an excuse. Libby followed the voice to a closed door, which she opened somewhat tentatively. She was not used to moving about the private parts of a client's house without a maid leading the way. "Come in, come in!" she heard in an imperious tone.

Eva Fowler was sitting on the edge of the bed, tying the sash on a dressing gown and looking flushed. Libby looked around the room and couldn't help noticing the sparse furnishings. Downstairs, the front rooms were decorated lavishly, but the upstairs of the Fowler's home told a different story about the couple's fortunes.

"Let me see what you've brought," Eva ordered, settling herself back under the covers. Feeling somewhat annoyed at being ordered about like a servant, Libby forced a pleasant expression as she opened her big carpet bag. Her good mood was gone, and she suspected she would once again be unable to get any useful information out of Eva. Pulling out a bolt of pale blue fabric, along with a roll of hyacinth velvet trim, she said, "I bought these for a new smock dress. That ought to be good when everything else is too confining." She smiled. "I thought they would look especially nice with your coloring."

Eva Fowler, surrounded as she was with pillows and blankets, regarded the seamstress sitting on the chair beside her bed. "It's very pretty. But what's the use? I won't be up and dressed and out of the house for a long time."

So much for Hiram's departing order to appear at dinner. Libby said soothingly, "I hope that's not the case. Perhaps this tiredness will pass soon, and you'll feel good as new. I understand things often change from week to week when you're expecting." Libby couldn't help but notice that Eva Fowler hardly fit the picture of a woman dealing with a difficult confinement. In New York, she had visited the bedside of more than one family friend or relative who had troubles during this delicate time in a woman's life, but they had looked wan and sickly. Mrs. Fowler's cheeks were rosy, and even lying in a bed she seemed full of energy.

She unwrapped the first of the old dresses she had altered for Eva, a rich butter-colored silk. Libby had hidden the new seaming where she had let the bodice out to allow for Eva's increasing girth with cascading loops of burgundy grosgrain ribbon. This would also help draw the eye away from the pregnant woman's belly. Eva reached over and pulled it toward herself. "Is this big enough? It still looks quite narrow in the waist."

"That's a trick of the cut," Libby explained, pride creeping into her voice. "With the right side seams and trim to divert the eye, a dress can be much more forgiving than it appears." She held up the second dress. "I made this next one a bit larger. I wanted to make sure that no matter what happened, you'd have at least one dress that feels comfortable."

Eva tossed the butter-colored dress back at her. "Please hang them both by my dressing screen, over there. I'll try them on later."

"If you feel up to it, I'd prefer to fit them now. That way, I can make any necessary small alterations right here, and they will be done."

Sighing, Eva sat up on the edge of her bed. "Oh, all right, I suppose I can try them on. But I will need your help."

"Of course." For several minutes, neither woman spoke, as Libby helped the larger woman into her corset, tying it loosely, and then Eva tried on each dress in turn. She stood in front of a dressing table with a large oval mirror, turning this way and that. She was obviously trying to assess how visible her pregnancy would be to a casual observer, and her hands instinctively cupped her abdomen. At one point, she opened a large jewelry box and held a few necklaces up to her throat experimentally. "I always used to wear this one with this dress." She held out a narrow gold chain with a locket. "But now that you've added the ribbon, I think the other one looks better. What do you think, Miss Seale?"

"You're right, the beads do look better against the lace. More contrast," replied Libby. Eva regarded the locket, as if trying to decide something. She seemed to come to some decision and snapped it open, removing the small picture that had been within it. Then she turned to Libby.

"Miss Seale, would you do me a favor? I don't have anyone else to ask, and I feel I can trust you." She twisted the gold chain around her fingers as she spoke.

"Of course, Mrs. Fowler. If I can do it, I will. What is it?"

Eva Fowler's voice lowered, even though there was no one else in the room. "I would like to sell a few pieces of my jewelry. To the kind of merchant who buys valuables for cash and doesn't ask any questions. Do you know the sort of place I mean?"

"A pawnbroker, yes," said Libby. She had never been to a pawnbroker in Portland, but when she was growing up, the ones in her neighborhood had done a steady business. Pawnshops had always struck her as repositories more for sad stories than expendable belongings. "I'm sure I could find one in downtown Portland, although I don't know of a particular one." She paused, realizing this gave her a perfect opening. "I suppose you used to have Matt to take care of these sorts of errands for you."

Eva continued looking in the mirror, but despite the lack of encouragement Libby plowed ahead. "It must be difficult for you, losing a member of the household you had come to rely on." She paused, not sure if she had said too much. "That is, I think Celia or one of the other staff mentioned that you used to pay Matt to run extra errands for you on his day off."

"Oh really? You shouldn't believe everything you hear, Miss Seale." Eva's voice was clipped. "I never paid Matt anything to run errands for me, despite what anyone might have told you, but if this is your way of asking for some remuneration for your labors, I will be happy to pay you a small stipend."

Libby was abashed. "Oh, no, I didn't mean it that way at all!" She scrambled to change the topic. "I just can't help thinking about how difficult it must have been for all of you lately. Especially with the further episode this week, someone shooting arrows at your brother."

"Hiram wasn't hurt, you know." Eva sounded almost disappointed, and certainly dismissive.

"But it still must have been quite shocking when he came in and told you all that had happened."

"I wasn't even there. I was at home when it happened. By the time I got to dinner, there wasn't really much to talk about. Hiram had sent word to the police, and that was that." Libby recalled that this corroborated what Celia had told her about the scene at the Rose house. She wished she could think of some way to mention Augustus, but Eva had sat back down on the bed looking at the picture from the locket.

Libby crossed to her and peered over her shoulder. "What a pretty picture! May I see?" Eva handed over the picture but made no comment. The somewhat faded image showed a child's face, wearing a very serious expression. "Your husband?"

"My brother," Eva said flatly. "The locket was my mother's, but I've never liked it. Please just take it." She handed Libby the piece of jewelry, taking the picture back in return. Carefully secreting the tiny photograph in her bedside table drawer, she lay back on her pillow and closed her eyes. "You can see yourself out."

———

Despite the discomfort caused by riding on a bumpy unpaved road, Half-Cent couldn't keep the grin off his face. Pittock, the delivery horse owned by the *Gazette*, swayed beneath him. John Mayhew had told him that they named the horse after rival newspaper publisher, Henry Pittock of the *Oregonian*, and Half-Cent thought it a fine joke. Every time he gave the horse a friendly slap on the neck he said, with his best John Mayhew impression, "Get a move on, Pittock!" and smiled again at the indignity of it. Henry Pittock wouldn't be pleased to know the *Portland Gazette* was delivered every day on an old nag that bore his name.

Half-Cent was enjoying being an investigative reporter . . . or at least assistant reporter. Riding a horse was a lot more exciting than hanging around the police station, and a secret pursuit of Hiram Rose was almost as exciting as a tale in *Boy's Own Adventures* magazine. Half-Cent avoided notice by keeping some distance between Pittock and Rose's mount, and as the turnoff to the Rose Paperworks approached, he slowed down even more. It wouldn't do to have Rose turn around and notice he was being followed; best to play it safe and give his quarry a long lead. Unobtrusively shadowing Rose in the hopes of catching his would-be killer was the biggest task Peter had given him. He didn't want to muff it up. For one thing, he enjoyed the chance to get out of the city, relishing the feeling of the wind on his face as he cantered through the mostly untouched landscape.

As he watched, Hiram Rose made the expected turn onto Papermill Road. Half-Cent came to a stop and, for the benefit of the few other riders and carriages on the road, pretended to adjust his saddle. After what he judged to be a suitable delay, he followed the mill owner. To his left was a narrow path leading up to a workers encampment, marked with a crudely painted wooden sign in Chinese characters, which, needless to say, he couldn't read. He hoped it didn't say "Trespassers will be shot" since he now turned onto the path and rode part way up the hillside. As far as he could tell, the camp ahead was deserted (it was the middle of the working day), but rather than risk being asked to state his business, he jumped down and tied the horse to a sturdy tree near the bottom of the slope. "Stay, Pittock," he murmured, and the animal seemed to whinny in agreement.

Keeping off the main road, he made his way through the brush to the large mill building. Smoke was pouring out of two prominent chimneys, and there was a nasty stench in the air. A large sign in front proclaimed The Rose Paperworks in fading red paint, with a small picture of a rose in place of the letter o. A small sign stating "Visitors" marked a wide staircase on the right. Seeing no one outside, Half-Cent sprinted through the yard and around to the back. A second-story porch ran the length of the building's rear, just as Peter had described, making a shadowed hollow beneath it. "It might be a good place to stay out of sight," the reporter had suggested. He figured here he would be able to see Rose whenever he left, as well as see anyone who entered.

Sitting on the ground, Half-Cent leaned against the cool stone of the mill's foundation and closed his eyes. Overhead, he heard doors opening and closing, and occasional footsteps. For what seemed like a long while, nothing happened. A few times he heard someone coming down the stairs, and each time he crept to the corner and stuck his head out to check, but it was never Hiram Rose. He was wishing he had brought something to read—and eat!—when somewhere above him a door slammed, and heavy footsteps made their way to the far end of the porch, right over his head. The voices were barely above a whisper, and Half-Cent had to strain to hear.

"Dammit, Kearney, didn't I tell you not to give me messages at the mill?"

"But he wanted me to get an answer from you today," the other man answered back just as fiercely. "How else am I going to meet with you?"

"Use common sense, man! After that accident on the catwalk, people are paying attention to everything that goes on around here. Police, reporters, all snooping around. The last thing I need is for my name to be linked with Manning at this delicate juncture!" There was a rustling of papers and a few sentences Half-Cent couldn't make out. Then the first man continued. "In the future, any communications between Mr. Manning and myself are to be delivered to my home. Never at the mill!"

"All right, all right, you've made your point. But we're here now, I need to bring him an answer. Shall I tell him you'll do it?"

"You know that I will. Now listen, here's what I want you to tell Manning . . ." Once again, the voice dropped to the point that the words were indistinguishable. A moment later, there was the distinct sound of a door opening and closing, and then overhead, the thunder of footsteps coming down the staircase. Half-Cent peered out and saw a man crossing the clearing to where a bicycle was chained to a tree. For a moment, Half-Cent forgot his original purpose, so intrigued was he by the newfangled conveyance. He had seen a few people riding them in the past several months, but they were still very much a novelty, these two-wheeled contraptions. One sat astride, like on a horse, but powered the thing by pedaling with one's legs. Soon enough, he remembered that the more important thing to note was the man, not the bicycle. He assembled a description in his head to report to Peter later: the man was short, with sandy hair getting a bit thin on top, a brown-checkered suit, and he carried a trilby hat. As Half-Cent watched, the man pedaled away up the road toward Portland.

For a moment, he toyed with the idea of abandoning Rose to follow this fellow, but decided to stay put. Peter would surely find the events of the past several minutes interesting, but Half-Cent's assignment was keeping watch for anything suspicious directly related to Hiram Rose. He would tell Peter about the overheard conversation later.

Half-Cent went back to his seat against the wall and tried not to doze off as morning turned into afternoon. The rest of the day was uneventful, and after seeing Rose leave for the day, he set off back to the *Gazette*, hoping his next day's work as a spy would prove more interesting.

———

There was a ringing in Elliot Rose's ears, and his legs felt so weak that had he not already been sitting down he would surely have collapsed. Dimly he was aware that his father was still speaking to him, or more accurately at him, going on about all the salutary aspects of the Ulysses S. Grant Wilderness Academy—how it was located on the flanks of Mt. Hood, and how each morning the cadets set off on a bracing three-mile hike (before breakfast), through some of the most stunning scenery Oregon could offer.

His mother was in the room too, but she looked as shocked as Elliot felt, and had yet to utter a single syllable. This was confirmation, as if he needed it, that this heinous plan was his father's idea. Elliot managed to find his voice and interrupted his father. "Why are you doing this to me? Am I being punished?" Unfortunately, the manly tone he had been aiming for was somewhat undercut when his voice cracked on the word "punished," making him sound twelve years old.

"Punished? Nonsense, son," Hiram Rose boomed, exuding false bonhomie. Whenever he called him "son" instead of Eli or Ellie, Elliot knew he wouldn't like what he was about to hear. "This school is one of the most exclusive in the state. Do you have any idea what strings I had to pull to get you enrolled in the middle of the spring term? You're a lucky young man! Around here you can't seem to spend enough time in that foolish garden, fussing with the flowerbeds, and now you'll have the majesty of the Oregon wilderness all around you, to loll about in to your heart's content."

If every morning started with a three-mile hike, Elliot highly doubted there was much lolling of any kind, ever, at the Grant Wilderness Academy.

Adele finally spoke up. "You can't send Elliot away, Hiram. He needs me."

Rose wheeled on his wife. "What Elliot needs is a little less of your pampering and babying. That's why he's been acting so superior and rude of late. Refusing to help out when he's expressly asked, and always off somewhere, doing God knows what. The Academy will make a man out of him."

"But what will I tell Mr. Avenier? Elliot can't just stop his painting lessons. Not when he's been making such progress . . ." Adele was now near tears.

"That's just the sort of nonsense I'm talking about. Of what earthly use is painting? Elliot is going to take over the Paperworks when the time comes. And it's my job as his father to see that he grows up into a fine, upstanding businessman. Let's hear no more about this painting business." Hiram rose to indicate the discussion was at an end. "Someday you'll thank me for having given you this opportunity, son. Now, your train leaves at seven in the morning on Tuesday, so I suggest you go and start getting your things ready."

Hiram left the room, leaving behind mother and son, the first weeping silently, the second sitting in stony silence. "Darling, let me help you pack," Adele sniffled.

"No." Elliot got up and headed for the door. "Leave me alone. I can do it for myself." The hurt look on his mother's face pleased Elliot. He wasn't sure why he wanted to wound his mother, but right now he wanted everybody around him to feel hurt. And if she hadn't been such an ineffectual crybaby she would have found some way to defy her husband and save him from that awful school. He slammed the door to the study, just to make sure everyone in the house knew how unhappy he was, and trudged up the stairs to the third floor.

At least here, in the suite of rooms under the eaves that housed the Rose boys and the household staff, he felt safe from further indignity. His father never ventured upstairs and his mother only rarely. He found the sanctuary of his room and threw himself on the bed. If there were any kind of justice in this world, it would be his father who would be sent away. Forever. Elliot buried his head in his pillow. Why, of all the people in the world, was he chosen to suffer so? Couldn't his father see that he was destined for greater things than climbing up mountains? He was going to make art that astonished people! But nobody understood. Not even his mother, even if she pretended to. She didn't know good art from bad art. He was completely and utterly alone, and he felt like the universe had conspired to place him in a family where he would always feel a stranger.

He felt tears wanting to come, but he ruthlessly pushed them back. Hauling himself up, he headed to the closet for his trunk. He wasn't going to cry, even if no one could see. That would be like admitting his father was right. That would be like letting his father win.

He was halfheartedly sifting through shirts a few minutes later when his brothers appeared in his doorway. "What are you doing?" said Izzy. Izzy was the older twin by just minutes, but he always took the conversational lead when the twins were together. Fussy seemed happy enough to let Izzy do the talking, but Elliot suspected that some of the duo's more mischievous schemes originated in the quieter twin's devious mind.

"I'm packing," Elliot said, annoyed. Even a seven-year-old should be able to tell that much.

"Why?"

"For school."

"But it's Saturday. There's no school on Saturday." Izzy's logic was impeccable.

Elliot went on with his packing, doing his best to ignore the questions. "I'm going away to school from now on. In the mountains."

"The mountains? Wow! You're lucky." The twins clambered on the bed, upsetting a stack of socks. "Will you get to climb on rocks and things?"

"Get off my socks," Elliot said peevishly. Izzy grabbed the socks he'd been sitting on and threw them on the floor.

Fussy spoke for the first time. "Elliot? When you're on top of a mountain, can you touch the sky?"

"No. No mountain is that high." He stooped to pick up the socks, hoping that the twins would get bored and leave him alone.

Fussy frowned. "But if you piled two mountains on top of each other, then would it be high enough?"

"How can you stack mountains on top of each other?"

Fussy shrugged. Despite his mood, Elliot smiled and took pity on him. His brother was only seven after all. "I'll tell you what, Fussy. I'll give it a try when I'm at school, and when I come home I'll tell you the answer." This seemed to satisfy the little boy, and without another word both twins wandered off to get into trouble. He looked after them a little wistfully, then reason reasserted itself. He must truly be lost if he was now getting sentimental about his annoying little brothers.

He wandered over to the corner of his room where his easel and paints were set up. Should he pack art supplies? They probably wouldn't let him paint at school, he decided, but he wrapped a few of his favorite brushes in a paint-spattered rag to tuck in his trunk anyway. The scent of linseed oil clung to the little parcel, and he could take it out and smell it when he wanted to remind himself what his true goal in life was.

He stepped back and critically assessed the half-finished picture on the easel, wondering if he would ever finish it now. It was an attempt at painting in a modern style (despite his teacher Mr. Avenier's dislike of all things modern—Mr. Avenier always made him copy from classical models, claiming it was the only way to train) and showed the view from his bedroom window. Elliot had to admit he didn't know whether it was terrible or just right. The truth was he didn't know what it was supposed to look like, having seen very little modern art in person. Most of his knowledge came from reading about the salons in Paris and Vienna where new artists were trying to redefine what a painting could be. The modernists infused their canvases with a rainbow of colors, applied in tiny daubs, broad strokes, or thick slashes, trying to pin down their impression of a place. Their aim was to reveal the emotional subtext of a setting, rather than simply making an accurate facsimile of it on canvas.

In Elliot's version of his backyard, the woods looked dark and foreboding as if enemies were hiding within, replete with blue and greenish-purple shadows, while the garden shed was picked out in yellows and pinks, as if a dawning sun were rising just behind it. The colors didn't make any logical sense, and the scene certainly didn't look like the actual view from his window. It didn't help that Elliot had messed up the perspective on the shed so it looked like the walls were buckling. Still he liked the way the shed looked happy, as if it existed in a dream.

Suddenly Elliot hated his painting, and picking up a palette knife, he slashed at the canvas until it hung in ragged strips from the frame and his hands were smeared with half-dry paint.

He leaned his forehead against the cool glass of the window. The day outside was bright, for the first time in weeks, and the midday sun beat down on the empty yard. It would be a perfect day for him to paint, if only . . . He wished it would rain. Wished it would storm. That would match the way he felt—the sky crying for him and his pitiful life. But no, today the sun was shining, the universe signaling that Elliot's feelings didn't matter at all in the grand scheme of things.

The garden shed, bright in the winter sun, somehow managed to look forlorn to Elliot's eyes. Never again would he sneak a cigarette with Matt in there. All the plans they'd talked about in that shed, all the dreams that had now come to nothing. There Elliot had longed for the day when he would no longer have to worry about what his father said or wanted him to do. And now it was Matt, his only friend, who was gone while his father was still very much here. That had been the worst day of his life—finding his favorite person in the world gone forever. And no one had cared. His mother thought of Matt as just an ignorant handyman, and his father treated Matt like he was one of the horses.

If Matt were here, he'd never let my father do this to me, Elliot thought. Matt had been his protector. He had joked with Elliot, held Elliot when his father made him cry. He had treated Elliot like a man. The hot tears that he had been trying to hold back finally sprang to his eyes. Staring out of the window, he sobbed until he had no more tears to shed, and a new resolve filled him. Matt was gone, but Elliot was still here, and he still had a chance to make the dreams they'd discussed come true. His father was wrong if he thought he could just ship Elliot off to military school and forget about him. No matter how they tried to break him at the Grant Academy, he wouldn't let them. Hate would keep him strong. Hatred of his father.

———

Shortly after Libby arrived, Adele had scurried off to deal with some sort of crisis with Elliot, promising to return in a few minutes. It was now almost half an hour later, and Libby was still waiting in the Rose's fashionably overstuffed dining room. She had used the first few minutes alone to carefully remove the lace runner from the big mahogany table, as well as the cut glass fruit bowl from its center, and then she had laid out six bolts of fabric she had brought for Mrs. Rose to choose from. Everything was in readiness now . . . all that was missing was the mistress of the house, and then Libby could get down to work.

Libby glanced around again, wondering if there was anything useful she could glean about the household from the room. It was large, but dark, filled with too much furniture (obviously of good quality and shipped out at great expense from back East). All the carved surfaces, with their scrollwork and floral garlands, were partly what made the room feel smaller than it was. That, and the fact that so little light got past the heavy draperies (velvet over satin, swagged over lace). All in all it was a depressing room, but, unfortunately, sparked no insights about the attacks on Hiram Rose.

Finally Adele reappeared, her eyes rimmed with tears. Libby suppressed a sigh. Tears were becoming something of a feature of her tenure in the Rose household.

Libby gestured to the fabrics on the dining room table. "I brought you a few different styles to choose from, Mrs. Rose. I know you were set on green for the party dress, but I brought a few patterns in tones of gold that I think might be very flattering on you."

"I'm sorry, Miss Seale, I can't possibly think about that today. My mind is in such a muddle there's no way I could make a decision. I only stopped in to tell you that you'll have to bring them back tomorrow. We can decide then."

Libby looked with obvious dismay at the six large bolts of fabric. "Are you certain? Perhaps you can just take a glance and narrow your choice down to two or three that I can cart back tomorrow." She knew she was allowing her frustration to be evident in her tone of voice. And she shouldn't have used the word "cart" in that sarcastic way, implying as it did that the task was an onerous and unwelcome one. But she was miffed at having been made to wait so long, only to be told she wasn't needed at all. She tried to temper her tone. "Or . . . perhaps I can leave them here overnight?"

Anger at the temerity of this lowly seamstress in making such a fuss flashed in Adele's eyes, replacing the tears. "And where are we supposed to eat dinner? In the kitchen?" At the doorway, Adele drew herself up and attempted to look down at Libby, a difficult feat as Libby was a few inches taller than she. "You may go and tell Stubbins I said he should hitch up the carriage. He can drive you home, with all your parcels."

"Thank you, that's most kind of you," Libby offered, but Adele had gone from the room. As quickly as she could, she packed up the fabrics and shoved them awkwardly under her arm alongside the basket she always carried with her needles, tape measure, spools of thread, and the like.

Outside the day was bright, but there was a chill wind that reminded Libby spring was not here yet. She knocked on the half-open barn door. "Mr. Stubbins?" she called out, and poked her head inside. It wasn't a large building, but there were stalls for four horses and room for at least two carriages in the center. Libby looked around, wondering if she should be searching for clues. Could Wilmer Stubbins possibly have been Matt's accomplice in the household—after all, he was the one who had worked almost every day beside Matt. Then she recalled that Wilmer was with Hiram during the arrow attack, and realized that he was the one person who couldn't possibly have shot at him.

"Yes, Miss?" A voice from the shadows startled her, but it was swiftly revealed as belonging to an aging Negro man with a friendly face. Obviously Stubbins. One glance at his slightly stooped back and arthritic hands, and she laughed inside to think she had been trying to cast him as a would-be assassin.

"Mr. Stubbins," she began.

"Oh, call me Stubbins, Miss. No need to be fancy." His soft voice had the warm, honeyed flavor of the deep South in it. Just listening to it made the drafty barn feel warmer.

Libby smiled. "Mrs. Rose said to ask you if you would mind hitching up one of the horses and driving me home. As you can see, I'm carrying quite a lot!"

"Here, Miss. Let me help you with those. Let's put 'em in the carriage, and then I'll hitch Frieda up and have you home in no time at all." Swiftly the parcels were placed on the carriage seat, and then Libby followed Wilmer to the stalls.

"Which one is Frieda?" she asked. She was hanging around, hoping to switch the topic to Matt, but there was genuine interest in her question as well. Libby loved horses, though she was rarely around them anymore.

"She's the Bay over here. She's Mr. Rose's favorite . . . mine, too, I don't mind saying. But since Mr. Rose is home for the day, we can use Frieda to pull the carriage." He began to put the bridle on her. "You partial to horses, Miss?"

"Yes, as a matter of fact, I am. My father had a horse to pull his fruit cart. When I was a little girl I used to tell people she was my best friend." It was a happy memory, and Libby glowed. "Her name was Gvaldik."

"What kind of a name is that? That a word in Jewish? I know a couple, but I don't know that one."

Libby looked at him in surprise. "Yes it is. It means mighty. It was a kind of joke on my father's part. Gvaldik was just an old work-horse, way past her prime, but I thought she was the greatest crea-ture in the world. How is it you know some words in Yiddish?"

"Oh, I learned 'em as a little boy, on the Maiers' planta-tion . . . that was Mrs. Rose's family name, you understand, before she married. Miss Adele, she didn't have no use for Jewish, but her grandfather was a great man for horses, and he didn't speak nothin' but. And so I picked up a bit here and there, around the stables."

With a start Libby realized that Stubbins must have been born a slave. He was clearly at least in his sixties, and the slaves had only been freed thirty years before. She had never met anybody who had been reared in bondage, just like her ancestors had been all those millennia ago in Egypt, and she was suddenly filled with questions for him. Only . . . that would be tactless, wouldn't it, to ask about what it was like to be a slave? She couldn't, and besides (she suddenly remembered) she was supposed to be asking about Matt.

Without attempting any sort of subtle conversation shift, she did just that. "I expect there's much more work for you now. I mean since Matt was . . . since Matt died."

"Yes, Miss, there sure is." He continued putting the bridle on Frieda.

"Tell me, do you believe it? That Matt was attempting to kill Mr. Rose? That's what the police are saying, isn't it?"

He cocked his head. "No one has asked my opinion about it one way or t'other. I guess . . . well, to speak truth, I didn't know the young fella too well for all that we worked together for over a year."

"What exactly did Matt do around here? It seems as if every person remembers his duties differently." Libby sighed, "He's been described to me as the gardener and the coachman, and oh, I don't know what else."

"That's about the shape of it, Miss. He did whatever needed doing. Well, most anything that needed a strong young lad. I'm not as spry as I once was, and Matt was strong enough, all right. But not . . ." Wilmer paused, as if trying how to decide what he was trying to say. "He wasn't strong in the mean, rough kind of way, and he didn't seem to care that what Mr. Rose paid him wasn't half what he could make over at the mill. No, Matt preferred to be with the horses and his flowers. I 'spects that's why he didn't join his pa and his brother over to the Paperworks. Not cause he wasn't up to the work, but he didn't want to be cooped up all day inside."

Libby digested this, then asked, "Did he seem any different those last few weeks of his life? I mean, if he was leaving threatening letters for Mr. Rose and planning to kill him surely there would have been some signs. Maybe he was talking about leaving here?"

"He maybe seemed a bit distracted right before he died, but he wasn't planning on going anywhere. Right around St. Valentine's Day, bitter cold it was and I was grumbling about it—never have gotten used to these Oregon winters . . . cold and damp just gets right into my bones—anyway, I was grumbling, and Matt, I remember him saying it didn't bother him. He had this sort of satisfied smile, and said how this situation suited him fine. 'I got me a good thing here, Wilmer,' he says. That's how he put it."

Libby waited, but apparently Stubbins had exhausted the subject of Matt Karlsson. He didn't seem to wonder why Libby was so interested, and so she didn't offer any explanation. After a pause, though, Stubbins turned to her and said, "I'll hitch Frieda up to the carriage. It'll be a few minutes. You might as well wait for me in the drive and enjoy the sunshine while we've got it."

Libby nodded, and without further comment exited the barn. Cutting across the lawn, she wandered alongside the towering laurel hedge that separated the Roses' yard from the Fowler's and headed for the front drive. As she came to the end of the hedge, she heard a jingling bell and caught sight of a man on a bicycle just as he was turning off of the drive onto the main road. She caught a glimpse of fair hair, but could see little else before he disappeared. She thought he had probably come from the Fowler's house.

She peeked around the hedge to see Augustus Fowler on his front porch, confirming her suspicion. He was reading a letter, which presumably the man on the bicycle must have just delivered. As Libby started toward the porch to say hello to Augustus, she noticed the bright noonday sunlight picked out an elaborate watermark as it shone through the notepaper in his hand. It looked like some sort of bird . . . one with a large beak. A crane! That was it. "Mr. Fowler, it is a lovely day, isn't it? Too nice a day to be cooped up indoors."

Augustus Fowler looked up startled. He had been so focused on his reading he had not heard her soft footfalls across the grass. "Good day, Miss Seale," he said, shoving the paper into his jacket pocket. He didn't sound nervous, but she could have sworn he didn't want her to see the note he had been staring at so intently.

"How is Mrs. Fowler feeling today? Better, I hope?"

"Somewhat better, yes. Thank you for asking after her." He shifted a bit nervously from foot to foot, "Actually, I best get inside to see if she needs anything. You will excuse me?" Without waiting for a reply he went back into his house and closed the door.

She wondered what the note could have been about that had him so wound up. It probably had nothing whatsoever to do with Matt or the attacks on his brother-in-law, but she made a note to mention it to Peter nonetheless, the next time they spoke.

Then Wilmer pulled up in the carriage, and she got in, thankful at least to avoid the long walk and then trolley ride back to Mrs. Pratt's.

EIGHT

THE LAST RAYS OF the little-seen March sun filled the street with a deep yellow light. Peter was lounging outside the door, enjoying the first hint of the spring to come, as Libby's figure appeared halfway down the block from the *Gazette* office. He was thus afforded time to gaze at her uninterrupted, with a stare that would have been rude had he tried to do it across a table or during a conversation. The sinking sun burnished her hair, giving it a corona of gold, and as she neared him, her soft brown eyes glimmered with flecks of amber. It was a very flattering light, that was for sure. But was it merely the light that made Peter think she was the most appealing woman he had ever known, or was it simply that she was Libby?

He gave a lopsided grin as she reached him, a little out of breath, and the moment was perfect. For the moment he didn't care about the fact that she had a husband. He didn't care that all she could offer him was a sisterly sort of affection. He just wanted to be near her. He had been looking forward to this meeting ever since his departure from Mrs. Pratt's boardinghouse two days before. Now that she was here, he wanted to speak of anything but Dutch Karlsson and Hiram Rose. So he cut off her first comment with a wave of his hand, and doffing his hat in a comically elaborate gesture, said, "Dinner first, milady. Business after."

"Dinner?" she queried. "Peter, you don't need to—"

"Yes, I am taking you out to a first-class dinner. It's the least I can do, since you're the one doing me a favor. I know how you like to argue, but this is one argument you'll lose. You might as well accept my hospitality with grace."

She laughed. Peter could always make her laugh, and that was what she had missed more than anything in the weeks they were apart. She took his proffered arm and they began to stroll toward whatever restaurant Peter had chosen. She didn't ask, she didn't care. She let herself be led and tried to forget that they weren't a courting couple on their way to a dinner date.

It turned out they were headed for a restaurant she had heard of, Jake's Crawfish House, at the corner of 10th and Washington. They entered through a front bar and made their way back to a smaller dining area traced with dark wood beams against plain white walls. The waiter, a spotless white apron reinforcing the atmosphere of cleanliness and modernity, seated them at a table by the back and handed them large cards printed with the day's bill of fare. Libby, who was quite hungry, made up her mind quickly and laid her menu to one side. Peter, on the other hand, perused his carefully, apparently reading every entry before making his mind up and raising his eyes to meet hers.

"Now may I tell you what I've learned?" she asked with a gently mocking smile.

"Oh, I suppose so. But just until the waiter comes to take our order."

Quickly she outlined the basic facts she had uncovered about the whereabouts of the household during the arrow attack on Hiram Rose. "I don't see how I can get any further regarding Eva and Augustus Fowler's whereabouts. She claims she was in their house, preparing to head over to the Roses' for dinner, and he hadn't yet returned from the mill. But I will find out where Miss Baylis was. I haven't had a moment to speak with her yet."

"I'm sure you will. What about the eldest boy? Elliot, right?"

Of course he had noticed that in her list of suspects, she had left Elliot out. "No one seems to know where he was. It's odd about Elliot . . ." She hesitated. She liked Elliot, and more importantly, she pitied him. She was afraid that what she had to tell Peter might cause him to wonder if Elliot was involved somehow in the attacks on his father. She wished she could honestly say she didn't wonder herself. "Elliot seems to be the only person in the household who spent any time with Matt. Certainly he is the only person I have seen who appears to be mourning Matt's passing."

"So Elliot is your pick for Matt's accomplice?" He whistled quietly. "That's something all right . . . if he's the one attacking his own father."

"Peter. I didn't say that." She felt compelled to add, "I think his father might be afraid of that very scenario, though. Hiram is sending the boy away to some sort of military school. But that might have nothing to do with Matt at all."

"If he's being sent away to school that must mean something."

"Well, his father is not thrilled that his eldest son wants to be an artist. It may mean no more than that."

The waiter reappeared beside the table to take their orders. After they had given him their entrée selections, Peter cocked his head at Libby and asked if she'd share a plate of salted almonds and sardines as an hors d'oeuvre. She nodded, and that (plus a bottle of white wine) completed their order.

Once the waiter's back was turned, before Peter could joke any more about not discussing the investigation over dinner, Libby returned to the subject of Matt. "What strikes me as notable is that nobody in that household will admit to knowing Matt well except Elliot. In fact, the household's silence regarding him is almost suspicious. Matt worked in that house for over a year! Surely his presence must have been felt somehow. And yet all I get are bromides—how sweet Matt was, how good-looking, how kind to animals. And then it occurred to me," she leaned forward, excited, "if Matt did have an ally inside the household, one with whom he was planning something nefarious, of course that person would deny the friendship! Which would point to one of the people who denies having been close to him. Elliot's very willingness to admit he was close to Matt argues that he's the one person who doesn't think it's an association he needs to keep quiet."

Peter listened carefully and read between the lines. Far from being Libby's prime suspect, Elliot was someone she was trying very hard to exonerate. Even to the point of extremely convoluted logic. He didn't say this, however, merely let Libby continue.

"For what it's worth, Mrs. Fowler denies ever having given Matt extra cash. Either your source was mistaken, or Matt was lying about where he got the money for his father's funeral."

"Or Mrs. Fowler is lying." He sighed, "Although why would she bother hiding an act of charity? I'll have to ask Anna again about

154

exactly what Matt told her." Libby noticed Peter had casually used Miss Karlsson's Christian name, and felt a pang that she sternly reminded herself she had no right to feel.

"Yes, there's also the fact that I don't think Eva Fowler would have had money to give Matt. She just asked me to pawn some jewelry for her, and from what I've seen, the Fowlers are struggling to maintain themselves in a fashion beyond their means."

"Well, that certainly sounds like a motive. If Hiram Rose were to die, I suppose Augustus Fowler would take over?"

"I suppose so. Even if Elliot and the twins are Hiram's heirs, they're too young. And Elliot, I know, has no interest. As for Adele, well . . . yes, I suppose Augustus would be in charge."

"And, needless to say," Peter concluded, "more financially solvent."

"Well, from what I've seen, I think we can conclude that Adele Rose has no desire to see her husband out of the picture. Celia, the cook, overheard them fighting, and Adele is most anxious her husband should get himself a bodyguard. Hiram is refusing."

"Mrs. Rose is right . . . that is, if the wrong man is in jail, then someone out there still wants Hiram Rose dead."

"There hasn't been another attempt since Dutch was put behind bars," Libby pointed out uncomfortably. She didn't want to seem as if she didn't support Peter's belief in Dutch's innocence.

"There will be another attack. I feel certain." He looked at her with a satisfied grin. "That's why I've set someone to trail Mr. Rose . . . unobtrusively, of course. If and when there is another attempt, Half-Cent will be there to thwart it and help capture the real killer."

"Half-Cent?"

Peter blushed. "It's just a nickname. His real name is Billy." Peter gave her the background of the name and the boy. She expressed her amazement that one so young should have earned Peter and John Mayhew's trust, to say nothing of the ear of the Portland police. She also said she hoped she'd get a chance to meet him soon. The hors d'oeuvres were placed before them—along with china plates, heavy linen napkins, and a delicate pair of silver tongs. Ignoring the tongs, Libby used her fingers to pick up one of the celery stalks garnishing the plate of sardines and almonds.

"That was very clever of you. I mean, thinking to have someone trail Hiram Rose. I hadn't thought that he might still be in danger until I heard about Hiram and Adele's argument." She bit into the celery, which gave a loud crunch. Embarrassed, she tried to chew quietly, unaware that Peter was enjoying her efforts to eat unobtrusively. She swallowed and said, "Tell me what you have learned," and reached for the salted almonds instead.

Peter looked thoughtful. Libby had learned a great deal in just a few days, while he felt as though he'd merely spun his wheels, following avenues that had not led anywhere. He reminded himself that she had specific suspects to target, whereas his investigation was open-ended. Besides, it wasn't a contest. Still, he wished he had more to tell her.

He quickly sketched in Dutch's continued refusal to provide an alibi, his return visit to the Karlssons (was it his imagination, or did Libby look bothered every time he mentioned Anna?), and his fruitless search at the Green Gale for the man he knew of only as Scotty. He left out the part about Phebe and Matt's brief fling, for reasons he couldn't quite explain, except perhaps that Phebe's brash outspokenness had embarrassed him, and he was a man.

Surely Libby would be just as uncomfortable were he to repeat what Phebe had said. "So," he finished lamely, "is there any chance that there is a Scotty who worked at the Rose house? Another of the male servants, perhaps?"

Libby finished swallowing an almond. "No. The only other male is the old stable hand, Wilmer Stubbins. All the rest of the staff is female." She reached for another almond and was horrified to find the little dish empty. She had been eating them continuously while Peter spoke, and hoped he hadn't noticed. She didn't think he had even tasted one. But he appeared to be only thinking about where their investigation could go next, and luckily their main courses arrived at that moment to further distract him.

For a few moments they were engrossed in their meal. Libby's boiled salmon, French peas, and creamed potatoes were delicious, and a welcome relief after the saltiness of the almonds. Peter was seated in front of two of the most monstrous looking creatures Libby had ever seen, like giant roaches with bright red shells. She was put in mind of some of the wilder inhabitants of Dante's inferno. Peter explained they were crawfish, the restaurant's signature dish. She had never seen one, though she knew they were related to lobsters. Crawfish were rarely served in New York. "Would you like to try?" Peter offered, then added, "I was thinking of getting the pork chops, but I wasn't sure if you might be offended." She didn't have the heart to tell him that, like all shellfish, crawfish were no more kosher than pork. Though that wasn't the reason, she still declined a taste.

The wine and heavy dinner took their toll, and a pleasant drowsiness overtook her. She and Peter had lapsed into a companionable silence as they ate, and neither one seemed eager to break the mood with further talk of murder.

Finally Peter spoke. "I will continue to look for Scotty. I'm sure those men at the Green Gale know something. Whether that's where to find Scotty or Dutch's whereabouts on the night of Matt's death, I'll get them to tell me somehow." Libby just nodded. "I need you to look further into Augustus Fowler's dealings with Matt and his relationship with his brother-in-law and the Paperworks. Half-Cent overheard a conversation over at the mill indicating someone there is communicating with Rose's chief competitor, Unsworth Manning. Right now Fowler seems the obvious suspect, but I have no proof of that."

Libby suddenly sat up, sleepiness gone. "I forgot . . . As I was leaving the Fowler house today I saw something that seemed slightly suspicious, but I didn't know what to make of it. A man on a bicycle dropped off a note for Augustus, which he didn't even wait to read until he got into the house."

Peter's ears pricked up at the mention of the bicycle. Half-Cent had gone on and on about the man he had supposed to be Kearney riding off on the newfangled contraption. "Did you see what was in the letter?"

"No, he tucked it in his pocket as soon as he saw me approach. I did see that there was a bird watermark in the paper. The sun was shining through and—"

"A great blue heron?" Peter asked excitedly.

"Well, it had a long beak. I thought it was a crane, but I guess it could have been a heron."

Peter could have kissed her. "That's the symbol of Unsworth Manning's Willamette Papers. It looks like you spotted a direct communication between Augustus Fowler and his brother-in-law's business rival! That's just the sort of proof I was looking for!"

Libby beamed, glad her hunch had proven accurate, that the note she had caught sight of was in some way significant.

Neither of them noticed the waiter approaching, so they were surprised to see him beside the table. "A sweet perhaps, to end the meal? We have a fine selection of cakes and pastries."

Libby started to demur, but Peter caught the glimpse of desire in her eyes and said, "We'll share the biggest, most decadent piece of chocolate cake you can rustle up." He grinned, then called after the departing server, "And two large cups of coffee, please." Then to Libby, "We have some planning to do."

———

Not only was Eva up and dressed the next time Libby saw her, she was astride a horse. Libby was walking up the drive when the clattering of hooves made her start, and the next thing she knew Eva Fowler was upon her, hair flying in the breeze, a wide grin on a face flushed with exertion.

"Miss Seale!" she cried gaily. "I didn't expect you this early. Or else I have lost track of the time. Please excuse me. I will just take the horse to the stable and meet you inside the house."

"I'm glad to see you feeling better, Mrs. Fowler. It must feel good to be out in the fresh air."

Eva Fowler agreed, and for a few moments, they discussed that most banal of topics, the recent warm spell in the midst of the rainy winter. Eva went on, "I am so glad the morning was clear! I can only ride when Augustus is away at work, or he chastises me. I suppose he thinks I am too delicate, in my present condition, for my usual activities. At any rate, I will see you inside, Miss Seale, I'll just be a moment."

She rode off toward the stables, while Libby continued to the Fowler house and let herself in. As she sat in the drawing room waiting for Eva, she looked around, wondering if there was any time for her to snoop. The house was obviously empty. Quietly, she walked around the perimeter of the room, wondering what, if anything, she might discover in this rare opportunity to look around undisturbed.

The room was nicely furnished, if small, and Libby was again forced to conclude that whatever money the Fowlers possessed went toward the public area of their home. The furnishings downstairs were of a much higher caliber than the ones she had seen in Eva's bedroom. There were two comfortable-looking, velvet-tufted armchairs, with a small embroidered tapestry footstool between them. Dominating the wall opposite the bay window was a large writing desk whose top was inlaid with marquetry. Libby wondered if this room served double-duty as Augustus Fowler's study.

Tentatively, she opened the top drawer, where one would normally keep writing paper and stationery. When she spied a slim, leather-bound volume bearing the label "Household Accounts" written in a fine, balanced script, she couldn't help herself. Pulling it from its resting place, she flipped it open at random to see a page full of meticulously marked entries. Next to each bill submitted by a tradesman was the date it arrived and the date it was settled. In each case (so far as she had time to see) the bills had been paid in full the very day they came in. It was exactly the opposite of what she expected to see. If the Fowlers were not short of funds, then how to explain the way their home was furnished?

And what to make of Eva's desire to pawn her jewelry? Realizing she had spent too long with the ledger, she hurriedly stuffed it back in the drawer, suddenly aware how it would look should Eva discover her in this position.

Her move came in the nick of time, because a moment later the front door opened, and Eva came in, tousled and ruddy. With a sigh of happy exhaustion, she sank into a chair. "You can't imagine how Hiram and Augustus coddle me . . . I had to sneak out for my ride this morning. I think my husband is afraid what may happen to the baby. As you know, we've waited so long. But this baby is going to be strong and sturdy . . . just like his mother. The world looks so bright today. I feel certain nothing will go wrong."

Libby smiled. Eva was certainly in a different frame of mind this morning. Reaching into the inside pocket of her cloak, Libby took out an envelope. "Before we begin, perhaps I should give you this. I did as you asked, with the jewelry."

Eva smiled gratefully as she reached out for it. "I appreciate your discretion, Miss Seale." She tucked the envelope into the pocket of her riding jacket. "I thank you for doing me the favor. I really didn't have anyone else I could ask. Sometimes Hiram is very generous with me when it comes to spending money, but other times I daren't ask for an extra penny. And Augustus . . . well, he insists that we need to save for the future." She placed a hand on her expanding belly.

Libby saw her opening. "I cannot imagine living next door to my brother, let alone having to share a household staff." Libby laughed inwardly, imagining the look on her brother Seymour's face if he could hear her talking about having a "household staff." As if there had ever been such a thing as a domestic servant in the

Seletzky home! "Sometimes one needs a little distance from one's relations."

"Oh, Miss Seale, I see you understand perfectly! Yes, of course I love Hiram and the children . . ." There was an almost imperceptible pause. "And Adele, of course. Why, Elliot seems to have grown up almost overnight, and the twins are so full of life! But . . ." she lowered her voice, "I do sometimes think it might have been better if my Augustus had not chosen to join Hiram at the Paperworks. Perhaps then we would not have moved into a home quite so close to them."

"Did Mr. Fowler grow up in Portland as well?"

Eva laughed, and Libby realized that she was almost treating Libby as a friend and confidante rather than an employee. Libby could only ascribe the changed attitude to the fact that she had just done Eva a favor. "Augustus? No, I met him at a party. At that time, he was a recent transplant to our city. He didn't even have a job." The memory made her smile. "Oh, Hiram was most displeased that I dared fall in love with someone he hadn't personally chosen for me, someone suitable. After all, he went all the way to Atlanta to find Adele, because it was so important that he marry . . ." She trailed off. "Oh dear, Miss Seale, I'm certain this is more than you wanted to know."

"Your brother was concerned that Mr. Fowler was not Jewish?" Libby wondered if she had gone too far, but she needn't have worried. Eva Fowler seemed in sore need of a confidante, and she went on almost enthusiastically.

"Yes! I should have known you would understand. My sister-in-law told me you are also a Jewess, although I would not have known it from your name and manner."

Libby thought of several responses to this, but she held her tongue as Eva continued.

"It's funny, when I was a girl, Father and Mother made such a fuss over the fact that we were different from other people in Portland. When I was in school, I always wanted to go to church on Sundays with my little friends, and Father would have to explain all over again to me that our people did not worship like everyone else. But my parents passed away before I came of age, and once Adele was in charge of the household, we stopped lighting the candles and saying the prayers at mealtime. She always said that all that 'mumbo jumbo' was just nonsense . . ."

Eva stopped. "Oh my, I am sorry. I hope I haven't insulted you, Miss Seale. I just realized that I have no idea if you are observant."

Libby was torn. On one hand, it was tempting to remind this woman exactly what it was she had thrown away so carelessly, to make her recall the storied history that bound them to a line of heroes and scholars that stretched back into biblical times. And yet, an internal voice reminded her, she mustn't stray too far from her original task, which was to find out more about this household. Reluctantly, Libby set aside her desire for frank conversation in favor of more duplicitous small talk.

"No insult taken, Mrs. Fowler. I appreciate hearing the details of your childhood. You and your brother must have been close, growing up as you did. How much older is your brother than you?"

"Almost nine years! My parents had quite a wait before I came along. So I suppose there is some sense in how long Augustus and I had to wait." She seemed to have only this moment had this realization. "Adele and Hiram had no such problems." Her smile was wry. "I always rather thought Adele felt this was my comeuppance for marrying a gentile." Eva's tone indicated that there was little love lost between the sisters-in-law.

After a long pause, Libby gently prompted, "I know that it can be difficult when two people marry who are of different faiths. Did you speak to . . ." She stopped, unsure if she was crossing some line. She had been going to ask if Eva and Augustus had met with a rabbi or priest before their marriage. Was that something she and Peter would have to do, if they ever did find a way to . . . oh, but this was silly to think about. As if she and Peter would ever be able to marry!

"Miss Seale?"

Libby realized she had been sitting silently, mouth open, mid-question. "I'm so sorry, I lost my train of thought."

Eva continued, as if there hadn't been an awkward pause. "You know, I had no idea when I married that religion would be any sort of issue. Augustus, when we were courting, used to say that out here in the west we had the freedom to be whatever we wanted. That we needn't be constrained by the prejudices of the Old World. And yet, as Augustus has gotten older, he has developed a longing for the comfort he gained from his church as a child. He started to go to services every Sunday, and I know he was praying that we would be blessed." She touched her bulging belly again. "I guess his prayers were answered. He asked me if I would mind if we had the baby christened, and I didn't see how I could refuse him. But when I mentioned it at dinner recently, you should have seen the steam coming out of Hiram's ears! He was quite upset, and I hadn't even realized he might care at all!"

"It is often surprising how people react when it comes to matters of faith and tradition," said Libby, thinking of Peter's unexpected reaction, weeks before, when he had first learned she was Jewish. If she was honest, her own feelings about marrying outside her faith were conflicted, too. Perhaps it was just as well she could not consider marrying Peter. If it weren't for Mr. Greenblatt, she might be forced to make a difficult decision between faith and love. And she truly couldn't say what her choice would be.

Eva leaned in conspiratorially. "But I think things may change soon. Perhaps it is because of the baby and the need for space, but recently Augustus has been hinting that we may soon be moving to our own house. Someplace bigger, he says, and not so close to Hiram and Adele." She paused. "Do you have a large family, Miss Seale?"

"No. Just one brother and one sister."

"But you know what it's like to be close to someone who has known you since you were a child . . . to love him dearly and yet to want to get away at the same time."

Libby's thoughts turned to her own brother. She missed her whole family, of course, but at times she thought she missed Seymour most of all. He had been the one who encouraged her love of books and learning after her father had told her that reading was wasted on a girl. And she never laughed so much as she did when Seymour and she were whispering in the corner of a big family celebration, making gentle fun of their many aunts and uncles under their breath. But all she said was, "I do miss my brother, very much. And yet, I do understand how fine a line it can be between sibling friendship and meddling." Libby wondered how on earth she could bring the conversation back to matters related to more current events. "You mentioned Mr. Fowler was a newcomer to Portland when you met him. It must be a credit to your husband that he has advanced so quickly through the ranks of the papermaking business."

"But not fast enough. Oh, I shouldn't tell you this . . ." Libby leaned in. Eva hurried on, her hesitation having only been a polite fiction. "My husband and brother have not been in agreement about the direction of the paper mill for some time. You see, when I became engaged to Augustus, Hiram suggested he would make him a full partner in the mill. But, after our wedding, Hiram changed his mind and gave my husband a simple managerial position, one without any real clout."

Before Libby could form an answer, the topic changed abruptly, as Eva cried out "Oh!" and lay a hand on her belly. "I think I just felt the first fluttering!" Her eyes were shining, and a glowing grin lit her face.

With a jolt, Libby realized that her first reaction was a stab of jealousy. All this time, she had set aside thoughts of starting her own family—she wasn't even sure it was something she wanted, and yet she couldn't deny that seeing the sheer joy before her gave her a pang of desire so strong she almost gasped out loud. Eva was blissfully unaware of any change in Libby's expression, so wrapped up was she in her own moment. "Miss Seale, do you want to feel it?" She laughed girlishly. "Give me your hand."

Delicately, Eva placed Libby's hand on her midsection, but Libby felt nothing. "Oh, now he's stopped . . . Maybe it wasn't anything." Eva smiled. "I suppose I am overly excited. Perhaps I let my excitement get the best of me. It's early yet to feel the baby, isn't it?" She looked at Libby for confirmation.

Out of her element and terribly disconcerted by all of the complicated responses she was feeling, Libby could do little more than shrug. Turning away, to hide what she was sure was an embarrassed blush, she rearranged her sewing basket and steered the talk back to alterations.

NINE

"Please, have a seat, Mr. Eberle." Unsworth Manning stood with his back to Peter, staring out at the darkening evening, but the bright lamps in his office turned the window glass into black mirrors that reflected the scene behind him, allowing the mill owner to observe his guest's movements. Likewise, Peter could see the reflection of Manning's face. Despite the tone of his cultured voice, he didn't appear pleased to see Peter again. "You wish to discuss something with me?"

Peter took a moment to decide how to begin. The weather had turned bitterly cold again, and the reporter could hear the distant rattle of sleet striking the mill's tin roof. It made a popping sound like the hissing and sizzling of a hot frying pan, imparting a menacing character to the silence in the office. A clock ticked. Peter waited, letting the tension mount. Finally Manning turned back to face his visitor, and crossed to his desk.

"Is this still about that business with Hiram Rose? I gave you my word I had no hand in the attack on him, and have nothing further to add." Manning settled into his leather chair. Even seated, his height and bearing gave him a regal air that challenged Peter.

"I'm afraid you were not completely honest with me at our previous meeting, Mr. Manning. You may not have had a hand in the attacks on Hiram Rose, but you most certainly wish him ill. And you are taking steps to destroy him professionally, if not physically."

Manning steepled his fingers and waited to see what Peter would say next.

"It seems odd that you should be so close to Augustus Fowler, second in command over at the Rose Paperworks. So close that you are in the habit of communicating with him not only at home, but through Hiram Rose's own personal secretary, Mr. Kearney."

Unsworth Manning leaned back in his chair. "Ahh." That seemed to be all he was going to say at this juncture. Peter continued.

"Now, I will admit to not knowing exactly what your plans are, but I feel certain the Portland police might be interested in learning of a conspiracy between you and these highly placed men inside Rose's mill. At the very least, I think it sheds a new light on the plot against Hiram Rose, one that requires further investigation."

"Mr. Eberle," Manning still spoke in his measured, silkily cultured way, "I have assured you that my business relationship with the Rose Paperworks bears no relationship to the attacks on Hiram Rose's life. But I can see that my word is not good enough for you." His tone implied the loss was Peter's. "May I speak plainly?"

"Of course."

"I am at a delicate juncture, business-wise. If knowledge of my plans becomes common knowledge it could wreck everything I have spent the last few months trying to achieve. If I tell you those plans, can you assure me the facts will go no further?"

Peter nodded. "Assuming they are no more than business plans."

"I assure you I mean Hiram Rose no bodily harm. But believe me, if I have my way the man will be destroyed."

———

Another Monday, and Andrew Matson was sick of it: the ancient machinery, the workers not showing up for work, even the smell of those strange dumplings the workers insisted on bringing. All morning long their lunch pails sat waiting at their feet for the lunch break, stinking up the whole place. In fact, everything about dealing with the damned Chinese bothered him, all their creeping around, their guttural language that sounded like screeching fishwives gossiping.

"Matson!"

He looked up. Fowler was coming toward him, looking grim. "Yes, Mr. Fowler?"

"I need to speak with you about something confidential."

Andrew Matson felt uneasy. There was something about his manager's face, a dark determination, he hadn't seen before. "What is it, sir?"

"Not here. Meet me at the Anchor . . . a half hour after the closing whistle." He lowered his voice to almost a whisper, which made him sound almost menacing. "It may be that you can help me, and I, in turn, can help you. The Anchor. It's in your best interest, sir. I can't say more now, but I'll see you then."

Fowler strode off toward his office as Matson watched him walk away. For the first time, he wondered if perhaps the rumors were true. Had Augustus Fowler engineered his brother-in-law's accident? A few of the men over at the Green Gale had the idea that Fowler wanted to kill Rose because he would presumably inherit the Paperworks and finally have a chance to run the show. This had never seemed credible to Matson, because, unlike the rest of them, he knew that Fowler had no financial interest in the mill. The business would no doubt go to Rose's sons in the event of his death. Besides, Matson figured the police would have turned up something by now if it was Fowler who had been involved in that catwalk tampering. Still, he couldn't shake the feeling that there was something darker than normal in Mr. Fowler's demeanor just now. Puzzling indeed.

The remaining hours of his shift dragged on. A container of lye spilled, necessitating a heavy cleanup job for Smirnikoff and his crew, and then the roller they used to finish their highest-grade paper got stuck, which meant a whole batch had to be started again. He was so caught up in this late burst of work that he was surprised when the whistle blew. The Chinese workers filed out in their usual orderly manner, and then he closed up the mill and headed out into the dark and cold.

By the time he got to the Anchor, Augustus Fowler had already half finished the pint of beer in front of him. Matson didn't recall ever seeing his boss drink before. Then again, why would he? It wasn't like he normally socialized with the likes of the Roses or the Fowlers. Augustus's vest was unbuttoned and his necktie had been loosened . . . there was something that seemed almost unhinged about him. Matson slid into the booth.

Fowler's first words startled him to his core. "I won't mince words, Matson. I'm leaving the Rose Paperworks and starting a new papermaking concern. Wood-pulp cellulose—it's the wave of the future. We—Unsworth Manning and I—want you to come on board as our foreman." He paused. "Needless to say, this is completely confidential, and I expect you won't tell anyone about it."

"Of course not," Matson agreed, a slow smile forming on his face. "That sounds like a good idea, boss. Wood pulp. If there's one thing we got plenty of in Portland, it's trees."

"Exactly. I think we'll all do quite well. I don't have to tell you, the rag paper process is expensive and unnecessary. Once we get the new machinery and convert Manning's mill over to the wood-pulp process, we'll cut production costs in half. We'll be able to sell paper substantially cheaper than anyone else in the Willamette Valley. And we won't need to hire some cheap, foreign-born workforce to do it!" He finished his drink and slammed the glass down. "But you don't even have a drink yet! Let me get us a round." He crossed to the bar and spoke with the bartender, and as Matson watched the man, he realized Fowler was a bit unsteady on his feet, as if he had been drinking all afternoon.

Returning with two glasses filled with amber-colored liquid, Fowler settled back into the booth. "Now then, where was I? Leaving Rose, Hiram Rose, that's it." He laughed, although he hadn't made any kind of joke. "I tell you, Matson, old friend, Hiram Rose is about to get his comeuppance. He thinks he's so smart, firing all those men to save a few dollars here and there, playing games with his rag suppliers to get the best deal he can, but it's not going to make a damned bit of difference when Manning & Fowler opens for business. Let me tell you something, Matson . . . Do you want to know what kind of man Hiram Rose is? Do you?"

The question hung between them, but Matson sensed Fowler wasn't waiting for an answer. Both men drank, and when Fowler had finished his drink, he went on. "He was happy to let me and his precious sister live like beggars. Oh, he always had to be lord and master, deciding when we eat dinner, when we could get new furniture for our house. I tell you, it wasn't right. Who should control the purse strings in a marriage . . . the husband, that's who! I tell you, sir, my wife is far too close to her brother, and it's high time I get some distance between them."

"Sounds like it's time for you to make a move, then."

"Damn right!" Fowler slapped his hand down on the table. "So, are you in?"

Matson didn't have to think twice. The chance to get away from all those damned silent Chinamen. "Count me in, sir."

Fowler reached across the table and shook Matson's hand, and his grip was tighter than Matson would have guessed. "Good, good, good." Fowler finally let go. "Now that you're part of the team, I'll let you in on a little secret." As Fowler spoke, Matson became uncomfortably aware of the beer on the other man's breath, and realized that Fowler had been leaning progressively closer to him as he spoke. "I've been saving, scrimping and saving, all these years. It was hard, don't think it wasn't, to watch my Eva living like a pauper, and it made me feel terrible. But I knew I had to save my stake. My stake, you understand. A man needs a lump sum to do anything in this world, you know. So now, now I have a secret. My secret money." His voice was filled with glee. "Just you wait! When my wife learns that her quiet mild-mannered husband is part owner in a new paper mill and owns a new house across town, well, let's just say I think she'll be very, very happy."

He stood up unsteadily. "Shall I get us another? No, no . . ." He shook his head as if to clear it. "I need to get home. I've got to get to the Rose house to sing for my supper. Not for much longer though."

Matson realized he had very little concrete information. "What next, Mr. Fowler? When is all this happening?"

"You just bide your time, my friend. When the time is right, you'll know about it." Fowler tidied his suit, put on his coat, and wrapped his silk muffler neatly around his neck. Once again, he looked like the moderately prosperous businessman that he normally was. "Messages will either come from me or from Mr. Kearney. Got it? No one else is to know about this, for now."

"Who would I tell?" laughed Matson, more relaxed now. "It's not like those Coolies speak a word of English!"

"Right enough!" The two men shared a laugh, and Fowler was still grinning as he wove his way out of the bar.

Matson sat at the table, considering whether to get another pint. Who would have guessed it—Scott Kearney actually had a backbone! And Augustus Fowler, all those years playing second fiddle to his brother-in-law, and now here he was poised to bring the whole Rose Paperworks down. Matson almost felt sorry for Hiram Rose, alone in the world and about to be ruined. Fowler has Manning and Kearney and me. Who does Rose have? No one but those inscrutable Orientals, he thought, and what use would they be when all his customers had jumped ship as well?

———

"Miss Seale, I insist this dress be taken in. Look at me, I'm practically swimming in it!" In fact, the dress Adele Rose wore flattered her figure far more than her usual style, which required tightening her corset to within an inch of its life and thereby accentuating every bulging curve of her ample body. In comparison, the new party dress Libby had made hugged Adele in all the right places but was loose enough in the others to give the illusion that the woman wearing the dress had a proportional waist, something Adele usually lacked despite all her machinations.

Without meaning to, Libby let out a small sigh. "I think it looks lovely on you, Mrs. Rose, and is quite becoming to your figure. And green does bring out your fair coloring. Perhaps later, you could solicit the opinion of your husband or your sister-in-law? It's often so hard to judge ourselves in a new outfit." Libby found that people were often resistant to changing anything about what they considered their personal style. Even if a style were wildly unflattering, it had the advantage of being familiar. Adele Rose was not her first client to resist abandoning the familiarity of a bad design for a much more suitable one. "How about you keep the dress, as is, for a few days and think about it. If you decide you are still unhappy with the size, I will be happy to alter it next week in whatever way you desire."

"Oh, very well." Mrs. Rose gave herself one final glance in the half-mirror above the sideboard and turned to Libby. "But I am fairly sure, Miss Seale, that I have never had a dress fit quite so . . . loosely in the bodice. I fear it makes me look less delicate."

"Izzy, slow down!" Miss Baylis' voice heralded the arrival of her two young charges who raced into the room, reminding Libby of nothing so much as a pair of kittens. Obviously fresh from their baths, the two boys clambered over the couch and jumped up on their mother, as if she were a particularly interesting tree they had happened upon.

"Mama, mama! It's bedtime, but we don't want to go to bed!"

"Is that your new dress?"

"Why is it green?"

"I think you look like a frog!" The twins laughed merrily together, and despite being their object of ridicule Adele smiled indulgently.

"Isadore! Adolphus! Get down off your mother this instant!" Miss Baylis stood in the doorway, and looked apologetically at Mrs. Rose. "They do get excited right before bedtime."

Their mother leaned down and gave each boy a hug. "Now, off to bed with you, boys! You heard Miss Baylis, it's time for little boys to go to bed and have sweet dreams." The twins made no move, and Adele looked helplessly at the governess. She seemed to have forgotten Libby was even there. "It's bedtime, darlings!" she said again, trying to disengage herself from the boys.

"But we don't LIKE bedtime!" screamed Izzy at an earsplitting volume. Adele cringed.

"Why doesn't Elliot have to go to bed?" asked Fussy, ignoring his brother, who was starting to cry.

"That's enough," said Miss Baylis, swooping in and taking each child by the hand. "Bedtime, now." Her authoritative tone seemed to work some kind of magic, for immediately the twins let themselves be led from the room. As the door closed behind them, Adele seemed to remember her seamstress.

"Miss Seale, I trust you can see yourself out."

"Of course."

"Thank you, and we can discuss the further alterations to this dress next time you are here. I believe you still have several commissions for my sister-in-law in progress, is that correct?" Libby allowed as it was. "Good. That should keep you busy for the moment." With that, Adele swept out of the room, leaving Libby to pack up her sewing supplies.

As she stood in the foyer, putting on her cloak, Libby listened to the wind howl outside. It appeared the rain of the earlier evening had turned to sleet, or could it possibly be hail? She could swear she heard little taps at the window as the storm outside raged. If only Miss Baylis would hurry! Libby had arranged to fit Mrs. Rose after dinner today specifically because she wanted to try and finally catch the governess alone. She planned to walk to the streetcar with her, but as the weather was getting worse by the minute, she was growing anxious to be on her way. Home was the only sensible place to be on a night like this. Finally she heard footsteps on the stairs.

"Are you leaving now as well?" Miss Baylis was bundled up in a plaid wool coat with an upturned fur collar. Libby fussed with her own collar, pretending she had just this minute become ready to leave.

"Yes, here, let me get the door." The rush of cold air hit her immediately, and for a moment the two women stood side by side on the wide porch girding themselves for the walk. Indeed the precipitation appeared to be hail, mixed with an icy, sleety rain. Their coats wrapped tight, they set off in the same direction.

"Do you take the streetcar?" asked Libby, though she knew (from Celia) that was exactly what Miss Baylis did.

"Yes, Mother and I live past the last stop on Thurman."

"Oh, you go the other way from me. I take it all the way through downtown and over the river. I live on the east side." They trudged along silently until they were almost at the point where they would part ways. Miss Baylis wasn't in a talkative mood, but Libby realized this might be her only opportunity to find out if the other woman had an alibi for the arrow attack on Hiram Rose.

"I understand you missed all the excitement recently, when someone shot at Mr. Rose arriving home from work," she managed. Her words formed puffs of icy vapor in the wet, frigid air.

"Yes, that was my day off."

"Were you home with your mother, then?"

"Oh, heavens no, I spend every Thursday in classes at the teacher's college. The classes run from noon until eight o'clock . . . it's quite a long day, but since I can only go the one day a week, I have to schedule all my classes then."

"One of my sisters is studying to be a teacher," said Libby proudly.

"I'm halfway through the certification course. Only one more year and I'll be able to find work at a school." She looked at Libby with some surprise. "Surely you didn't think I wanted to spend my life watching children like the Rose twins forever, Miss Seale!"

Libby smiled. "Please, call me Libby."

Miss Baylis nodded. "Evangeline."

Libby went on, "Of course not, Evangeline. I must say, you do seem to have a way with them. It's amazing how they listen to you."

"They're good boys, really. They just get overly excited sometimes, and they need a firm hand." She stopped at the corner. "Well, I need to cross to my trolley stop. Good night, Miss . . . Libby!"

Miss Baylis' trolley arrived first, and she gave Libby a wave from across the street as she disappeared into its warmth. Soon the streetcar disappeared as well. Libby stood in a doorway, trying to stay dry as she waited for her own ride. She realized that neither she nor Peter had taken Miss Baylis seriously as a suspect, and after speaking with her she was even more convinced the governess knew nothing about the attack. Still, she figured Peter ought to check that Miss Baylis had actually been in her classes that Thursday, and then they could cross her off their list of suspected marksmen positively.

TEN

Several men suspected of being behind a series of local robberies were arrested yesterday in connection with their latest theft. Police had dubbed the men the "Cinderella Gang" because of a cap left at the scene of one of the crimes, and indeed this is what led to their apprehension. The cap, which had the initials of one of the men embroidered inside, led investigators to Les Wooley, unemployed mill worker. He and his confederates, a loosely organized collection of unemployed layabouts, were behind a series of robberies around Portland in the past month which targeted warehouses, grocers, and butchers. The Cinderella Gang's crime spree culminated in a three-night campaign last week during which the aforementioned cap was accidentally left behind.

PETER STOPPED READING AND looked up at John Mayhew, who was standing by the press, proofreading a piece for the next day's paper. "Who wrote this story?"

Mayhew thought for a moment. "Warner."

"I wonder, do you suppose I could see his notes?"

Mayhew shrugged. "I don't see why not, but you'll have to ask him." He turned toward the doorway that led to the back press area. "Fred, are you still back there?"

Froedrich Warner shuffled into the front room, looking every inch the typical newsman. His hair was mussed, and he wore a rumpled suit, a bit tight around the middle. "I was just eating a late breakfast," he explained, brushing crumbs from the vest that strained to cover his oversize belly. "What was it you needed, John? Peter! Good to see you. Been busy out on the trail of a story?"

Holding the paper out, Peter pointed to the large headline: Police Catch Cinderella Gang. "These robberies . . . I need to see your notes."

Warner smiled. "Are you checking up on me?" He laughed.

"No. It's fine. I mean it's wonderful. You know that I wouldn't ask unless it had bearing on—I wanted to find out more because I think I may have been speaking with these men . . . the Cinderella Gang . . . just a few days ago, about another matter entirely."

Warner looked interested. "I'll get my notes."

Mayhew immediately saw where Peter was heading. "So you think this might clear your man Karlsson, the one you say is unfairly in jail for killing his brother?" He rubbed his chin thoughtfully, and Peter suppressed a smile at a blot of ink on the editor's chin. "Could be, could be." He turned when Fred reentered the room. "Well, Freddie?"

"Well, I tell you, those men were busy. Three nights in a row! And the murder attempt at Rose Paperworks was the same night as one of the robberies." Of course, Warner knew Peter was following the Hiram Rose murder attempts, and he too had quickly caught on to what was being asked. Now he leafed through his notebook as he excitedly filled in more details for Peter. "You understand, we have limited room on the front page, it didn't seem important to mention all the names, but I have them here somewhere. Let me see what else. . . . Ah, this is interesting. They were not professionals, these men . . . yes, that's right! The police say there were eight of them, at least, but there may be even more. There was this Les Wooley fellow, the one who left his green cap with his initials at the warehouse." He raised an eyebrow for emphasis. "Not the brightest criminal mastermind, our Mr. Wooley, and there were others from the Rose Paperworks; all of them ex-employees. They say the ringleader was Daniel McFerley, the one they call 'Plug.' Odd name," he said, almost to himself.

Peter said impatiently, "Was it all fellows from the Rose paper mill?"

"Oh no, I hope I didn't give that impression. I believe I mentioned that several were other unemployed men from the area. You know as well as I do, Portland has a lot of men out of work these days, trying to feed their families." He turned a few more pages of his notebook. "Ah, here is the list of names . . ." All the names of the men listed sounded familiar to Peter, and he was now more certain than ever that the Cinderella Gang consisted at least in part of the group of Dutch's friends he had met at the Green Gale. His certainty was sealed when Fred said, "They all know each other, these men, apparently from some bar called the Green Gale, where they drink together in the evenings."

So, thought Peter, his mind whirring, it stood to reason Dutch had participated in the Cinderella Gang's robberies, too. That explained not only where he was the night his brother was killed, but why he wouldn't say so to the police. By admitting his own part in the robberies, he would have been selling out his friends to the police as well.

Fred was still talking to Mayhew, who was looking interested. "I do hope that the police are somewhat lenient. All these men ever stole was food. They never took anything else, just food." He shook his head sadly. "It's hard times when a man cannot put food on the table to feed his family without resorting to something like this."

The editor jumped in. "Fred, can you get me an editorial ready for tomorrow's paper? Saying what you said just now. About how these men were driven to crime, and yet they are certainly guilty of breaking the law. How should we, as a civilized society, mete out their punishment?"

Peter knew his two coworkers could easily be there all day discussing the law and how it should be applied to men who only stole to feed their families. So, interrupting Mayhew, he thanked Warner and set down the copy of the *Gazette*. "I'm going to go," he told Mayhew, "see if I can find any hard evidence that Dutch Karlsson was in on these robberies."

Mayhew grinned. "Heading over to the Green Gale again, eh? Give my best to Scotty!" At Peter's blank, confused look, Mayhew went on. "You must have met her the last time you were there. She runs the place. She's the bartender too. Got a lot of—" he gestured vaguely in the area of his chest, "vim and vigor, shall we say! She and I once had a bit of a time together, back when I first came to town."

"She told me her name was Phebe," Peter said, feeling foolish.

"Yes, that's her first name. Phebe Scott. But everyone just calls her Scotty." For once, Peter was speechless. Mayhew went on, not noticing his reporter's uncustomary silence. "Tell her I said hello, will you?"

———

It was another frustrating day at the Rose house for Libby. Adele had taken to her bed with grief as soon as she returned from the train station where she had seen Elliot off to boarding school. Eva Fowler was apparently out running an errand of some sort and had not left word when she might be expected back. So Libby, with no clients to make use of her services, took the opportunity to bask in the warmth of the kitchen before heading back out into the soggy, blustery day. Celia had made her a cup of sweet, milky tea, which she was sipping slowly. A giant pot of boiling chicken broth on the great cast-iron stove filled the room with its appetizing aroma, while Celia stood at the wooden table in the center of the room, her hands busily shaping flour dumplings. Every so often, when the plate was crowded with them, she would cross to the stove and toss them in the pot to cook. Libby figured if she dawdled long enough the cook would have to offer her lunch before she went back to Mrs. Pratt's.

As usual, Celia's mouth was as busy as her hands. "Just took off in the carriage and dressed to beat the band in that new red dress you made for her. Which, if I may say so, is very becoming on her, especially with her winter cloak, and just the sort of cheery color one likes to see with the weather so gray."

Libby accepted the compliment with a smile. "That's just the way I feel. And I do think Mrs. Fowler looks wonderful. I was so relieved to find her up and about when I was here on Saturday."

"Yes, she's a strong woman. I knew she'd be up and about in no time. Even as a girl you couldn't keep her down. Oh, the scrapes she used to get into! Would drive Mrs. Rose . . . the late Mrs. Rose that is, Hiram and Eva's mother . . . into a frenzy. There was a time I thought we'd never see her settled, and now here she is about to become a mother herself." Celia sighed, "That's another thing I thought we'd never see—"

Libby was quite certain that Celia would have gone on in this vein for quite a while longer had Wilmer Stubbins not poked his head in through the kitchen doorway. "Mrs. Jackson? The butcher's boy is out in the yard . . . ?"

Celia looked annoyed, whether at being interrupted or because Wilmer seemed to be making a question out of a simple statement, Libby didn't know. "Well, tell him to put his order in the icehouse and send him away, Stubbins."

Wilmer said patiently, "I asked him to. He says he needs to be paid first. So I came in to get the money from you."

The cook sighed. "Well, that's no good. I don't have it. You know the master locked up the money box, and I don't have the key. You'll have to tell the boy to come back later, I suppose."

"He won't like that." The elderly stable hand clucked his tongue.

"Well, I don't like it either! You can thank whoever decided to help himself to a little extra cash." She shot an almost accusatory glare at Wilmer, and he backed out through the door and disappeared.

"What was all that about?"

"It's typical of Mr. Rose not to worry about a silly little thing like how I'm supposed to stock the larder when I can't pay the local tradesmen. I'd enjoy seeing the look on his face if I told him there was nothing for his dinner but soup."

"Doesn't Mrs. Rose have a key to the household money box? Perhaps she can help."

Celia looked at Libby oddly, as if wondering why she wanted to know about such a domestic matter. But, in the end, a desire to vent her frustration won out over her desire not to air the family's dirty laundry. She plunked herself down on a chair beside Libby's and rested her beefy arms on her knees. "Oh, I still have a key to the money box . . . it's just that the box itself is now in the safe in Mr. Rose's study, and nobody has the combination to that except him."

"What a silly system!" Libby blurted, then looked embarrassed at having insulted the running of the household. But Celia nodded, so she added, "Why did he lock the box away?"

"Someone in the household had light fingers. The first time it happened, when we noticed ten dollars missing from the household cash, we just put it down to one of the delivery boys who had been in and out of the kitchen that week. But a few weeks later, another ten dollars disappeared, and this time I had just counted it the night before, and so I knew there had been no one around but the regular staff."

"And the family, of course," Libby added helpfully.

Celia snorted. "That doesn't make sense! Why would any one of the Roses steal from themselves?"

Libby thought. "It could have been Elliot . . . some art supplies his father wouldn't allow him, perhaps."

Celia said grudgingly, "Well, I suppose that's possible. I hadn't thought of that. In any case, the staff were the ones blamed, though I'd swear on my life it wasn't one of my maids. I feel certain it was one of those stable hands, Stubbins or Matt—" She stopped short, and feeling guilty for speaking ill of the dead, crossed herself quickly. "It was probably Stubbins."

"In light of what later happened with Matt, I would think him the likelier suspect." Libby frowned, "When exactly did all this happen? I mean, when did the cash box get locked away?"

"That would have been . . . middle of February, I guess. A few weeks before Matt . . ." The older woman stopped herself again. "It's all water under the bridge. This is the way things are now, and we haven't had a lick of trouble since. But I must remember to ask Mr. Rose for enough to cover the butcher's bill soon, or we'll be dining poorly come the weekend." Celia heaved herself up from her chair and went back to making dumplings.

Libby thanked her for the tea and left the kitchen and then the house. She wasn't sure if Celia's story of the household pilfering had any connection to the attacks on Hiram Rose, but she found it more than a bit suspicious that the thefts had occurred during January and February when the Karlsson family was slowly starving. And, she suddenly recalled, Matt had told his sister that he had gotten the money for their father's funeral from Mrs. Fowler, a fact that Eva had denied. Where had that money come from? From the household cash box? And was it just coincidence that, shortly after that source of money was cut off for good, Matt had been killed while crossing the catwalk leading to Hiram Rose's office, where the office safe held a fortune? Could Matt have been at the mill to burgle Hiram's office? If so, then who had sawed the catwalk?

Her mind teeming with questions, Libby lowered her head against the stiff wind and headed for the tram.

ELEVEN

Anna Karlsson stood just outside the Portland police station, feeling afraid to enter. When she had left her house, she had been full of purpose, sure she would arrive at the jail, get them to free Dutch, and save the day. Now that she was here, actually confronting the authorities felt like a foolish idea. She had been there before, of course, visiting her brother, but this was the first time she would ask to speak to a detective, and she was nervous. Did they even talk to women, those detectives? Or would they just laugh at her—or worse, not even acknowledge her?

In her hand was a folded copy of that day's *Portland Gazette*, with the article about the Cinderella Gang on the front page. Carefully unfolding it, she glanced once more at it, as if to remind herself why she was there, then pushed open the heavy glass doors and entered the empty waiting room. In two wide steps, she stood in front of the desk sergeant. He looked her up and down appreciatively, and she squirmed under his gaze. "I know you," he said. "You're here to see Karlsson, right?"

"I'm here to see that he is released at once. I saw right here," she held the paper out for emphasis, "about those robberies. These men, they are all friends of my brother. It's obvious that he was just covering for them, that's why he wouldn't say where he was the night our . . ." She was unable to finish the sentence. "The night of the accident at the mill."

From behind her came a new voice, unable to hide his amusement. "Oh ho! What have we here? Callahan, did you know Karlsson's sister was a detective too?"

She spun around. "Are you the detective?" she asked, holding her ground.

"Officer Macon," he introduced himself. "I don't think we've had the pleasure, but I've seen you around the station, Anna, isn't it? That is—" he made a small bow, mocking her. "Miss Karlsson. I'm sorry to inform you that your brother has not been implicated in the robberies. Which means, of course, that he will continue to be held here, pending trial for the death of Matthew Karlsson and the attempted murder of Hiram Rose."

"But it's obvious! Those were all his friends, Plug McFerley, Les Wooley . . . surely you can see it plain as day that . . ." Se bit her lip, started again. "My apologies. With all due respect, sir, if you only ask him I think you'll see this new information answers the question of where my brother was the night of the accident at the Rose Paperworks."

"I'm sure you believe that, Miss. And we've heard from your brother. He's thinking along the same lines you were. When he heard his friends were all arrested, he jumped up and claimed he was with them all along. Convenient, that . . . provide himself with an alibi, and plead guilty to the lesser crime. Naturally it would be to his advantage to take the opportunity to sidestep the charges of attempted murder and manslaughter."

Anna could feel the tears welling in her eyes. But she was damned if she was going to give this nasty policeman the satisfaction of seeing her cry. "What about the others? Won't they confirm that Dutch was with them?" Macon just smiled and shrugged.

It was at this emotional juncture that the front door opened, and Peter Eberle walked in, notebook in hand. In a second, he took in the scene before him, desk clerk looking vaguely amused, Macon looking smug, and Anna Karlsson looking upset. Ignoring the policemen, he addressed himself to Anna. "Miss Karlsson, are you here to see Dutch? The robberies, I saw the news as well. It looks like we finally know where he was that night!"

Afraid to speak, lest she cry, she nodded her head.

Peter turned to Macon, who once again laid out his impeccable policeman's logic, the gist of which, Peter realized, was that as long as they had a plausible suspect in custody for the attempts on Hiram Rose's life, they weren't about to let him out, regardless of any evidence to the contrary.

Peter put a gentle arm on Anna's back and led her to one of the wooden benches in the waiting area. "Will you wait here for me for a few minutes? I want to speak to the police and see your brother, but then I'll walk you home."

"Yes, Mr. Eberle. Thank you."

Peter asked Macon to bring him back to the holding area. "I just want to speak to the prisoners for a moment. No long interviews, I promise, I just want a quick quote for tomorrow's paper."

The detective obviously didn't want to allow him, but the desk sergeant (Callahan, was it? Peter couldn't remember) chimed in,

"The Portland police department always tries to cooperate with the press. You can go back for a couple of minutes, but that's all." Macon pushed open the heavy door that led to where prisoners were kept, and Peter followed.

At the very edge of the room, he could see Dutch sitting on the floor close to the bars of his cell, talking to the other men in the next cell over. They were all too far away for Peter to hear what they were saying, but a burst of laughter indicated that at least the prisoners were deriving some comfort from their close proximity. As Peter drew closer he saw that each cell but Dutch's had four men crammed in it. Some faces he recognized, some not. He saw Plug McFerley, Les Wooley, and several other men who looked familiar, as well as a few he didn't recognize at all. He looked carefully to see if Alex Smirnikoff or Andrew Matson were among those in the cells, but didn't see either of them. But why would they be involved, he thought wryly. Unlike these men, they still had legitimate sources of income.

When the men saw Macon and Peter making their way down the corridor, all laughter stopped at once. "Listen here, men," said Macon, sounding more authoritative than Peter expected. "Your statements have been copied out. As soon as you sign your name to 'em, you can apply to be released on bail. But I won't have exact bail information until tomorrow, so don't ask. For now, you stay here." He turned to face Dutch. "There won't be any bail for you, Karlsson. Or rather, nothing the likes of you can afford. The rest of you, we'll be taking in to look over your statements again. Two at a time." Seemingly out of nowhere, deputies appeared, and Peter imagined they must have been standing silently on the other side of the doorway just waiting for their cue.

Macon seemed to have forgotten all about Peter, which suited Peter just fine. He made eye contact with Dutch and maneuvered himself over to the tall, blond man's side. As Macon and the other policemen were opening cells and carefully leading the first prisoners down a hallway, Peter said quietly, "Your sister Anna is here. She looks quite upset. I'm going to walk her home now, but don't worry, we'll get you out of here soon."

Dutch nodded. "Is she all right? And have you seen my boy? How is Pim?"

But before Peter could answer, Macon noticed him. "I thought you wanted quotes from the infamous Cinderella Gang? Anyway, your time is up. Better luck next time." He gestured to the door they had come in. "You leaving, Eberle, or do I need to get a guard here to assist you?"

Peter nodded to Dutch to indicate that everyone was fine at home, and then spoke loudly to Macon. "On my way, Officer."

———

The walk home with Anna was mostly quiet. Peter could tell she was very unhappy. He didn't know her well enough to know if she was the sort of woman who wanted to be coaxed into talking about a problem or whether she preferred to stew about it (like a certain other woman he could think of). Deciding to err on the side of caution, he matched her silence, and the walk stretched on with both of them lost in their own thoughts.

When they arrived at the Karlsson house, Peter walked her to her door and hesitated on the threshold, unsure if he should enter. Tilda was outside, sweeping the porch, and Pim was sitting at her feet, playing with what appeared to be a new wooden toy train. Peter crouched down beside the boy and smiled widely, pointing to the toy. Pim made a sound halfway between the noise of a gurgling brook and the caw of a seagull, which Peter interpreted as a happy noise, gleefully showing off the way all the wheels on his locomotive spun in unison, like magic. Peter nodded and gave the wheels a powerful spin before rising and greeting Tilda.

Anna held out her hand. "Thank you for walking me home," she said, primly. Turning to Tilda, she said flatly, "They don't believe he was with those men who were stealing food. He's not getting out."

Tilda sighed, but looked as if she had expected this bad news. Surprisingly, she invited Peter in for a cup of tea. As the day was chilly and wet, he agreed, hoping to establish more of a connection with the sweet, sad Anna than he had been able to muster on their walk home. Tilda requested his help in carrying in a new load of firewood, and he readily agreed. He couldn't help noticing that to the left of the porch was a huge stack of obviously new firewood, still smelling of sawdust and resin. He wondered if their neighbors had chipped in to help them afford it.

"It's good to have a man around the house," Tilda said, pointing for Peter to put the wood down by the hearth. She ushered her son onto the rug beside the fireplace and filled a kettle for the stove while Anna hung back, silent, standing behind her mother's chair by the window. Peter wondered if she wished he had not agreed to join them for tea. He didn't know what to say to her, so he contented himself with greeting the elder Mrs. Karlsson, who nodded distractedly in reply and went back to her knitting. Pim was rolling his train happily by the fire now.

"Would you like some gingerbread with your tea, Mr. Eberle?" Tilda's tone was so much more pleasant than he had ever heard from her, he wondered whether it was the same woman. He was about to refuse—how could he take food from these people when they had so little?—but then he noticed the cabinets were filled with food. It appeared the Karlssons were not as bad off as he had feared, and so he accepted the offer.

Peter, Anna, and Tilda sat at the table. Peter spoke first. "It's true, the police refuse to lose their prime suspect in the Hiram Rose attacks, but eventually they will have to see reason and admit Dutch has an alibi. The *Gazette* is one hundred percent behind him on this," he said reassuringly, wondering if John Mayhew would actually let him write an article attacking the police's handling of this matter. Keeping cordial relations with the police department was crucial to the running of a daily newspaper, and as yet he had no actual proof to disprove their theory.

"I hope you're right," said Tilda.

"Oh, Mr. Eberle, we do so appreciate that you believe in Dutch, like we do!" Anna spoke softly, but fervently. Her china-blue eyes looked deep into his, and with a murmured excuse Tilda moved across the room and began a conversation with her mother-in-law in low tones.

Uncomfortable meeting Anna's gaze, Peter smiled and watched Pim play with his toy engine. "I commend you in stretching your household budget to allow toys for the boy. He seems to love that new train."

Anna's look turned cold. "What are you saying, Mr. Eberle?"

He was surprised at her tone. "I meant nothing by it. It just appears to me that your family is managing quite well to make ends meet despite your troubles."

"Why don't you just come out and ask, Mr. Eberle?" she said brusquely, and Peter was flummoxed by the sudden change in behavior. "You must be wondering where all the food, and the new toy, is from. I assure you, they are not part of Dutch's ill-gotten gains."

"I hadn't meant to imply . . . I simply meant to say . . ." Peter sputtered.

"For your information, Dutch may have been with those men who were stealing, but I don't believe he took anything for himself. If I know my brother, he was probably trying to be sure no one was hurt, to make sure they didn't do anything foolish." She was more animated now, and he noticed, despite himself, how pretty she looked when she was fired up. Her hair, still damp from the rain, curled in tendrils around her face as she spoke. "I'll have you know that the toy, the firewood, all of it, we owe to a benefactor who kindly gave us a substantial sum of money this week." She paused, searching his eyes to see if he believed her. "There are still kind people in the world, Mr. Eberle. Surely you know that." She seemed to have exhausted her flare of temper. Her tone was more gentle now. "I'm sorry. I shouldn't have gotten so worked up. Of course you know there are kind people . . . you are one of them yourself."

"Who was it?" he asked, genuinely curious. Had the regulars at the Green Gale taken up a collection for the destitute family? Or was there someone else who had a vested interest in making sure the Karlsson family didn't starve?

"They asked that I not say. And I feel I should honor that wish."

He tried to make a joke of it. "This is off the record, Miss."

But she refused to tell him, despite his entreaties, and it was in a slightly sour mood that Peter thanked them all for the tea and stood up to leave. What bothered him was not so much her refusal to name the anonymous benefactor, although he was quite interested. It was that the trust and closeness he had felt toward Anna had somewhat evaporated. A little voice of doubt pricked at him. Was it possible this seemingly kind and open family was not as honest as he gave them credit for? Had their air of sincerity blinded him to the most obvious answer of all: that Dutch was in fact guilty as charged?

———

"Ouch!" Libby had been poked with one of her own pins, but it was not her hand that did the pricking. "Give me that pincushion, Fussy."

"I'm not Fussy," said Izzy, as though that invalidated her request.

"It's not nice to stick people with pins," Libby said tartly, grabbing the pincushion from the little boy's hand and stuffing it back into her basket. She supposed that it was her own fault, attempting to get any work done while babysitting the twin terrors. Though this was not one of the duties for which Mrs. Rose had hired her, she had been unexpectedly pressed into service. Miss Baylis was home with some family emergency. Adele had managed to be almost sweet when she beseeched Libby to look after the boys. Libby had thought she might be able to use the extra time in the house to finish off some sewing odds and ends, and then snoop around. A foolish hope, clearly, since it was going to take all her energy and attention making sure Izzy and Fussy didn't cause bodily harm to themselves or anybody else. She quickly packed her work things, including the shirtwaist she was hemming, and stowed them all in her carpetbag. Just for good measure she buckled the big leather strap, so as to deter small hands from seeking more mischief within its confines.

When she looked up, one of the twins was climbing out one of the windows. "Izzy, get down from there!" They were in the boys' nursery, on the third floor, and it was a long way down to the ground.

"I'm Fussy. And I'm allowed . . . Miss Baylis lets us play on the roof." Libby highly doubted that.

"Well, today you can't." Fussy reluctantly clambered down off the windowsill. "Let's see if there is another game you'd like to play." Libby made the mistake of turning her back to scan the low shelves that ran along one wall for possible games she could offer to play with the twins. A crash caused her to whirl back around. Two very guilty-looking little faces looked up at her. Between the two boys, lying on the floor, was the heavy, framed alphabet sampler that a moment before had hung on the wall. Thank heavens the glass hadn't shattered.

"Which one of you is responsible for this?" she asked, leaning the picture against the wall, hating the fact that her voice sounded like a spinster schoolmarm.

"It wasn't me!" said Izzy. Or was that Fussy?

"We were just standing here and it fell," said Fussy. Or Izzy . . . she didn't know.

She had to find some way to keep them still. "Come here and sit by me, and I'll tell you a story." She grabbed both of them and propelled them to a stout, leather-clad, padded bench by the fireplace. "Now, what do you want to hear a story about?"

"Tell us about the monster who lives under the mountain," said one. She'd never be able to tell them apart. She resolved just to think of the one on her left as Fizzy One, and the right as Fizzy Two.

"All right . . ." she said dubiously. She wished they had asked for a common story, one she knew. "Once upon a time, in a kingdom where—"

"The monster doesn't live in a kingdom," Fizzy One stated authoritatively.

"I'm sorry, where does he live?"

"He lives under Mt. Hood. When Papa takes us to the park, we can see Mt. Hood from there."

"All right. Once upon a time, deep below Mt. Hood," she smiled a bright false smile, "there lived a monster. One day, as the snow swirled down from the sky—"

"You're telling it wrong," Fizzy One piped up again.

"I don't like this story." This was Fizzy Two. "Where are your children? Can we play with them?"

The question took her aback. "I don't have any children."

"Why?" Fizzy Two looked at her, wide-eyed. "Were they bad? Did you send them away like Elliot?"

"No. Some grown-ups simply don't have children, and I am one of those grown-ups." She hoped that would be the end of this line of questioning.

"But you could get some children. Like Auntie Eva and Uncle Augustus. They didn't have any children and now they are going to get one. Mama told me," he finished proudly.

"Yes, that's right. Your Aunt Eva is going to have a baby." She smiled and ruffled his hair. "Where was I? Once upon a time—"

"Are you going to have a baby?"

"No."

"Never?"

She didn't have an answer for that. It was a question she didn't even want to try to answer. "I have a new idea. Why don't we play hide and seek? You go hide, and I'll count to a hundred and then try to find you." Before the final words were even out of her mouth, the boys were off the bench and heading for the door.

"Don't peek!" called Fizzy One over his shoulder.

"And count slowly!" added Fizzy Two.

Then they were gone, and she breathed a sigh of relief to be alone. But the boy's last question seemed to echo in the empty room. Would she ever have a baby? Did she want to? Even if she did, would she be able to?

This was something she had never even considered when running away from New York. Then, all she had been concerned with was getting herself as far away as possible from Mr. Greenblatt's fists. And also, she was forced to admit, to in some way punish her father and mother for forcing her to stay in a marriage that was so obviously a mistake.

But Libby no longer bore her parents any ill will. That much was past. She understood why they felt the way they did, and she missed them terribly . . . to say nothing of the rest of her family and friends. But what did that mean, in terms of having a family? What was she hoping would happen? Was she just waiting for Mr. Greenblatt to die? True, he was very much her senior, but he was still only a man in his late fifties—he could live a long time. And even if he lived only into his seventies, her time for having babies would have passed. Already her girlfriends, like Rivka, had little ones of their own, and she had nothing. She flashed on the incandescent smile she had seen on Eva Fowler's face just a few days before, when Eva had felt the baby inside her flutter, and she felt a pure envy. She wanted to know that feeling. Of course she wanted the baby inside her to be that of a man she loved . . . Peter's baby inside her. The thought made her feel simultaneously jubilant and bereft. It was a lovely thought, but she couldn't see how it might ever come to pass.

She heard a sniffle from the doorway. A Fizzy stood there, with tears in the corners of his eyes and a red face. "You said you were coming to look for us." Good lord, she'd lost track of time. She must have had time to count to a thousand by now. Would she be as bad a mother as she was turning out to be as a governess?

"I'm sorry. You hide again, and I promise I'll come look right away. Where's your brother?"

"Fussy's better at hiding than me. I can't find him anywhere!"

"Let's go look together," she said gently, and took Izzy (for now she knew this one must be Izzy) by the hand and went into the hall. They peered into the twins' bedroom, looked inside the linen press, and even peeked into the maids' rooms (which were so small and sparsely furnished that even a seven-year-old couldn't have found a place to hide in them). For one awful moment she thought Fussy might have thrown himself down the laundry chute to the basement, but Izzy assured her that they had tried that once, and their papa had spanked them so hard they promised not to try it again. There was only one door left in the upper hallway, shut firmly. Libby reached for its handle.

"We can't go in there. Eli gets awful sore if we go into his room when he's not here."

"I'm sure he meant if you're alone, and look, you're not alone. Besides, Elliot is far away and won't be back for some time." Why was she trying to reason with a small child? She was an adult, and she could open a door without justifying herself. "Come on, let's look." She cracked the door open, and they tiptoed into the room.

There was no Fussy in the wardrobe, or behind the draperies at the window, but the rug beside the bed looked suspiciously askew. Libby put a finger to her lips in a "shhhh" gesture, and pointed under the bed. Izzy plopped down on his hands and knees and yelled delightedly, "Fussy!"

"Ha, I win!" came a muffled voice.

"Come out now," Libby said.

"No, I'm going to live under here from now on."

"I think you'd get awfully hungry living under a bed, Fussy." She was forced to get on her hands and knees, and started feeling around under the bed. Finding a small ankle she began pulling the squirming child out.

"No! No!" But before too long a dusty-faced Fussy slid out from underneath the brass bedstead, his arms wrapped around a flat package. Whatever it was, it was wrapped inside a tattered and stained old towel.

"What's that you've got there?"

"I don't know. It was just under there. It was going to be my new bed." Fussy jumped up, "Let's play again!"

Libby didn't answer. As she unwrapped the threadbare towel, she saw that it contained a painter's canvas. Now why would Elliot be storing one of his paintings under his bed? She nearly gasped when she saw the half-finished painting. It was a nearly naked young man, heavily muscled. He had the look of a Greek god, with just the merest scrap of a loincloth, looking none too secure, draped across his nether regions. Though she was a married woman, a blush rose to her cheeks at the sight of so much exposed male flesh. Perhaps that was partly because, despite the formal setting (the ruins of a Roman temple and an Italianate landscape sketched in with red chalk behind the main figure), the man looked highly contemporary. He had pale blond hair parted in the center, a handsome pair of sideburns, and an astonishingly intense pair of blue eyes. One lock of straw-colored hair tumbled over his forehead, and he gazed out at the viewer with a frank and almost mischievous look, despite the fact that he was bound to a pillar and pierced in more than a few places with arrows. Arrows! Libby's mind immediately went to the attack on Hiram Rose. Had Elliot painted this picture as some sort of rehearsal for shooting his father? She dismissed the idea as ridiculous . . . clearly the man in the painting was nothing like Hiram Rose. Still the connection bothered her.

"That's Matt!" she heard behind her. She hadn't even realized the twins were still in the room.

"Why is he shot with arrows? Is he playing cowboys and indians?" The twins began to argue it among themselves.

Libby broke in. "What do you mean, that's Matt?" she asked, although she already knew the answer.

"The man in the painting. He used to be Matt, who worked outside," one of the Fizzys said.

"He's dead now," said the other, as if daring Libby to contradict him.

"Was he shot with arrows?"

Libby said distractedly, "No, he wasn't shot with arrows. That's just in the painting. Why don't you go hide again." They started to run out of the room. "And stay away from the laundry chute!"

She returned her gaze to the painting. Why hadn't Elliot finished it? Though she wasn't an expert, she thought it was very good—a vast improvement over the mawkish landscape that Adele had hung over the dining room mantle. The figure in the center pulsed with a youthful vitality, and the flesh looked soft and pliant. And those eyes . . . she couldn't bring herself to gaze into them for more than a moment. They seemed to beseech her to solve the riddle of his death. She realized she had never seen Matt, not even in passing, though she had started working for the Roses during what would have been the last few days of his life. She'd have remembered if she'd seen this man. No wonder everyone commented on how good-looking he had been. It broke her heart to think that this beautiful young man would never have the chance to grow and mature. How devastated his mother must be! Was there anything worse than seeing a child cut down before his life had really even begun? Libby didn't know why, but gazing at the painted portrait of Matt she suddenly found herself siding with the Karlssons. Surely this sweet and pretty boy would not have been trying to kill Hiram Rose.

"Stop it!" she told herself. She had no reason to believe in Matt's innocence other than that his appearance makes him seem so pure. Perhaps it was just Elliot's talent, imposing on Matt an aura of saintliness because of the friendship they shared. But was Elliot a good enough painter to do that?

She wrapped the painting back in the towel and shoved it under the bed once more. She knew she would tell Peter about it, but was disinclined to show it to Adele or, god forbid, Hiram Rose. Still feeling disturbed, she pushed herself up from her knees and went to look for the twins.

———

"Why didn't you tell me you were Scotty?"

Peter had headed directly to the Green Gale that evening upon leaving the *Gazette*. He had not wasted a moment on small talk, accosting Phebe Scott as soon as he was through the door. However, if he thought to catch her off guard, out from behind the bar, with no barrier between them and no time to prepare a dishonest answer, he was sadly mistaken. In retrospect, he should have expected no less than he got.

"It was an honest mistake. You said you were looking for a fellow named Scotty." She placed her arms on her hips, threw her shoulders back, and brandished her ample cleavage at him like a weapon. "Do I look like a fellow?"

He plunked himself down on a barstool. "I'll not dignify that question with a response."

She crossed behind the dark wood bar, wiped down the space in front of him, and smoothly poured a shot of one of the better brands of rye for him. "Here, on the house. You look like you could use one. Besides," she continued, as if there had been no interruption, "I figured you'd catch wise sooner or later and then you'd be back. Maybe I just wanted to see you again," she added with a wink.

Peter wasn't buying that, though he did take a sip of the rye. "I just came from a house where people are suffering. They've lost one son to the Rose Paperworks, and now it looks like they'll lose the other one to the hangman."

"You think I don't care about Dutch's family? You have some nerve, Mister. I've known them a lot longer than you, and . . ." She stopped.

Peter suddenly had a thought. "You wouldn't be helping them out? With money, I mean?"

"I do what I can, but Lord knows it isn't much." She grew sober. "That boy needs Dutch. It isn't right . . . I wonder if he even knows what's happened to his father."

Seeing her soften, Peter tried again, asking gently, "Why didn't you tell me you were Scotty?"

"I was just playing with you. I was honest with you about Matt, told you everything that could've made any difference. Though I didn't, and still don't, see what that has to do with Dutch. If Matt had something to do with those attacks on Hiram Rose, I never knew anything about that. That all happened long after he and

I stopped . . ." She left the end of the phrase to Peter's imagination and switched gears. "Surely, now that the Cinderella Gang is behind bars, you can figure out why Dutch wouldn't say where he was the night of Matt's death. I did know that, and I'm sorry I couldn't tell you, but I'm loyal to my customers." She raised her head and jutted out her chin. "I'd do the same thing again."

Peter looked around him. It was after working hours, when the bar should have been crowded, but it seemed to him the bar was much emptier than it had been on his previous visit. Of course, some of the customers he had seen were in jail, but that alone couldn't account for the shortfall. He wondered if people were staying away because of the Green Gale's association with the Cinderella Gang. Despite the fact that she had tricked him, he found himself hoping that Phebe Scott's business wouldn't suffer because of her now infamous clientele.

Peter tossed back the rest of his rye and asked for another. "Yes, I believe that Dutch was with them during the robbery that night, but the police don't. They say that Dutch had nothing to do with the Cinderella Gang and they're sticking with their original scenario. It looks like Dutch is on his way to being tried for the attempted murder of Hiram Rose and involuntary manslaughter when it comes to Matt."

"But that's outrageous! I could give you the names of a dozen men who'll back Dutch up, starting with those eight locked up downtown."

"Unfortunately the police aren't listening to them. After all, they're confessed criminals, and according to police logic, criminals lie for each other."

Scotty's nostrils flared, and she looked like nothing so much as a bull getting ready to stampede. "Those men are not bad men. They were trying to feed their families. That doesn't make them liars!" She gazed at Peter and said in a deadly serious tone of voice, "We need to do something."

"What?" Peter answered dully. The rye was working its magic, and his tension had ebbed. With it, however, had gone his fire. All that was left behind was a deep weariness and a sense of hopelessness.

"I don't know." The words could have signaled defeat, but Scotty's eyes were blazing, and she was ready to take on a battalion.

Suddenly, though his mind was dulled by the drink, he saw something he should have seen before. It came to him clear as day, with the certainty that drunken thoughts sometimes have. "You love him. Dutch." It wasn't a question. *In vino veritas*, indeed.

She didn't directly answer him, but she didn't deny it either. She gave a half sigh, half rueful laugh, and he could see that he had struck her in a tender place. "He's a good man. I can't just stand aside and see his life ruined."

Peter felt a kinship with the barmaid. He understood what it was like, loving someone you couldn't have. "Join me in a drink, Scotty?" His tone was warm, his eyes were smiling, and he winked as he added, "If I may call you Scotty?"

She smiled in return, but not flirtatiously. "Maybe one. But then I've got work to do." She poured the shots and lifted her glass. "To Dutch."

He concurred. "To Dutch."

"His family needs him. And his boy needs him." She frowned and looked thoughtful. Something was in her mind, but she would say no more. Peter could see she was forming some sort of plan, and could only hope that whatever it was it wouldn't make things any worse.

TWELVE

Hiram Rose was on the run! Well, that might be putting it a bit melodramatically, but for the first time since he had begun trailing the irascible businessman, Half-Cent felt his pulse race. Rose had just rushed out of the mill and into the stables, long before he usually left the mill for the day, his hat askew and his overcoat bundled under one arm. Half-Cent scrambled to where he had left Pittock, again tied halfway up the path to the Chinese workers' camp. He would have to hurry if he was going to get mounted and on the road before his quarry had disappeared. Something had obviously upset the man, and it was Half-Cent's job to find out what. Perhaps he might finally be able to learn something that would prove really useful! Most of his time spying on Hiram Rose had been spent under the moldy porch, munching chocolate bars to pass the time and watching an intermittent stream of commercial travelers and salesmen ascend and descend the stairs up to the executive offices of the Paperworks.

He had a sudden flash of realization. It must have been that woman who had upset the mill owner! The one with the rusty red hair and that strange hairstyle with looped braids over her ears like earmuffs. Half-Cent tried hard to remember anything else about the last visitor who had descended the stairs shortly before Hiram Rose had left his office in such a rush. She had stayed there for quite a long time and must have been kept waiting before being allowed to see Mr. Rose. Either that or their meeting had gone on for over two hours. Half-Cent had noticed her right away, partly because it was so rare for women to be at the mill (unless you counted the little Chinese girls), but partly because she had dawdled in the mill yard, looking unsure of which entrance to use. Finally, after peering up at the signs posted on the side of the building, her pale face had registered determination, and she had gone up the stairs to the visitor's entrance where Rose, Fowler, and the accountants all had their offices.

Astride Pittock now, Half-Cent gingerly made his way out of the scrub and onto Mill Road. There was almost no traffic at this time of day, and he had to be careful he wasn't spotted by Hiram Rose. Luckily, he was just in time. The mill owner didn't see him emerge, because he was already turning onto the main thoroughfare that would take him into the city center. Half-Cent spurred Pittock along at a fair gallop, and, turning onto Harbor Drive, he was able to see his quarry not too far in the distance. There was more traffic now, and he relaxed as he was able to simultaneously keep watch on Rose and stay far enough back to remain inconspicuous among the wagons and carriages that filled the roadway. He assumed Rose was heading into Portland, and once in those smaller streets he would need to move in closer and stay alert, but for now he had the freedom to let his mind wander.

If he could only find out something important! Then Mr. Mayhew would give him a permanent job at the *Gazette.* He imagined himself in five years, every inch a newspaperman—dressed in a snappy suit, notepad in his hand, and with his bowler cocked rakishly over one eye just the way Mr. Eberle wore his. He could afford to move out of that moldy closet of a room he rented by the docks, though God knows that was an improvement over the years he had spent sleeping in doorways. He intended on having a fine home, with lots of food and someone to cook it. He pictured a plump older woman with a white apron slaving away at all hours of the day and night, making an endless stream of sweets and whatever else entered his mind. Every morning he would give her a list, and when he got home from being a reporter she would be waiting with roast beef and dumplings, with cherry pie and chocolate cake to follow, and then he would sit in his leather armchair and munch on licorice and—yes!—he would smoke a pipe! He would have a telephone in every room, so he never needed to get up, and . . .

He was so wrapped up in his dreams of the future he almost missed seeing Hiram Rose turning off onto Everett Street. The mill owner must be heading home, not into the city at all. Why would he be going home? He never went home in the middle of the day, at least he never had before. What could be so important there, and what could it have to do with the woman at the mill? Could he just be heading home for a late lunch? Billy's heart deflated at the thought that perhaps he would learn nothing important to tell Mr. Eberle.

In any case, he had to make a decision quickly. There was no way Rose wouldn't spot him if he turned onto a residential street in broad daylight! But if he was wrong about Hiram Rose heading to his own house, then by the time he tied up Pittock in the churchyard around the corner and made his way to West Hill Lane on foot he would have lost his quarry completely. No, he decided, Hiram had to be heading home. That was the only thing that made any sense, although the reason still escaped him.

Half-Cent disengaged from the traffic and turned into the deserted churchyard, nimbly hopping down off the horse as he did so. "It's all right, girl, I'll be back in just a few minutes," he whispered to the horse, patting her on the head and loosely looping the reins through the ring in the hitching post.

Pittock stood with placid unconcern as the slender figure of her rider melted almost soundlessly into the trees and was soon lost in the gray gloom of the woods.

———

The offices of the *Gazette* were just as Libby had remembered them. She had come to feel somewhat at home there during the intense investigative experiences she had shared with Peter and John Mayhew back when she worked at the Portland Variety. Now she passed swiftly through the plain front room without ringing the bell, and poked her head through the archway that led to the heart of the paper's operations. The large, cluttered room was home to a few battered desks, but it was dominated by the printing press that rose and fell with a clack and a whoosh as paper rolled through its complex machinery. The only men she saw in the room were Peter, another reporter she had been introduced to once (a German fellow whose name was something like Fred or Freed), and the editor himself, who was busy scanning the type cases ranged along the walls, each filled with hundreds of individual letter forms in different fonts and sizes. Libby caught the tail end of a question, something like, ". . . decided to hide all the uppercase 24 point Courier D's?"—which made no sense to her—when John Mayhew spotted her head in the doorway.

"Miss Seale!" His cheerful voice boomed over the clatter of the printing press. "Visits from you have become as rare as sunny days." He left what he was doing at the type case, and soon his solid frame enveloped her in a bear hug. "Bet you're here to see Petey, huh!"

Peter jumped up from his desk. "Yes, we have some business matters to discuss, John." He seemed intent on making sure Mayhew know this was not a social call. "Libby . . . Miss Seale, you remember Mr. Warner?" He gestured to the German, who returned Libby's encouraging smile with little more than a grunt and a "Ja, ja, hallo," before returning to his sandwich.

"It's a pleasure to see you again," Libby said, trying not to laugh at the portly reporter's dedication to his gustatory pleasures. "Where is Half . . . I mean, Billy? I was hoping to be able to meet him, too. And thank him, of course, for helping us."

"Half-Cent?" Mayhew mused, "Not sure where he is. Haven't been seeing much of him since Petey here promoted him to junior reporter."

Peter cut in, "I believe he's out watching Hiram Rose, Libby. But I'm sure you'll get to meet him soon." He glanced about. "Shall we go sit in the front? It's quieter out there . . ." And more private, his look added.

"Yes, yes, of course. I have to be at the Rose house in less than an hour," Libby replied. Peter headed toward the reception area, but she hung back, and smiled, "John, it was a pleasure seeing you again."

Mayhew gave her a big grin in return, and then she turned her back and joined Peter, who had settled himself on the bench to the left of the front door. Sitting here, they were screened from view by the battered wooden counter that ran across the room.

She was about to say how good it was to see him, when he briskly said, "Tell me, what have you learned?"

So she outlined what she had learned about Miss Baylis, and her whereabouts during the arrow attack on Hiram Rose. And, as she had anticipated, Peter volunteered to confirm the governess' alibi with a source of his at the teachers' college. Next Libby told him about the portrait she had discovered in Elliot's room. She actually blushed as she described the almost nude man pierced with arrows, but Peter just laughed.

"Libby, I realize this is something that probably fell completely outside the bounds of your education, but it sounds to me like all you found is a classic portrait of St. Sebastian. He's always pictured tied to a post, in a loincloth and with arrows by the bushel piercing his torso. Didn't you mention the Rose boy was attending St. Sebastian's Academy downtown? He probably just copied it from somewhere."

Her face burned with the false importance her ignorance and imagination had ascribed to those arrows, to say nothing of the skimpy loincloth. "Don't forget, though," she said hotly, "it was

Matt Karlsson whom Elliot chose to paint as St. Sebastian. That might be significant."

Pete waved the thought away. "We already knew they were good friends. I don't think it's significant that he used his friend and household servant as a model. So, is that all?"

"No!" Her tone was tart, and she reminded herself that Peter hadn't meant to be rude. What was important was finding the truth, not which of them came up with the answers. She went on in a more composed voice, telling him all she had learned about the household pilfering that had gone on in the weeks leading up to the attack at the mill, and the interpretation she had put to it. "So," she finished, "if it was Matt who stole the household cash, as a way to support his family, that would explain why Eva Fowler knows nothing about the extra cash Matt's sister told you he was bringing home. It might also explain what he was doing at the mill that night. Once Hiram had locked up the household cash box, he was forced to contemplate breaking into the safe at the mill."

"Yes," Peter said dubiously, "assuming he wasn't there to help booby trap the scaffolding. We must accept that still seems like the most obvious option."

Libby nodded silently, feeling she couldn't say that. Having seen a portrait of Matt, she was now as convinced as his family that he was innocent of any wrongdoing other than perhaps stealing petty cash to feed his family.

Peter continued, "Whatever the source of the extra money the Karlssons acquired, it appears not to have dried up with Matt's death. I was just there and couldn't help noticing new supplies, a new toy for the little boy, and . . . well, I wouldn't necessarily have thought much about it except that Anna Karlsson was surprisingly defensive when I remarked on it in passing. I'm sure she's keeping some sort of secret, though I have no idea what it could be. I fear I may have been wrong to be so trusting of Matt's family."

Libby couldn't suppress an unworthy shiver of happiness that Peter seemed to have lost his infatuation with the pretty Karlsson daughter.

"Oh, I haven't told you the most important thing." Peter leaned in toward Libby and lowered his voice. "I haven't mentioned this to John, and I gave my word to Unsworth Manning that I wouldn't let the news out." He explained what he knew of Manning and Augustus Fowler's partnership, and their plan to open a new wood-pulp paper mill. "That explains much of the behavior we didn't understand, but unfortunately I believe it takes two suspects away. It's unlikely they are behind the murder attempts on Hiram, since they are on the verge of ruining his business."

Libby was shocked, and she wondered if Eva knew anything about her husband's plan. She would never have guessed Augustus Fowler had the gumption to stand up to his brother-in-law, and she wondered where the money was coming from. The Fowler home was positively spartan. "Peter, did Manning say whose money was financing this new venture? Why would Eva Fowler have asked me to pawn her jewelry if . . ."

Peter cut her off. "It's very important you not discuss this with Eva or Adele. I don't know whose money is behind this—Manning claimed not to know how Fowler came up with his stake, and not to care—but the very fact that Eva asked you to pawn jewelry would seem to indicate she doesn't know that her fortunes are about to rise, while her brother's are about to fall."

"All right, Peter, I promise. I expect all will be explained when Manning and Fowler make their plans public, which you said should be soon. Now I really need to get to work. Unless . . ."

Peter waved his hand to indicate he had nothing further to tell her. "Stay dry!" he said as a farewell.

"Vain hope!" she replied, and hurried out of the office. So, Hiram Fowler was about to get the comeuppance he so richly deserved. Picturing the Roses destitute, she made a mental note to get paid in advance for any future work.

Peter headed back into the print room. John Mayhew had a worried look on his face. "Petey, do you know where exactly Half-Cent was going today?"

Peter frowned. "No, John." A shadow crossed his face. "Has something happened? Do you need to locate him quickly?"

"It's the darnedest thing. Pittock just came back . . . just wandered back into the yard, still saddled up . . . but without a rider. I'm afraid something might have happened to the boy."

A prickle of guilt began in Peter's abdomen. If something had happened to Half-Cent he'd never forgive himself. "We've got to go look for him!"

"Let's not jump to conclusions. Perhaps Pittock just threw him and he's on his way here right now, walking. Besides, where can we look? It's not like we have any idea where he was riding when he got unseated."

"We don't," Peter said, grabbing his hat and heading out the door, "but Pittock does. Maybe he can lead us to Billy."

Mayhew sighed, but grabbing his coat and hat, followed Peter out into the yard.

Officer Macon sat at his desk, cursing the new system of paperwork that had been instituted by his superiors. Every one of the men involved with the Cinderella Gang required three separate forms, listing everything from date of birth to collar size, as well as one master entry to be placed in the official "Mug Book" of all criminals in the county. He was half surprised he hadn't been forced to open their mouths like horses and inspect their dental work before releasing them on bail, and it wasn't like he didn't have enough else to do to fill his busy days. On top of his regular reports, the mayor had recently decided to fill the city's coffers with a new source of revenue, dog licenses for all pet dogs, and Macon was supposed to be preparing a detailed census of the canine population of Portland. He sighed. At least with the robberies, he would get some credit for helping clean up crime instead of counting animals.

As he bent over his work, the feeble light from the central electric lamp was hardly a match for the office's gloom. The police department had proudly, and with great fanfare, switched the building entirely to electricity a year before, but as far as Macon was concerned, progress wasn't all it was cracked up to be. At least the old gas brackets had made it easier to see what you were writing. He was distracted from these discontented musings by a commotion coming from the front entryway. He looked up, debating whether to go see what was happening. Probably one of the beat officers bringing in a drunk. But before Macon could decide whether to abandon his work, Officer Bray came running back to his desk, looking flushed. "Sir, Mr. Rose is here and demanding to see you."

Macon stood. "Rose? What does he . . ." But before he could finish his question, Hiram Rose himself came barreling back into the office area. "Macon, dammit, man, there's been another attack on my life!"

Macon set down his pen and regarded the man before him. "What happened, sir?"

"A boulder, rolling out of nowhere, as I was riding by! It almost crushed me!" Macon was already reaching for his waistcoat, draped over the back of his desk chair. He was only slightly ashamed that his initial reaction was pleasure that the mountain of paperwork was going to have to wait another day.

THIRTEEN

THE HOSPITAL WAS ARTIFICIALLY bright and smelled of carbolic acid and soap. Peter sat on a hard-backed chair in the waiting room, twisting his hat around his hands until he realized his fingers ached. John Mayhew was talking to him in a reassuring tone, but none of the words registered; the man might as well have been reciting the local phone directory for all the meaning his words held.

Peter's mind was racing. Everything that had happened in the last hour seemed incomprehensible. He had ridden Pittock to the police headquarters at Second and Oak, Mayhew following close behind. While Mayhew waited with the horses, Peter went in to find out if there had been any reports of an accident that could have involved Half-Cent. "I'm sure the boy's fine," called Mayhew, as Peter rushed up the stone steps two at a time.

Out of breath with worry, Peter asked to see Officer Macon, and was told he was out on the scene of a crime. There had been another attempt on Hiram Rose's life, a rock fall which nearly crushed him. He wondered if Half-Cent had seen anything—perhaps he could catch the boy heading back into town on foot, so he could get the full story. But then his blood began to run cold as the policeman continued with the news that an unidentified young man had been found in the path of the boulder, close to death. The boy, said the officer, was now being taken to Portland Hospital.

Before the officer could say any more, Peter ran outside and jumped on Pittock, relaying the awful news over his shoulder to Mayhew. The two men raced across town to the hospital, pulling into the grounds just as a police wagon was discharging its occupant, a battered Half-Cent. His left leg was a tangle of blood and bones that made the color drain from Peter's face. He had to turn away, literally sickened. How could anyone survive an injury like that? How long had the boy lain abandoned and bleeding before the ambulance had come to take him to the hospital? Had he been awake and aware of what had happened? The blood rushed back into Peter's face as he considered that Half-Cent would never have been there at all if it hadn't been for him.

Now, he and Mayhew sat waiting. A nurse had spoken briefly to them, telling them that a doctor would be out shortly, but an interminable amount of time had passed since then. The clock ticked on the wall, a slow trickle of mostly sad-faced souls shuffled past them—some entering the hospital with flowers or little gaily-wrapped parcels, some leaving the hospital in quiet tears. The hard bench grew less forgiving to their tense bodies and still there was no sign of any medical personnel. The hospital might as well have been a church, it was so silent and grim.

"Eberle! Are you in there?" Peter realized with a start that John Mayhew was patting his arm and trying to get his attention. "Now, Pete, don't blame yourself." The words rang hollow. How could he not? He was the one who asked Half-Cent to take on what had turned into such a dangerous assignment. He had been excited, but he was only fourteen, still a boy—of course he was excited! Peter was an adult. He should have had more sense. His editor went on in a soothing tone, "I can't stay with you, I have to go set tomorrow's paper, but I don't want you to worry about anything else. Just stay here as a representative of the *Gazette* and make sure Billy's all right." He placed his hand on top of one of Peter's, and the oddly intimate gesture snapped Peter out of his torpor for a moment.

"Oh, John . . . what have I done?"

Mayhew patted Peter's hand awkwardly, but said no more before rising to leave. At the door of the waiting room, he turned. "I'll be at the *Gazette* offices all night, Petey. Come tell me as soon as there's any news."

Peter had no idea how long he sat there alone. The waiting room had one window, and the sliver of sky above the buildings opposite went from blue to grey to black. Sometimes, in the distance, he could hear voices, the clattering of pans, footsteps. Twice, a confused-looking nurse poked a head in the door, looked around, and scurried backward, obviously not seeing what she was looking for. Once, Peter went to the nurse's desk and asked about Billy, but the sister behind the desk told him to wait. Someone would see him as soon as possible, she said. She didn't know anything more.

Finally a nurse approached him. Her white apron was spattered with dark stains—Half-Cent's blood?—and her voice was so quiet he had to lean in to hear her. "Mr. Eberle, is it? I'm Sister Jerome. The doctor needs to see you."

Peter clutched her arm. "How is he? Billy . . . is he awake?"

She shook her head. He started to ask another question, but she cut him off. "The doctor would like to speak to you. Come with me."

She led him to the side of a bed. A shallow line of hills and valleys barely disturbed the surface of the sheet—somehow Billy's lanky frame had been reduced to this inert, fragile thing. He was in a room with space for four patients, but only one other bed was occupied, by a man who kept moaning in his sleep. Peter found it disconcerting. A doctor, wearing a white coat, stood beside Half-Cent's bed. The doctor turned to Sister Jerome.

"Is this his next of kin?"

Peter jumped in. "No, sir. I am his . . ." he hesitated. Why had he never realized that he had no idea if the boy had any family? Uncles or aunts? He didn't even know where Half-Cent lived. "I am his friend and employer. The boy is an orphan." At least Peter knew that much was true. Billy had told him when he first started coming around the *Gazette* that his parents had both died. Why did I never ask him where he slept? I never asked him anything about himself.

The doctor looked solemn. "This young man is very ill. In addition to the head trauma, his left leg was crushed beyond repair. If we are to have any hope of saving his life . . ." Peter blanched and turned away, ". . . we must amputate at once. Are you able to give your permission, Mr . . ."

"Eberle, Peter Eberle." Amputation? Peter's head reeled. Little Billy with one leg, using crutches for the rest of his life, or worse, in a wheelchair. He closed his eyes for a moment, then reopened them, hoping against hope it would all be a nightmare. But when he looked, the suddenly frail-looking body of what had been such a bright and energetic boy still lay in the bed, the sheet covering his injured leg but his face a mass of bruises. Peter was overcome, and tears began to fill his eyes until the image blurred. "Do what you must to save him, Doctor."

He walked back to the now-familiar waiting area, his heart heavy and his mind spiraling between guilt and a burning sense of helplessness. Finally, Sister Jerome came back and told him Half-Cent was in the recovery room. The operation was over, and insofar as they could tell, a success. He stood before her, the news-paperman in him wanting to ask her for more information, and wondering in what way losing a leg could ever be termed a "suc-cess." But he said nothing.

"I'm afraid his fever is very high. That isn't a good sign, but we are doing everything we can. There is nothing you can do by stay-ing here. He won't wake before morning at the earliest. You should go get some rest, sir. Come back tomorrow." She was urging him toward the door. "Your boy is in good hands."

His boy. Peter's heart contracted, but he managed to nod. "Thank you, Sister."

He stopped at the first bar he saw after leaving the hospital and had a stiff drink to steady his nerves. That helped so much that he stopped at the second bar he saw as well, and then the third. This time he just shoved a five-dollar bill at the bartender and said, "I'll take the whole bottle."

Out in the street once more, he took a mammoth swig that made his throat burn. He stared into the streetlamp, letting the glare sear his eyes. Anything to blot out the memory of Half-Cent lying in that bed, his chest barely rising and falling with each shallow breath. He blinked, then squeezed his eyes, partly to shield them from the light, and partly to try and hold back the tears that the liquor had brought to the surface. Inside his head, one thought throbbed, over and over like the sound of a locomotive's wheels chugging across a plain. "Must find out what happened. Must find out what happened. Must find out—"

He stopped and pulled his pocket watch from his vest. It was only five minutes past nine. Unbelievable. He felt as if he'd lived days since the moment in the afternoon he had bid Libby farewell. Surely Hiram Rose couldn't be in bed yet. It was too late for a social call, but this call wasn't going to be social. He had to find out exactly what had happened on that deserted stretch of road near the Paperworks. How else could he find out who had done this horrible thing to Billy?

A brisk fifteen-minute walk, and he was facing the front of the Rose home. Lights still burned in the lower windows, indicating that indeed the household had not retired for the night. He straightened his tie and tried to button his coat, belatedly realizing that the half-filled bottle in his pocket made that impossible. The walk had cleared his head a little, but he could still feel the effects of the alcohol, which (on the whole) was not a bad thing. He took one more healthy gulp of the liquid, which now went down with an easy warmth, and tucked the bottle behind the rosebush just inside the front gate. Perhaps he still wasn't strictly presentable, but he felt ready to take on the world.

A maid answered his knock. "Yes, sir?" He could see she smelled the liquor. "Can I help you?"

With as close an approximation of sobriety as he could muster, Peter made sure his words came out clearly. "I need to see Mr. Rose." The maid looked doubtful. "It's an urgent matter, or of course I should have waited until tomorrow morning."

"Who is it at this hour, Maisie?" Hiram Rose appeared at the back of the hall, wearing a belted smoking jacket. When he saw Peter his face showed confusion, and then recognition dawned. "You're that reporter."

"Peter Eberle, sir. We met the day of the accident at the mill, here in your home . . ."

Hiram cut him off. "I'm not giving any interviews to the press."

Maisie started to shut the door. "Please, Mr. Rose," Peter stuck his foot in the doorway. "It's urgent I speak with you about what happened today. The young boy who . . ." Peter felt a sob rise, and quashed it immediately. "The young man who was injured in the rock fall. That was an apprentice of mine. I'm afraid he was following you on my orders."

Hiram gazed at Peter, and then glanced at the maid, who was staring openmouthed at the reporter wedged in the doorway. Well, at least Maisie was enjoying herself. As if deciding that, perhaps, what was being discussed should be kept from the staff, Hiram grunted, "All right then, come in. I'll give you five minutes." He waved the maid away and gestured to Peter. "My study, sir. This way."

Afterward, Peter couldn't remember anything about the room Hiram led him to, except that it seemed overstuffed and overheated. Sweat was trickling down the back of his neck as he tried to explain what Half-Cent had been doing out on that stretch of road, spying (as it were) on Hiram as he went about his business. Rose didn't take it well, and Peter felt like a schoolboy being lectured to by an irate headmaster.

"What gave you the right to have me followed? I have a right to my privacy!"

"I just . . ." Peter could tell his alcohol-fuzzed brain wasn't working at top speed. "I wanted to prove the police arrested the wrong man. And I feared there would be another attempt on your life, and so I told Half . . . Billy . . . to watch you."

"What did you expect the boy to do if someone made another attempt on my life? Stop them single-handedly? A fourteen-year-old boy? Did it never occur to you to come to me to warn me you believed I might still be in danger?" Hiram didn't pause between questions, and it was clear he didn't expect Peter to answer. "You weren't worried about me. No, why should you be? That boy was just supposed to watch me die and then give you the scoop for the *Gazette.*"

"No, no, that wasn't what I wanted to see happen . . ."

But it was true, wasn't it? Peter hadn't cared if a new attack on Hiram Rose's life would prove successful, as long as it cleared Dutch Karlsson's name. And what could he have expected Half-Cent to do if he spotted an ambush? Peter felt like an idiot, and because of his idiocy a boy lay in the hospital near death . . . and with only one leg. Peter wanted to sink into the floor.

Salvation, as it were, came in a most unlikely form. Hiram was about to renew his verbal assault on Peter when Mrs. Rose rushed into the room, waving a slip of paper. Peter realized he had heard the front doorbell ringing during Rose's harangue, but had ignored it. "Hiram! We just got a telegram!" She apparently didn't notice the reporter sitting in the chair. "Elliot has run away from his school. They say they haven't seen him since yesterday. Yesterday! They claim they were sure he would turn up, and so they waited until now to tell us."

"Let me see that," Hiram barked. Tears streaming down her face, Adele handed the slip of onionskin paper over. "My poor boy! He could be dead in the woods or on some remote road somewhere." She turned an accusing finger at her husband. "I knew sending him to that military academy was the wrong thing to do. He's such a sensitive boy, but you insisted, and now . . ." Her words were lost in a flood of tears.

Hiram looked past his crying wife. "Mr. Eberle, I'll thank you to leave now. I have my own boy to think of." Adele turned a surprised face toward Peter, but didn't speak. "See yourself out, please," his voice was like ice, "and don't return."

Peter stumbled to his feet, out through the hall, and out into the night. Elliot lost, Billy in the hospital. It was a bad night to be a boy in Portland, Peter thought, weaving his way down the street. He was a good twenty yards from the house when he remembered his hidden bottle. Turning back to fetch it, it occurred to him that it wasn't such a great night to be a man either.

———

Libby bolted awake and sat upright in bed. Something had woken her. She lay there, listening intently. Had it been a dream? No, there it was again, a faint rattling at her window, then nothing. Reaching for her robe, she sat up and crossed the small room. There was no tree outside her window, and she was at a loss to think of what could be causing the sound. Could a bird be outside her window in the middle of the night? Gingerly, she pulled the corner curtain aside, but she saw only dark sky and a sliver of moon. She dropped the curtain and turned back to bed, when what sounded like a volley of hail hit the window, followed by a faint whisper.

"Libby!"

Pulling back the curtain once again, she looked down three floors to the backyard garden. It was a man, hardly able to stand. No, not just any man . . . Peter. But he didn't look like himself. His coat was open and he was disheveled. No, she decided, as she watched him stagger a few steps then fall to his knees in the mud, not disheveled—drunk. He was drunk.

She opened her window a crack. "What are you doing here?" Frantically, she waved her arms in the universal signal for "go away," but if he understood what she was trying to communicate, he gave no sign of it.

She realized with a growing horror that he was crying. He knelt on the ground, a crumpled heap, unable to even form words. What on earth had happened? "I'll be right down," she whispered. Tiptoeing so as not to wake Mrs. Pratt and the rest of the tenants, she went down the two flights, then down one more to the cellar. It was darker than she realized, the only light the faint moonlight from a dusty window high up on the wall. She had only been down here in daylight before, once when she had moved in and stored her empty trunk, and a few other times to help Mrs. Pratt bring up canning from last summer.

Libby gasped and almost screamed with fright. A cobweb had brushed across her face, startling her. She waited a moment for her breathing to return to normal, then carefully ran her fingers along the chalky wall until her fingers brushed the hinges she was looking for. She had remembered there was a door that led outside to the backyard, and she figured this would be the most inconspicuous way to bring Peter inside.

Getting him upstairs quietly was no small feat, but at last they were safely ensconced in her room on the third floor, and since she was the only tenant up there, it felt fairly safe. She would have to sneak him out very carefully. Worry gnawed at her. How was she ever going to manage without Mrs. Pratt . . . No! She mustn't worry now. She would figure it out tomorrow.

Peter had stopped crying, but his cheeks were stained with a mixture of tears and dirt, and there was a bruise on his cheek. Had he fallen? Libby helped him remove his coat, and they sat on her bed, knees touching. "Oh, Peter, what is it?"

"Half-Cent . . . You know, I told you about him, Billy, the boy who . . ." He stopped, and she could tell he was fighting back tears. Bit by bit, the story came out: Half-Cent's injury, and Peter's deep raw feelings of self-blame that it had happened at all. "If only I hadn't asked him to . . . what was I thinking? And now that poor child is paying for my pigheaded stupidity with his . . . What have I done?" He wasn't even forming full sentences. She had never known Peter to be so inarticulate.

"Shhhh, shhhh." Libby held him to her, rocking him back and forth like a child. His arms wrapped around her tightly, and she could feel his ragged breaths on her neck. With a jolt, she realized her robe had fallen open to reveal her light nightgown. Peter's heavy form pressed against her, and she could feel the rough texture of his tweed jacket, the buttons on his starched shirt, and the heat of his body, almost as if she were wearing nothing at all. "He'll be all right," she whispered over and over like a lullaby, although she had no idea if this was the case. Peter slept at last, and beside him, Libby finally drifted off into a kind of half-sleep.

Dawn came, a faint light from the still-open curtain streaming in. Libby awoke from a light sleep to realize Peter's limbs were tangled around her, and as she moved, he moved too. He raised his head and looked at her, and then squinted at the light. He looked at her confused, and she could tell he was trying to put together a sentence. She waited, but instead of saying anything he kissed her. It felt like the most natural thing in the world that they were kissing, first lightly, then deeper. Slowly, he tugged at her robe, and as if in a dream, she let him. He buried his face in her, kissing her through the nightgown. Rattling noises from the street told her the milkman was making his early morning rounds; soon the rest of the world would be waking and, for a brief moment, reality intruded. She tried to push Peter away.

But she couldn't, he needed her. And she knew she needed nothing so much as his warm kisses, his caresses making her feel things she had never felt before, not with her husband, not with any man. As if she were watching herself becoming a different person, she peeled back his still-damp shirt, pulled off his pants, and then they were both naked, holding each other tightly, rocking back and forth as they had been when he fell asleep the night before. She felt an excitement welling up inside her, a pleasure she hadn't known existed based on her brief experiences in the marriage bed. Peter's hands ran up and down her back as he pulled her closer, and for the first time since she had moved to Portland, Libby Seale let everything fall away but the moment and surrendered herself to the bittersweet pleasure of a union with the man she loved and could not have.

FOURTEEN

When Peter woke again a few hours later, a deep golden sunshine fell across his smile. The smile was quickly wiped from his face as the most extraordinary series of emotions and recollections tumbled one after the other to the forefront of his emerging consciousness. First, there was the realization of where he was, in whose bed, and what had happened there just a few hours before. Then came the memory of the night that preceded coming to this bed, the amount of alcohol he had consumed, and the awareness of the dull throbbing headache that was his comeuppance. Finally, he remembered the reason for his inebriation, the embarrassing scene with Hiram Rose, and the image of a broken and perhaps dying Half-Cent looking lost on a narrow hospital cot.

These last thoughts made him take stock of the sky, and it dawned on him that it must already be fairly late in the morning. He had been resolute in his determination to begin investigating first thing—damn his lethargy. Well, better a late start than no start, he chided himself, and swung his legs over the side of the bed, squinting against the light. Why of all days did the weather have to be so fine today! His head protested against the sudden shift to verticality, and his stomach seconded the motion. With embarrassment he realized he was naked. Luckily he was alone in the room, though after last night he supposed he had no reason to be embarrassed in front of Libby. Still, if she had been there he would have blushed nonetheless.

The thought of Libby brought a smile back to his face as he gathered his clothes up off of the floor. It mingled with a confusion and the vague sense that they had irreparably changed their relationship. For his part, he hoped it would lead to something better, but he feared it might just make things unbearably awkward. Would she now be willing to acquire a divorce and marry him? She had told him, weeks before, that she intended to make Portland her home permanently. Didn't it follow, then, that the old-world ways of her parents and neighbors back in New York should loosen their hold on her? If she wasn't going to go back East then ... Not having had any sort of religious upbringing, he found himself baffled by her adherence to a set of laws that he knew so little about.

Once he was dressed, he slipped down both flights of stairs, careful to keep an eye out for Mrs. Pratt or any of the other boarders. He made it to the front hall unobserved, then opened the front door as quietly as he could and, slipping around to its porch side, knocked loudly, calling out, "May I come in? It's Mr. Eberle."

Libby appeared in the arched doorway to the dining room. "Mrs. Pratt has gone out. There's no need for a big charade," she said, her voice not exactly cool but strangely without affect. "We were lucky." Her voice didn't sound as if she felt lucky. She headed back to her place in the dining room, and Peter followed. "Would you like something to eat?" she offered.

Peter quailed at even the thought of trying to eat something. What he wanted was for Libby to laugh or grin or giggle, anything to show she wasn't upset. "No, thank you," he managed, and made a funny face, and was rewarded with a weak smile. "Libby, I'm sorry how I . . . last night I was . . ." She didn't answer. Did she think he meant he was sorry for what had happened this morning, in her bed? He hastened to correct that misapprehension, "I meant coming here drunk. And so late. I don't mean that I am sorry we . . . that is—"

"I got a letter from home," Libby interrupted, picking up some thin sheets of paper from beside her plate, sheets that bore the creases from having made their rough way across the width of a continent folded inside a small envelope.

"I hope all is well?" he asked somewhat awkwardly.

"My sister is going to college. She's going to be a teacher." She looked up, meeting his eyes for the first time that morning. "My parents are very proud."

The tone was self-lacerating, and Peter heard the unspoken completion of the sentence: "of her."

"Libby, what happened . . . what we did last night, it may not be something to be proud of. But I'm not sorry it happened. It was—"

"It was wrong, Peter. It was something we shouldn't have done. You were inebriated and I was foolish."

He leaned over the table and said warmly. "My being drunk isn't why I wanted you. Why I want you. I wanted to marry you before, and I still do."

236

Her look didn't change. "I told you. I am already married, and that's that. Which is why it was foolish of me to . . . no matter how much I may want you, too."

That admission cost her, he could tell. In that moment he loved her even more, if that was possible.

"It isn't foolishness, Libby. It's love. And I don't understand why, if you love me, you won't get a divorce." His voice went up at the end, in a questioning tone.

Libby carefully folded the letter from her mother and rose from her seat. As she talked, she drifted aimlessly around the dining room, focusing on everything except the man standing in the middle of the floor.

"Peter, even if I were not married, you know there would be problems. Problems with our religion, our families . . . with my family, certainly. But maybe, maybe if that were all, we could overcome it. But when it comes to my marriage, my faith is very clear. Divorce is strictly a husband's prerogative."

Peter's face looked blank, so she went on. "In Jewish law you need a decree called a Get, which is a legal statement from a man stating his intent to be divorced from his wife. Without it, I would still be considered married, no matter what a judge might say."

She picked up a vase on the sideboard, and to all intents appeared to be studying the intricate pattern carefully. Peter would have been willing to bet she wasn't even seeing it clearly. "If I were to remarry in that case, I would become an outcast. No Jewish home would be open to me. My parents would view me as dead."

The word seemed to hang in the air between them. Peter's headache was mounting a fresh assault, and he could barely assimilate this new information. "But surely . . . your husband, Mr.

Greenblatt, yes? Surely he'll give you this Jewish divorce? You're three thousand miles from him, and this must mean he can never remarry either."

She sighed. "It's not unheard of for husbands and wives to live apart. Divorce is something my parents and their friends simply do not consider. To them, the shame of it is far worse than any rumors of an unhappy marriage. Mr. Greenblatt has apparently told people I am away visiting a sick relative, and whatever they may guess privately, that fiction is enough to allow him to hold his head up high in temple."

Peter sat down. He had been so sure that last night had indicated a softening on Libby's part to the idea of marrying him. But if anything it seemed to have had the opposite effect, stiffening her resolve to stay her present course. Libby saw his distress, and she felt a pang of guilt. She had not been suffering the combined effects of emotional stress and too much alcohol the night before, and so the lion's share of blame was hers.

"Peter, I'm sorry. Last night I didn't think. I let my emotions rule my actions. It wasn't until I sat here this morning that I realized . . . I know what's right, now. I know what I have to do. And I need to listen to my head, not my heart."

"Libby, are you," he hesitated asking the question, afraid of what the answer might be, "are you going back to New York?" That was the only possibility that made any sense of this topsy-turvy speech.

She paused, then said quietly, "I don't know." Then, in a rush, "Maybe someday, but not now. But even if I stay in Portland, even if I decide to live here forever, I cannot live in a world where visiting my parents or my brother and sister—or having them come

238

visit me here—is not a possibility. I am not ready to decide that I will never see my family again." She paused, and he saw that her eyes were filled with tears. "It may not make sense to you, Peter, but breaking with my faith would mean an irrevocable rupture—if I do that then I never can go home, not even for a visit." She sat down next to him. "I love you, you know I do. But not enough to give up everything I know. Not if it means you would be all I have."

He stared at her. "Mr. Greenblatt could change his mind."

She stared right back. "I wouldn't count on that," she finally said. "In the back of my mind, I suppose I was holding out hope for just such a resolution, but the more time that goes on, the less likely it seems."

"But—"

"No, let me finish. Peter, please don't get mired in 'what-ifs'. I realize now that had I faced some unpleasant truths from the start, we would never have come to this. I should have told you I was married when we first met, and then none of this heartbreak need have happened."

He smiled then, bleak, but genuine. "You don't know me very well if you think anything you said could've stopped me from falling in love with you." He put his hat on and stood up. "I need to be going. I'm getting a much later start than I intended."

She persisted. "Peter, you need to find someone else. Give up all ideas of marrying me. You need to fall in love with someone who can give you the love you deserve in return."

"I need to start right away investigating the latest attack. Someone might have seen something." He wouldn't meet her gaze.

She sighed again, but dropped the topic. For now. Assuming a more businesslike tone, she said, "Yes. The most important thing is to find out who could have done such a terrible thing to Billy."

He turned for the door. "Oh, but I haven't told you. Last night I did make the time to see Hiram Rose, to see what he could tell me about the incident. That turned out to be very little. But, while I was there, Mrs. Rose came rushing in."

Peter consciously left out the details of the scene. It would surely not come as news that he had been drunk during the meeting, but it still embarrassed him to have been dressed down like an errant schoolboy. It mattered a great deal to him, even now, that she not think of him as a bumbling idiot. "It seems Elliot Rose has run away from that school he was sent to. So it appears he might be back in the picture."

Libby's face registered shock. "Do you really think he could have attacked his own father?" Belatedly Peter remembered the feelings Libby seemed to have for the teenager.

He backpedaled. "No, no, I'm sure it's merely a coincidence. But I wanted to tell you. Perhaps you . . ." He groped for a way to end the uncomfortable topic. "Perhaps you should go and see if you can comfort Mrs. Rose. She was quite distraught."

"How could I explain that I knew? Shall I mention the drunken reporter who overheard the news at her house?" Libby was teasing, and Peter smiled, too. He figured that if they could still joke with each other, then everything would be all right between them. Eventually, at least. Though his head still throbbed, he began to feel better.

"I should go," he said. Libby looked up at him again, and he thought he saw regret and sorrow in her eyes. Or was that just wishful thinking?

She said simply, "Yes."

——

Peter rode along Harbor Drive toward the mill. He was unused to riding a horse, but this morning he felt a certain odd comfort riding Pittock, as if it somehow brought him closer to Half-Cent. He had stopped by the hospital on his way out of the city, but the boy was still unconscious. The nurse on duty assured him this was normal for a post-operative patient, and warned him it could still be hours before Half-Cent woke. Assuming he did, her tone implied, though she was too polite to voice the thought. Peter hadn't stayed long.

As he approached the turnoff to the mill, he slowed down, wondering if he would be able to find the spot the policeman had described. He needn't have worried. A pile of rocks—one enormous boulder surrounded by numerous smaller ones—sat very obviously at the side of the road on his right. Behind them, several downed trees and a flattened path among the brush and weeds showed the trajectory of the rock fall. Peter dismounted and looked for a place to tie the horse up.

That done, he walked up from the debris, following the trail of flattened foliage. The boulder's path was clear, even with a day's rainfall to obscure it. As he crossed a footpath halfway up the slope, a large dark spot that was obviously blood made him shudder, but he continued upward, trying to determine where the

241

boulder had stood before it was pushed. Surely there was no way it could have been an accident? A boulder loosened by too much rain, and Half-Cent just in the wrong place at the wrong time? No. Someone had to have pushed the rock.

Occasionally he stopped and squatted, carefully examining the matted grass. What he was looking for, he didn't know. He only knew that he wanted to see every last detail in the hopes of finding some useful evidence. At the top of the incline he found the indentation where the largest rock must have once stood. The steep slope of the hill at this point would have made the assassin's job easy—it wouldn't have taken a lot of brute strength. One well-timed push probably would have done it. Unbidden, he pictured Billy, suddenly overtaken by a ton of tumbling rock. The boy probably hadn't even seen it coming, Peter thought.

Bringing himself back to the present, he found he was mumbling to himself—evidence, must find evidence. He began a methodical search of the area around the indentation, trying to reconstruct the scene. The would-be killer must have stood in the nearby thicket of trees, waiting for Rose to ride by . . . watching the road to determine just the right moment to impel the boulder on its destructive path.

Although the rocky ground beneath him hurt his knees, Peter crawled looking for anything useful. Sadly, the previous day's rain had covered any footprints with a layer of fresh mud, but his eyes combed the ground looking for any scrap that might have been left behind by the person he sought. But after a muddy search, in an ever-widening circle, he was forced to admit defeat. Suddenly, he was struck by another idea.

He had noticed a small, crudely lettered sign indicating the mill's Chinese workers' encampment lay just beyond the fringe of trees. Could Hiram's workers have engineered the accident? He considered that for a few seconds. Of all the people in Rose's world, the employed Chinamen were probably the last to wish him dead. But perhaps one of them had witnessed the attack.

He followed the arrow on the little sign until he reached an empty clearing, ringed with flimsy wooden structures. It was silent. Of course, Peter thought, at this hour all the workers would be at the mill. Boldly, he walked up to each building and peered in. Each one contained several beds and shelves, extra clothing hanging neatly from hooks on the wall. He was just deciding the search was a waste of time when he heard a clattering sound from the long, low building at the end of the row of cabins. Stepping over to it, he realized at once that it was a cookhouse. A vague odor of fish and rice hung over the rows of long pine tables and benches, and a fire crackled in a kitchen area in the rear of the single large room.

A gray-haired woman appeared, brandishing a frying pan, spouting a barrage of incomprehensible words. Peter held his hands up and tried the few phrases of Chinese he thought he knew. But she appeared not to understand, and what's more, she looked as if she'd enjoy beaming him on the head with her stovetop weapon. Shaking his head and waving his arms, Peter backed out of the cookhouse. The woman followed him as far as the doorway, then waved her arms with one last outburst and retreated back to her domain. Peter couldn't help noticing that the building had a distant but clear view of the exact spot where the rock had been pushed. If he could only find a way to communicate with the old woman, he might uncover something that could help him find Half-Cent's attacker.

———

An hour and a half later, Hatty Matthews was deep in animated conversation with the elderly Chinese cook. Peter and Libby sat silently to one side at one of the dining tables, watching and feeling useless. Hatty was a good friend, Libby's former boss during the time she had worked at Crowther's Portland Variety. Originally from Hong Kong (although she had lived in America for many years), Hatty was also the only fluent Chinese-speaker Peter knew.

The two Oriental women laughed at some joke only they understood, and finally Hatty turned to her friends. "I can only understand about half of what she is saying. I speak Cantonese, you see, and she speaks some dialect I'm not familiar with. I have to use what little Mandarin I know to try to talk to her. I think she just said something about how she ought to cook you some white people's food, but she doesn't have any spoiled milk." Hatty was unable to keep the slight smile from her face as she reported this. Peter and Libby turned to the wrinkled Chinese cook and made a show of polite laughter, though they failed to see what was funny. Hatty began speaking to her countrywoman again.

Now that she wasn't threatening him with bodily harm, Peter could see that the cook was really quite elderly, although she moved quickly for one of her advanced years. She was gesticulating wildly now and speaking quite loudly, frustrated that Hatty did not understand all her words. When they had arrived, Hatty had gone into the cookhouse first and somehow managed to make it clear that she and Peter and Libby were there as friends. But if the current problems were any indicator, communication had gone downhill since then. Libby turned to Peter, worried. "What if she did see something and Hatty can't understand her?"

"Worse . . . what if she saw nothing?" he said glumly.

Peter had foolishly assumed this interview would be like his usual work, he asking questions and getting answers, the only difference being a pause between questions as his translator said the words. But nothing about this was usual. The cook seemed unwilling to answer straightforward questions, and Hatty had made it clear that since she was not able to speak the same dialect, all she could do was let the old woman rattle on and then give Peter the gist of it. And so it was that Peter and Libby sat on the sidelines, watching but not interacting at all. This only served to highlight the awkwardness that lay between them. In the wake of recent events their usual easy familiarity had disappeared.

Peter turned to Libby, obviously grasping for conversation. "I'm glad it was not a problem for you, locating Hatty on such short notice."

"I know she's glad to help. And I've been meaning to stop at the shop where she's working, so this gave me a good excuse."

After this, there was another long pause as the two of them regarded the dining hall, noting all the details, from the low windows to the knotholes in the wooden walls. Hatty turned to them. "I think she wants to show me something," she said, puzzled. The cook held her arm and was pulling her toward the door. Jumping up, Peter followed them, Libby close behind.

The cook waved toward the hillside and appeared to be describing something. Peter couldn't help himself. He asked Hatty excitedly, "What is she saying? Did she see someone?"

"Shhh," whispered Hatty annoyed, not turning to face Peter. The old woman rattled off a long string of ominous-sounding syllables, then Hatty said something back. There was much gesticulation, and at one point the cook appeared to be miming a veil, like a bride might wear, waving behind her in the empty air. Finally, Hatty turned to Peter.

"Yesterday, she heard something, a loud noise outside, like something falling. She came out but didn't see what it was. Something about a woman wearing a sister-in-law . . . no, not that of course, I'm sorry, a cloak. The Cantonese word is so similar. Anyway, a cloak . . . something pale . . . tan, or maybe pink. I'm not sure. She seems to feel the woman looked like a ghost. She keeps saying pale."

"The woman? Or the cloak?" Peter turned to the cook, while Hatty did her best to express the question, but received only a noncommittal reply. "I'm sorry, Mr. Eberle, I can't make out everything she is saying. I think she said she couldn't see the person very well, the big light-colored cloak was hiding her. And she seems to feel all white women look the same. She describes them all as looking like flour dumplings . . . well, you get the idea." She brightened, "She did mention there was a carriage . . . the woman got into a carriage and then went away."

"What did the carriage look like? How tall was the woman? Did she actually see her push the rock?" Peter couldn't stop himself from firing a volley of questions, but Hatty only smiled and shook her head.

"I tried to ask what else she could tell me, but either my Mandarin isn't up to the task, or more likely, she doesn't know any more than she told me. She keeps repeating the same things, about a white woman, a light-colored cloak, and a carriage. I don't think there's anything else she can tell us."

Peter impulsively reached out and took the old cook's hand, looking into her eyes. "Thank you, madam." He bowed deeply, and the old woman cackled and simpered. No words were needed to convey her pleasure in receiving the attentions of the polite reporter. All her previous animosity seemed to vanish.

"We should go, then," said Libby, feeling somehow uncomfortable watching Peter charm the Chinese cook. "Hatty, thank you so much for your expertise." Hatty made suitable thanks and goodbyes to the cook, and then she, Peter, and Libby walked to where they had tied up Pittock, who was harnessed to the dilapidated newspaper delivery wagon Peter had used to ferry them all to the mill workers' campsite.

On the way home, Libby sat between Peter and Hatty. The plank seat was designed for one driver and one passenger at most, certainly not for three adults. The tight squeeze forced Peter and Libby into close proximity, making them acutely aware of each other's bodies. But Hatty's presence at least provided a distraction, and for most of the ride back to town, Hatty and Libby chatted about their respective sewing jobs and other gossip about people they knew in common through their shared work at the now-defunct Crowther's Theatre.

As they approached her home, Hatty leaned in and said quietly, so Peter wouldn't hear, "It is nice to see you are still spending time with your young man." Libby looked at her feet, but didn't answer.

Hatty, unaware of any awkwardness, went on. "Perhaps soon you will be asking my help in making you a wedding dress?"

Libby felt her cheeks turn crimson, and immediately cast about for a change of subject. Brightly, she said, "Hatty, we really must get together again soon, without any work in the way." As Peter gallantly jumped off and came around to help Hatty down, the two women promised each other they would meet again soon, and shop for fabrics together.

When he got back on the wagon seat, Libby had moved as far away from the driver's side as possible and was sitting stiffly, playing with the ends of her shawl. As she had watched him walk Hatty to her door, her mind returned to her actions of the night before. Why had she let it happen! Had she somehow engineered events so that she could have what she wanted while telling herself it was unplanned? Peter had been drunk, and was deeply wounded by the news of Half-Cent's accident, but she had been sober. She should have been able to remain in control.

She thought about her little sister back in New York. It now seemed like a chasm separated them. Rebecca would be heading off to a teachers' college in the fall, a credit to the family, while Libby . . . well, what she had done last night was nothing but shameful. Of course, she had not had the opportunities her sister was being given. She had not been offered the choice to pursue her studies. No, she had been forced into a loveless marriage. Perhaps if she had been allowed to go to college she would not have run away across the country! Lost in her own thoughts, Libby noticed the wagon was moving again.

Peter saw the frown on Libby's face, but he decided to ignore her obvious discomfort. After a moment's hesitation, he began speaking excitedly about all they had learned and what it might mean. She answered him, and slowly her contemplative look was replaced with her usual inquisitive expression. Soon they were talking as they always did, listing all the possible females who might be the woman the cook described.

Peter, still smarting from his last encounter with the Karlsson family, leaned toward thinking the mysterious woman in the carriage might have been Tilda, or even Anna. And, of course, Phebe Scott was in the running, having made it clear that she had a deep desire to see Dutch's name cleared. At least this latest attempt on Hiram's life had done that.

Meanwhile, Libby vowed to check into Eva Fowler's whereabouts. Adele and Miss Baylis, they decided, were less likely candidates. Since those two couldn't have committed the second attack—the one with the arrows—they seemed unlikely to be behind this latest violence. What motive any of the women in the Rose household could have had, however, Peter and Libby still had no idea. But at least it felt like they were finally making progress. They knew for sure it was a woman who had pushed the stone that had crushed poor Billy, and when they figured out who the woman was they could figure out why. And discover whether she had acted alone all along or had an accomplice in this campaign against Hiram Rose. Libby was just summing up as Mrs. Pratt's house came into view.

"So it's settled. You try to find out where Dutch's friends and family were at the time of the rock fall, and I'll do what I can to investigate Mrs. Fowler," Libby finished, all business. Peter reined in the horse, and she jumped in a rather unladylike fashion off the wagon before he could help, landing in a puddle of mud with a mutter of annoyance. "I'm fine, I'm fine," she said, and gave a false smile up at Peter, waving off the look of concern that immediately filled his face. "I'll talk to you tomorrow!" And with that, she ran into the house.

Well, if I had any doubt, thought Peter, I can see that she is uncomfortable being alone with me. He sighed, and gave the reins a rattle to get Pittock moving again. He wasn't uncomfortable with her, why did she have to be with him? Or was he? Her declaration this morning had certainly unnerved him. After the uncomfortable scene in church a few months before, when she had devastated him by turning down his proposal and admitting she had lied to him about being unmarried, he had sworn he would never again let Libby Seale get under his skin. And yet she had managed to do it again, pull the rug out from under him when he had least expected it. Perhaps it was time to give up. Perhaps he should listen to her and try to find someone else. But no one could replace Libby . . . he loved her, was in love with her. That was a fact. But it was apparently a hopeless fact, a fact without a future.

He couldn't think about this now. He couldn't face what making a decision, finally and irrevocably, might cost him. And there were others to whom he owed his attention and his focus. First he had to get whomever it was who had taken Billy's leg away from him—he pushed aside the possibility that Half-Cent might actually die—and then there would be time to determine what to do about Libby.

FIFTEEN

WILMER STUBBINS WAS IN a talkative mood. Which, from Libby Seale's perspective, was both a good thing and a bad thing. She had arrived at the Fowler door a few moments before, and upon receiving no answer to her knock, she had thought it best to check in with Stubbins to make sure Mrs. Fowler was indeed away from home. Unfortunately, having confirmed that Mrs. Fowler and Mrs. Rose were off shopping for baby things, she could find no way of breaking off the stream of reminiscence flowing from the elderly family retainer. The subject of pregnancy had gotten Wilmer thinking about Adele's first confinement, and to her amazement, Libby found that the stable hand was quite sentimental about Adele, whom he still referred to by her childhood nickname, which had apparently been Miss Addy.

"Oh, she had such a glow about her, she did, Miss Seale. You should have seen Miss Addy when she was working on her eldest boy. We could have lit the whole house without candles, she shone so."

Libby tried to switch the topic to Eva. "I suppose now Mrs. Fowler has much the same look. It's such a miracle . . . the greatest miracle of life, don't you think?"

"Yes, siree it is, Miss. Of course, I shouldn't say, but if you ask me, Missus Fowler doesn't have half so much a glow as Miss Addy did."

"Well, Mrs. Fowler is a much . . ." Libby searched for a proper euphemism, "heartier woman than Mrs. Rose."

"That she is, Miss. You're not wrong." He tsk-tsked disapprovingly.

"It amazes me she drives her own carriage too. I'm surprised you aren't driving them on this shopping expedition."

Wilmer looked pained. "I don't think it's right, but Mrs. Fowler insisted. A fine one for horses, she is. And, truth to tell, if I were to drive her everywhere she wanted to go, I wouldn't have five minutes in the day to get done all the other things I need to do around here."

Libby feigned amazement, and voiced the question she had wanted to ask all along. "Oh, were Mrs. Fowler and Mrs. Rose out shopping yesterday as well? I wondered why they couldn't meet with me."

"No, Miss Addy was here, all right. But she has been mighty glum since word came that Elliot ran off from school. She only went today on account of her husband said she needed to get out of the house, at least for a little bit."

"You mean Mrs. Fowler went out by herself? In her condition?"

The old black man just nodded sagely. "It wouldn't be my way, but nobody asks for my opinion, so I keep it to myself."

"Then maybe that was Mrs. Fowler I saw in Meier & Frank downtown yesterday afternoon. I tried to say hello, but I couldn't catch up with her through the crowd. Could she have been there around three?"

"Well," he said, drawing out the word with a long southern vowel, "she was out most of the afternoon. Left here just after Mr. Hiram came back for a bit around lunchtime. I didn't see her go, being in the kitchen and all, but when I finished my meal the carriage was gone. I guess she got her brother to hitch up the horse for her."

Well, it certainly appeared Eva Fowler at least had the means and opportunity to have pushed the boulder. Libby decided she should poke around further and see if she could find anything else that might turn out to confirm Eva as their prime suspect. "It's been a great pleasure speaking with you, Mr. Stubbins, but I suppose I should just leave these parcels with Celia and be on my way."

"A good day to you to, Miss." And with that he headed back into the stables and left Libby alone in the yard. She briefly toyed with the idea of doing what she had just told the old man she would do, but she feared that any trip into the Rose house would end in a long conversation with Celia. So, checking to make sure Stubbins couldn't see her from the half-open stable door, she darted through the gap in the laurel hedge and into the Fowler's yard. As she had suspected, the back door was closed but not locked, and within a moment she was standing inside the Fowler home, considering where to begin looking for some clue that Eva had been the woman spotted by the Chinese cook.

There was nothing of interest to be seen in the kitchen. The room looked almost barren and unused, unsurprising since the Fowlers took all of their main meals with the Roses next door. Libby put down the wrapped bundle of sewing on the table and headed out into the front of the house. She suddenly had an idea of what she could look for. The elderly Chinese woman had spoken of a pale cloak. As it happened, Libby knew exactly what Eva Fowler's main winter cloak looked like—it was a gay red and blue tartan, heavily trimmed with black rickrack braid, and Libby had made her a deep-red dress specifically to complement it—which meant, if Eva had been the woman spotted by the mill workers' camp, there had to be another cloak somewhere in the house. The front closet proved not to hold any such item, but Libby hadn't really expected it to. Surely a would-be murderess would be more careful than to stow an incriminating garment where any guest might catch sight of it. There was nothing for it but to go upstairs and search through Eva's room.

Halfway up the staircase, a whinny from out in front of the house reached her ears. Quickly she ran back down and peered through the lace curtains in the front parlor window. Damn! It was Augustus Fowler, and as she watched he dismounted and looped his horse's reins to the railing of the front steps. As silently as she could, she moved back through the parlor and dining room, out the kitchen door, and into the yard. She realized immediately that she had left her bundle of work on the kitchen table, but it was too late to go back inside the house now. She could only hope Augustus, like many men, rarely if ever ventured into the kitchen.

Hidden in the shadows of the hedge, Libby tried to collect her thoughts while waiting for her racing heartbeat to slow down.

That had been a close call. What could she have said if Augustus Fowler had found her rooting through his wife's drawers? Her instinct said to flee, but she reminded herself of that incriminating parcel on the kitchen table. She had to wait and hope Augustus would only remain a short time and she could get back in the house before Eva arrived home. But where could she wait? Both the Rose home and stables she dismissed—one would open her to the petty gossip of a loquacious cook and the other the long-winded reminiscences of the lonely stable hand. She spied the corner of the garden shed behind the barn, and realized with a start that she had never even seen the inside, and that was supposedly where Matt, the center of this mystery, had spent so much of his time. It would be the perfect place to wait, since with both Matt and Elliot gone she imagined it was never used.

The air inside was thick, with a musty, peaty odor. Very little light made it through the grimy panes in the small windows high along the back wall, but once her eyes adjusted she could see reasonably well. Tools stood neatly at the front, hoes and spades, plus some fierce-looking implements—a contraption made of iron wheels ringed with pointed tips, long-handled shears with blades curved like a bird's beak—at whose uses Libby could only guess. The rear of the shed appeared to contain the detritus of the household. A very dusty baby buggy stood next to a dented copper washing kettle, but as she got closer she could see that there was a clear space among the junk. When she reached it she saw it for what it was . . . a campsite of sorts, a nest. She realized at once that Elliot Rose had headed directly home when he ran away from military school, whether or not he had announced his arrival. A makeshift bedroll was neatly set to one side, a folded-up coach blanket forming a pillow at one end, and an old tan mackintosh folded back like a coverlet. Next to this lay the stub of a candle in a chipped saucer, and a small wrapped parcel. Libby crouched beside it and unwrapped what lay inside—a small collection of much-used, and obviously much-loved, paintbrushes.

What she spotted next made her blood run cold. Tucked between two crates, with the end sticking out within her reach, was an archer's bow and a few feather-tipped arrows. She pulled it from its place, and any hopes she had that it was merely a coincidence that it should be here were put to rest. It was quite free of the layer of dust that lay thick on most of the household junk, and, though worn, the bow was stretched taut and pinged when she plucked the string. Libby knew little about archery, to be sure, but she knew if this bow had been sitting forgotten for months or years the string would certainly have slackened.

Her mind tried to make sense of what she had found. If Elliot was the one who had shot at his father, then . . . But, of course. Why hadn't she and Peter seen the possibility that what the old Chinese cook had seen was not a woman but a slender teenage boy. He must have worn his father's old mackintosh, which he was using as a blanket. Designed to cover a grown man from rain all the way to his ankles, it would have billowed around Elliot's small frame, and so anyone might easily have mistaken it for a woman's cloak. But what about Matt? She remembered the painting she had found under Elliot's bed and wondered just what sort of relationship there had been between the handsome young servant and the lonely teenager. Had Elliot been there the night Matt was killed? Was Matt's death just a horrible accident or part of some plan of Elliot's?

She was still in a crouch, so deep in thought that she hadn't even registered the pain gathering in her stiff legs, when a shadow fell across her. She looked up to see Elliot backlit in the sliver of light from the open door. For a moment alarm and surprise registered on both their faces. Then carefully Elliot shut the door behind him with a soft click, as Libby struggled to her feet.

"Miss Seale," he said quietly, "you can't tell my parents I'm here."

———

As Peter entered the hospital, Sister Jerome greeted him placidly. "Mr. Eberle. May I have a word before you head into the patient's room."

Peter felt as if his heart was being squeezed by a vise, and he leaned on the counter for support. "Yes, of course, Sister." Amazingly there was no tremor in his voice.

"I should tell you that your young friend has awakened."

Peter's spirits rose a thousand feet in a second, and he couldn't help breaking in. "He's awake! He's alive!"

"Yes," the calm nurse said gently, seeing the elation in Peter's face. "He started talking just a few hours ago. But I must tell you, he is not himself yet." She started to say something else, but amended it to, "I'll send the doctor in to speak to you soon."

That didn't sound good to Peter. "He is going to be all right, isn't he, Sister?"

"He's still very weak, Mr. Eberle. In fact he's dozed off again, but it is not a deep sleep. And . . . well, I'm sure the doctor can explain things better than I can. Please, don't be alarmed."

Taking his arm, she led a slightly less euphoric Peter to Half-Cent's room.

At first, he looked the same as before, although the bruises on his face were slightly less pronounced. Sister Jerome told him to sit down and wait, that Billy would probably wake up again soon. As she backed out of the room, her eyes seemed to entreat him not to expect too much. Peter settled into the hard-backed chair beside the bed.

At the creaking sound, Half-Cent opened his eyes. "Mama?" he said, and Peter thought his heart would break. The boy tossed and turned a bit in the bed, mumbling, but then seemed to sink back into sleep.

Peter couldn't take his eyes off the shape under the sheet, or rather, the lack of shape where a left leg should have been. He felt sick. "I'll find out who did this to you," Peter whispered fiercely, laying his hand lightly on Half-Cent's. Unfortunately, he felt hardly any closer now than he had been the day before. After dropping Libby off, he had immediately gone to the Green Gale, where he determined from three separate sources that Scotty had been working behind the bar the entire time in question. Establishing the whereabouts of both Anna and Tilda had also been surprisingly easy, as it turned out the two women along with Mummo had been at a church rummage sale all afternoon. He hoped Libby was having better luck finding a likely suspect on her end.

Half-Cent began moaning, and Peter froze, not sure what to do. "Are you awake, Half-Cent? Billy Boy? I'm here, it's me, Peter, from the *Gazette*."

Suddenly the boy opened his eyes wide, fully awake. He stared at Peter, his brown eyes trusting and innocent.

"Where am I? Was there a horse?" Oddly, the boy began to laugh, a childish giggle Peter had never heard him make. "I seen the horse, Mister!" He gave a big grin.

"Do you know where you are, Billy?"

Half-Cent replied, "I like beets!"

Peter said, uncomfortably, "You're here in the hospital. You had a bad fall." As he spoke, he patted Half-Cent's hand.

"Something tastes funny. Is there soup? I want soup." He looked unhappy, and suddenly unsure of something. "People ride horses, don't they?"

"Shhh, shhhh. . . ." Peter looked around wildly. Where was the doctor? Sister Jerome had said he would be here soon. He let go of Half-Cent's hand, which he realized he had been patting all this time, and went to the door of the room. He was relieved to see the same doctor from yesterday, making his way down the corridor. Peter gestured wildly, and the man nodded that he would be right there.

The doctor looked at Half-Cent, opened his mouth and peered down his throat, then lifted the sheet and examined the dressing on his leg. He pulled a syringe from the pocket of his white coat and gave the boy a shot. Half-Cent drifted back to sleep. Turning away from his patient, he regarded Peter. "Mr. Eberle, is it?"

"How is he, Doctor? He was talking just now, but not making any sense."

The doctor didn't seem overly concerned. "That's to be expected with a trauma of this sort. The fright following an accident generally leads to disturbances of the nervous system. We call it traumatic neurasthenia, a sort of hysteria."

"How long will it last?"

"Not much longer, we hope. The surgery went well, but of course there is always the risk in these cases of infection." He paused. "He's quite lucky he wasn't killed outright. If that rock had been a foot or so to the left, he might have been damaged beyond treatment."

"You're saying there's still a chance he might . . ."

"Mr. Eberle, it is out of our hands. But I believe he'll recover. I have seen no sign of infection as yet, and the real risk is within the first day."

"Will he . . . How will he get around, with only one leg?" Peter had to concentrate on not letting his voice crack with emotion.

The doctor spoke in a chipper tone of voice Peter was sure had been honed in countless conversations such as these. "You would be surprised at how resilient people can be, Mr. Eberle. Hopefully by the time his mind has, er, cleared, we can start teaching him how to use crutches to get around. The boy is young, he will adapt." With that, the doctor made a quick note in a chart and snapped it shut with a cheerful, "Good day, sir."

———

Elliot had half expected that he might be discovered in the garden shed, but never in his wildest imaginings had it been Miss Seale who would find him. "What are you doing in here?"

The seamstress looked unsure of how to answer. "I found this with your things . . ." She gestured to the bow and arrow. "Elliot, did you try to shoot your father?"

"I couldn't stay at that school. My father was wrong to make me go there." He looked at her as if daring her to contradict him. "Fathers can be wrong."

Libby, who knew that well from her own experience, had no wish to contradict him. "They can, Elliot, and I believe yours was."

"But I didn't shoot him. I wouldn't try to kill him."

He sounded sincere. Libby believed him, though he hadn't satisfactorily explained the bow and arrows. She crossed to him and placed a hand on his arm. "Your mother is very worried about you. You must tell her you've come home."

"No!" Elliot wrenched his arm away. "She let him send me away. So let her suffer."

Libby didn't wish to be drawn into an argument about parental responsibility and family duty. "Elliot, what were you doing, or planning to do, with those?" She pointed an accusing finger at the weapons.

He stared at her, and then reacted the last way she would have expected, with a bark of laughter. "That's not mine. I found it hidden under some bushes out back the first night I came back here. I slept out there before I could sneak in here. I think they're my Aunt Eva's. She was archery champion at school when she was my age, you know." He looked glum. "I've certainly been told often enough. My father never misses the chance to tell me that even his sister is a better sport than I am." He flopped himself down on his makeshift bed.

"Is that why you seem so angry at your aunt?"

"No," he muttered. He wasn't about to go into that with her. She was silent for a moment, and he thought perhaps she would now leave him be in peace. He sighed with relief. And then her next words shattered his fragile calm.

"I found the picture you painted of Matt. Please, don't be angry." She explained the circumstances playing hide-and-seek with his little brothers, and told of her unwitting discovery of the hidden painting under the bed. "Did you and Matt do something bad together, Elliot?"

"He was my friend," the teen boy said, sounding younger than before. "Is that a bad thing?" He wished she would stop asking questions.

"No, no, that's not bad. But I had no idea your friendship was so close. Did he often pose for you?"

"No. That is, he didn't pose for that picture. The one you found. It was a copy of Saint Sebastian hanging at school." He wondered if he could make her believe it had just been a prank, a harmless exercise. "My teacher, Mr. Avenier, says the only way to learn is to copy. I didn't want to, but he said I had to. And I wanted to see if I could paint someone I knew. So I gave the figure in the painting Matt's face. It didn't mean anything." His voice sounded unconvincing to his own ears, and he knew he was talking too much but he couldn't stop. "I just wanted to see if I could. And then when he . . . when he died, I put it away because I felt guilty." The image of the painting came into his mind, the body so lovingly stroked with layer after layer of thin colored glaze, the brush going where he himself could never hope to touch. The truth was he had rolled it up and stored it under his bed weeks before Matt's death.

"You put it away because you'd had a fight with him. You told me as much that day in the pantry." Libby sat down beside him,

"But you wouldn't tell me what the fight was about. Will you tell me now?"

Elliot didn't answer. Libby said softly, "It was about your Aunt Eva, wasn't it?"

He looked at her in astonishment. "How did you know?" She just smiled a knowing smile. She hadn't bought his lies at all, and the whole story now poured out of him in a rush.

"I went looking for him one day. And when I found him, he was with her . . . with my Aunt Eva. They were in here together, and I could hear through the door sounds like people fighting . . . grunts, sort of, and exclamations like someone was trying to move something heavy. And so I moved over one of the garden chairs and stood on that, and then peeked in through the window and they were . . ." He didn't know what word to use with an adult, and a lady at that. He knew what words the boys at St. Sebastian's used when they would snicker out in the yard, but that didn't seem right, so he just skipped over it. "I was so surprised I fell off the chair. And they must have heard that because Matt came running out, fastening up his pants, but by the time he got around the shed I pretended I was just coming from the house, and they never knew I saw them." He barely paused for breath. "After that Matt was different, and he never wanted to spend time in the garden with me. I wanted to pretend nothing was wrong, but he didn't seem to like me anymore—he always seemed to be running errands for Aunt Eva, and so I started staying in the house, and when Matt said hello I would pretend not to even see him there, just like my mother does with Stubbins." He finished, all in a rush, and looked at her. "What I saw them doing . . . that was a sin, wasn't it?

Libby nodded, but her mind was frantically trying to factor in this new information. She had guessed that Elliot was jealous because his friend Matt had paid attention to his aunt, but she had not guessed that there had been more than a flirtation at most. No wonder Elliot had been so rude to his aunt. From his perspective she had taken his only friend in the household away from him. Something else clicked for her. "Elliot, when did all this happen? When did you see your aunt and Matt together in the shed?"

He thought about it for a moment. "I guess it was a few weeks before Christmas."

She mentally did the arithmetic. "So it's possible that the baby is not her husband's at all." She wasn't even aware she had spoken aloud until she saw the shocked look on the boy's face.

"Not Uncle Augustus's?" Elliot felt his cheeks go red, and he burned with embarrassment. The thought had not even occurred to him. Of course he knew where babies came from, well, mostly. He knew that it took a man and a woman, but he had not connected what he saw in the shed with that. He knew that what he had seen was fornication, but the nuns at school said that fornication was what happened between men and women who were not married. Babies were born to married people. It was a little confusing. "Does that mean that Auntie's baby won't be my cousin?"

Libby shushed him. "Elliot, it's very important that you not tell this to anyone. Promise me you'll keep this secret, at least a little while longer."

"Of course, Miss Seale."

While she could not yet piece together the whole puzzle, she felt sure this new information would prove to be the key. Eva Fowler must have been Matt's accomplice in the plan against Hiram Rose, and it couldn't be coincidence that the attack had started shortly after she must have learned she was pregnant. Did Augustus know, or suspect? There was much still to figure out, but first she must see Peter and tell him. Together they would make sense of it. She was so lost in thought Elliot had to say her name twice before she realized she was being addressed,

"Miss Seale, will you please do something for me in return? You mustn't tell my father that I'm here." He looked at her, his eyes beseeching her to take pity.

"All right," she agreed, but added dubiously, "I still think you should let your mother know you're safe."

"I can't go back to that school. I won't." With his chin stuck stubbornly out he looked older somehow, and for the first time more than a bit like his father.

"I will keep your secret, Elliot. But you can't hide from problems indefinitely." She crossed to the shed door. "Trust me. I know."

SIXTEEN

"The last thing I remember is that woman with the braids, and then Mr. Rose left right afterward." Half-Cent closed his eyes as if trying to summon more information, but he opened them again and shook his head. "I just don't remember what happened after that. I do remember that the woman had her hair wrapped on the side of her head like earmuffs. Does that help?"

Peter smiled. "There's only one person I can think of who fits that description. You did a good job, son." He tried to speak to the boy as he always had, but it was hard to contain his joy that Half-Cent was once again lucid, and the relief in his voice was palpable.

"I'm sorry, I don't mean to interrupt . . ." Libby Seale appeared in the doorway of the room. She held a package under one arm and looked flushed and damp from her long trek in the rain, since she had gone looking for Peter at the newspaper offices before John Mayhew had directed her to the hospital. She leaned over the bed and introduced herself to Billy, telling him what a brave boy he was, and Peter could see the youngster visibly preen at the praise from a lovely woman. Taking off her coat, she pulled over a chair from beside another bed in the room and sat beside Peter. "I heard you mention a woman with braids. That must be Tilda Karlsson, right?"

"Yes, that's what I think," Peter said in response to Libby's question. "I'm not sure why Tilda would have been visiting Rose at the mill, but it obviously upset him enough to leave shortly afterward."

From the bed, Half-Cent made a low moan of pain, then stopped himself, teeth gritted. Peter started to rise, mumbling something about getting a nurse, but the boy stopped him. "I'm fine, really," he said, although his features said otherwise.

Peter leaned in, suddenly serious. "Now Billy, I want you to know I am so very sorry I asked you to do this in the first place. I understand if you're angry at me, you have every right to be . . ."

Half-Cent cut him off. "Gosh, Mr. Eberle, it's not your fault that I was dumb enough to get run over by a rock. And I was happy to be doing that, following Mr. Rose, being a reporter. You didn't force me to! You and Mr. Mayhew are the only real friends I have."

Peter smiled, but he had tears in the corners of his eyes, and Libby knew how much he felt responsible for this boy's future. "I'm proud to have you as a friend, Billy. And my friendship is something you can count on forever. Believe that. Mr. Mayhew, too, you know."

"Sure, I know." The boy smiled, then sighed. "I do wish I could remember some more, but I'm so tired. Maybe I'll remember more tomorrow." He added, almost offhandedly, "You will come visit again?"

"Of course."

Half-Cent looked at Libby. "You too?"

She nodded. "Of course, I'll look forward to it."

———

Outside the hospital, Libby and Peter stood under the overhang of the main entrance, watching the rain, which had come back again that morning as if it had never left. Libby avoided Peter's eyes, though she pretended not to. Peter looked at the waterlogged street glumly, watching horses slip in the mud. "They're saying the Willamette may overflow if the rain keeps up," he said to Libby. To himself he said, You're an idiot. Is this all we can talk about now—the weather?

Without replying, she motioned at a small restaurant across the way. "Shall we make a run for it?" Before waiting for his answer, she was off like a shot, and he watched her for a few moments, unable to keep a smile from lighting up his face, a memory of the first time he saw her crossing his mind. So much of what she did was unexpected in a woman! Pulling his collar up, he joined her in what felt a bit like a race. He caught up with her as she was shaking off her cape before opening the restaurant door. "You had a head start, you know," he said.

"You have longer legs," she shot back, but with a glibly bantering tone. God, how he loved her. He shoved the thought away.

They settled in at a table and ordered cups of tea. There was a lovely, fragrant smell wafting out from the kitchen, and so they decided to split a piece of the cook's freshly made apple pie. Peter grew quiet again. It was almost as if he had to keep reminding himself of the terrible situation they had just left at the hospital, lest he start to enjoy his life too much. It didn't seem fair that he could still run across a street, enjoying the feeling of power in his limbs, while Half-Cent would never know such pleasure again. "Do you think Billy will really be all right? With his . . . without his . . ." he faltered.

She looked at him with wide eyes. "It is a terrible thing that happened to him, but it seems like he will come through it all right in the end. People are very resilient, you know. They handle all sorts of things you wouldn't expect."

He said wryly, "You know, the doctor said almost the same words to me the last time."

She was looking into space, stirring her tea, suddenly lost in thought. When she spoke, he had to strain to hear her words. "When I was only six years old, my brother Benjamin—he was two years younger than me—ran into the street when my mother wasn't looking, and he was run over by a cart horse. At first they thought they could save him, but he . . . he died the next day."

"Oh, Libby." He reached for her hand.

Her eyes welled with tears, but she rubbed them away almost angrily. "No, I'm not telling you this for your sympathy, although it is a terrible thing, and I know my mother thinks about Benjy every day. I'm telling you about this because I want you to acknowledge that, yes, sometimes terrible, awful things happen to the people we love, the people we are supposed to be protecting. Now you can either wallow in self-pity, or you can decide that from this point on you will make sure we find out who killed Matt and maimed poor Billy." She was suddenly all business. "I didn't want to ask you in the hospital, but what have you found out?"

Peter had to admit to himself that he liked it when Libby took the lead. He dutifully reported to her all his dead ends, the Karlsson women's church sale and Phebe Scott's well-observed afternoon in the bar. She had an expectant look on her face.

"You look about ready to burst," he said. "I take it you found something out at the Rose home?"

"I saw Elliot. In the garden shed."

All at once, she couldn't speak quickly enough. She hadn't wanted to tell him about Eva and Matt at the hospital, thinking it was not suitable conversation for a convalescing Billy, and then she had somehow forgotten it until this moment. But now, between bites of pie, she told him how Elliot had discovered his aunt in flagrante delicto with the handsome servant, and shared her suspicions about the parentage of Eva Fowler's unborn child. Peter interrupted a few times to clarify this or that detail. She polished off the slice of pie, Peter having only one or two bites while the two of them puzzled over what it all could mean.

"Let's think this through," said Peter. "Why would Eva want her brother dead? Did he know about her and Matt and threaten to. . . . to what, tell her husband?"

"But she was his sister! Wouldn't his loyalties lie with her?" countered Libby. "And why was she pawning her jewelry? I can't figure out how that fits in." She paused, thoughtfully. "Unless . . . perhaps she and Matt needed money to run away, and he was trying to rob the mill."

Peter leapt in. "This could explain where he got the key! Eva stole the key from her brother, and then Matt snuck into the mill to steal from the safe."

Libby interrupted him. "But if robbery was why he was there, why would he set a booby trap to kill Hiram Rose?"

"Good question," said Peter. "Also, once he had accidentally died in the attempt, why did Eva Rose continue the attacks on her brother?"

For several minutes, they stared at each other, drinking their tea and pondering Eva's possible motives. A few times one of them started to say something, but stopped with a shake of the head. No matter how they tried to put the pieces together, every possibility raised more questions than the last. Had Eva Rose wanted her brother dead because if Hiram died Augustus would take over the mill? Had she been with Matt at the mill the night he was killed, helping him set the trap? Perhaps she and Matt had assumed that if Hiram died on the scaffolding the theft of the money from the safe would somehow have escaped notice . . . or at least not have been the focus of an investigation.

Finally Peter spoke. "We don't have all the answers, that's for sure. And yet, the by process of elimination, we are left with the fact that Eva Fowler must be the woman in the light-colored cloak who started the rock fall that nearly ended Hiram Rose's life."

Libby sighed. "Should we talk to the police?" she asked. "I know it's not much to go on, but at least we can give them a new line of inquiry."

"And we've seen how well that has worked in the past," Peter replied sarcastically, sounding more curt than he meant to. "I'm sorry, Libby, I don't mean to snap at you. I'm trying to figure out what to do, and I can't help thinking of something Hiram Rose said to me the other night."

His voice grew quiet, and she could tell he was embarrassed, but despite his discomfort, he went on. "He said I should have warned him he was in danger, instead of sending a small boy out to follow him, and you know, although I don't like the man one bit, he was right."

"What are you saying?"

"I'm saying that I think this amateur detecting has gone far enough in secrecy. I think it's time we contacted Hiram Rose and told him who we suspect, so he can take precautions as he sees fit."

"Shall I go with you to the Rose house?" asked Libby. "I have a few things needing fittings, so I was going there anyhow."

Peter reddened, remembering his last disastrous visit to Hiram Rose. Sheepishly, he admitted that Hiram Rose had told him in no uncertain terms not to return. "I think the only thing to do," he said, "is use the telephone at the *Gazette* to ring him at the Paperworks. That way, he has to take the call, and hopefully I can impress upon him the importance of our suspicions."

"He won't like hearing that his sister is trying to kill him," replied Libby, matter-of-factly. She was already gathering her coat and scarf and preparing to leave. "I'm coming with you. This is a telephone call I don't want to miss."

———

"Peter Eberle! At the *Portland Gazette*!" For the third time, Peter was yelling his name into the telephone mouthpiece. "I must speak to Mr. Rose immediately!"

As he waited, he turned to Libby and said in a much quieter voice, "I think the fellow said he is bringing him to the phone. These connections! I think I'd do better standing on the roof of the building and yelling." He listened intently, then spoke. "Yes, Mr. Rose, it's Peter Eberle." He paused, and Libby could clearly hear Hiram's yelling over the wires. Peter tried to get a word in, but his attempts were almost comical. Libby was able to hear both sides of the conversation, as Peter realized he could hold the earpiece quite far away and they would both hear Rose's booming voice.

"I thought I told you to stop bothering me."

"But sir, I have some important information. I believe you are still in danger, and as you pointed out the other night, I believe I owe it to you to warn you."

"Of course, I'm still in danger! Do you think it escaped my notice that a rock nearly ran me down two days ago?" He sounded pompous. "That is not news, Mr. Eberle. If that is all you have to tell me, then good day, sir."

"No!" Peter almost lunged at the telephone apparatus, as if somehow he could stop the other man from ending the connection. "I am trying to protect you—"

"Thank you, but I am listening to my wife's advice and getting myself a pair of bodyguards. No disgruntled ex-workers of mine are going to scare me into hiding away!"

"I believe you are mistaken about it being ex-workers, Mr. Rose. I don't think that the man who the police have in custody ever had anything to do with the attacks. Nor any of his acquaintances either. In fact, well—the truth is, I have recently found out some information that I think points to someone in your own household."

There was silence. For a second, Peter was worried Rose had ended the call, so he was relieved to hear the other's voice. "Well, I suppose you had better tell me what you know and be done with it. What have you learned?"

"As I said . . . I believe it is someone close to you, who you probably have not suspected, who is trying to hurt you." Peter lowered his voice. "I would rather not say who on the phone."

"I can't hear what you're saying, sir. Either speak up or I will break the connection."

Peter looked at Libby, confused. He faltered. "Can I possibly come there and speak to you? This connection is not very secure, and I don't think you will want this information to be overheard. I can come to the Rose Paperworks right away."

"Not now!" barked Hiram. There was a substantial pause, and then the mill owner spoke lower. "This is the middle of my workday, and I have work to do. And, as you say, there are too many people around. Come after the mill has closed."

"All right. Doesn't the mill close at seven?"

"After seven, yes, and . . ." The rest of Rose's sentence was garbled by the bad connection.

"What is that, sir?"

"As I say, if it is someone in my household who is behind these attacks, then this is the only safe place to have a conversation. Use the side entrance, and don't be late." With a click, it was clear that this time, Hiram Rose had hung up the phone.

"What do you make of that?" he asked Libby, as he placed the telephone's mouthpiece back in the holder.

"I'm not sure," she said thoughtfully. "He sounded almost nervous. Perhaps he already suspects that someone close to him wants him dead. I wonder what he will say tonight when we tell him it is his own sister."

"We?"

"Surely you don't think I'm going to leave you to go face him alone. Besides," she said, with the tilt of her head he knew so well, "I've always wanted to see what the inside of a paper mill looks like."

———

If Hiram Rose's face registered displeasure when he opened the door to the mill offices for Peter that evening, it quickly became a look of pure fury when he saw the figure of Libby Seale standing just over the reporter's shoulder.

"Miss Seale!" He took in the two of them, as if trying to ascertain how these two people he knew from very different circumstances were connected to each other. Then he snorted in disgust, turned on his heel, and marched through the open door to the inner office, calling over his shoulder, "So, Eberle . . . it wasn't enough that you set a boy to follow me wherever I went, now it appears you've been bribing my household staff to obtain information as well."

Libby and Peter hurried to follow the irate businessman, and did not wait to be asked before settling themselves in two hard-backed chairs facing Hiram's imposing desk. "Now wait a minute, Mr. Rose," Peter began, but Libby cut him off.

"Mr. Rose, my friendship . . . my association with Mr. Eberle predated my employment by your wife." She stressed the word association, as if to remind him that she was not exactly a part of his household staff. "—as a dressmaker to her and your sister." It was astonishing—they had not been here sixty seconds, and already the mill owner had managed to rile her. He really was unbelievably obnoxious, and that was especially galling when she considered that she and Peter were only there to try and help him. "It was pure coincidence that, when Mr. Eberle needed me, I happened to be in a position to keep an eye on you and your family. And a good thing, too, since . . ."

It was Peter's turn to cut her off. "Let's all calm down. I believe we should explain more calmly what we came here to tell you."

"Get on with it. I'm a busy man," Hiram grunted. He seemed distracted, glancing over at the black and gold safe that dominated the corner of his office.

Peter cleared his throat and began in a measured tone. "We have reason to believe that your sister Eva has been behind the attacks on you from the very beginning." He paused, but if he expected Hiram to look incredulous, he was disappointed. The portly man's face remained impassive, as if waiting for some proof to back up the accusation. "We have learned that her relations with Matt Karlsson were somewhat more intimate than merely servant and employer. It is even possible that the baby she is carrying is not her husband's, but Matt's."

After a moment, Hiram said laconically, "I'm not sure how you found out, but yes, I am aware the baby is Matt's."

Libby's mouth hung open with surprise, and while Peter managed to remain more composed, he stopped speaking. Into the gap, Rose injected flatly, "She's my sister, and I like to think I know what goes on under my own roof. So, how much do you want?"

"Excuse me?" Peter managed.

"I assume that's why you're here, and with your little hussy in tow. Forget this foolishness about warning me—obviously you've guessed that I don't wish this information about my sister's child to become public, and I am willing to pay to ensure that it does not."

Libby controlled her anger at being called a hussy, but she still sounded somewhat harsh as she broke in. "It is not foolishness, Mr. Rose. We do believe you are in danger. Your sister was seen by . . . a reliable witness." She somehow doubted Hiram would be reassured if she told him it was the elderly cook at his workers' camp. "This person saw Eva pushing the boulder that nearly missed you the other day. Additionally, I have located the bow and arrows she used to shoot at you. We do not know why she has acted this way, but I'm afraid there's no other conclusion. Now, thus far all we've uncovered is circumstantial proof, unfortunately, and since we were afraid the police might choose to disregard it, we have come to warn you personally, out of basic human concern." She rose and gave him a haughty look. "Keep your money."

She started for the door but Hiram stopped her. "Please, Miss Seale, wait a moment." He rose, walked to a closed door in the wall behind him, and opened it. "Eva, will you please come out here?"

Eva Fowler, enveloped in a fawn-colored cloak that Libby immediately recognized as the one the Chinese woman must have seen, stepped into the room. For the second time that evening Libby was stunned into silence. This meeting was not going at all the way she and Peter had planned. Hiram said, "Would you please tell these people that you are not trying to kill me?"

Eva raised her chin and dutifully declaimed, "Kill you? That's utterly absurd. You're my brother, and I would never harm you."

"There," said Hiram, turning back to his guests, "are you satisfied now? Or are you going to take the word of your young friend in the hospital over my sister's sworn oath that she is not trying to kill me?"

Libby couldn't stop herself. "Billy wasn't the witness. In fact, he has yet to recover his memories of what happened that day." She addressed Eva, "You were seen by someone else. Someone who specifically mentioned seeing a woman in a light-colored cloak get into a carriage and drive away after the rock fall."

There was silence. Suddenly Peter, who had been sitting there with a look of deep concentration during the preceding conversation, piped up with a question. "Mrs. Fowler, may I ask you something? Did you ever see any of the threatening letters your brother received? Or, rather, claims to have received?"

Eva looked blank. "What?"

Hiram Rose began, with a warning edge to his voice, "Eberle—"

But Peter went on, heedless of the interruption. "It's only, seeing how close you and your brother are, it's logical that, if he had shown them to anyone, it would have been you." Eva and Hiram looked so much alike standing side by side, ready to sail into battle together to protect their family honor. As he looked at them, something had clicked for Peter. It should have occurred to him, or to Libby, that if Eva was in cahoots with anyone, it was most likely to be her brother. "It strikes me as odd, Mr. Rose, that no one but you ever saw those letters. In fact, we have nothing but your word to suggest there ever were any letters."

Hiram sat down on the edge of his leather desk chair. "I told you I didn't show them to anybody."

"Ah, but if we assume, just hypothetically, that there never were any letters, then perhaps it follows that no one has been trying to kill you at all. So I am willing to believe your sister's avowed denial."

Hiram said without a trace of humor, "That's big of you, since it's the truth."

Libby sat down again too, confused. "Peter, how can you say no one has been trying to kill Mr. Rose?"

Peter went on, addressing Libby. "Well, he seems to have had the most remarkable luck in escaping from every attack made on him. Which either means that his would-be assassin was completely incompetent, or that he wasn't killed because he wasn't intended to be." He directed his focus back to Hiram. "In fact, now that I think on it, I believe the only person who was ever intended to die was the only one who did die . . . Matt Karlsson. And, furthermore, I believe you, Mr. Rose, were the one who planned to kill him."

Hiram didn't directly address the accusation, but if the mean-looking revolver he pulled from his desk drawer and leveled at Peter and Libby was any indication, the reporter's hunch was correct.

Eva was the first to react. "You can't kill them, Hiram. This has got to stop."

Rose wheeled on his sister. "What would you have me do? I can't let them walk out that door. I'm not happy about it, either, but we wouldn't be here if it weren't for you. Let's not forget who started all this."

"I never asked you to kill Matt!" Tears were filling Eva's eyes. "Why didn't you just give him what he asked for and let him go?"

"Once they start, blackmailers never stop. And no matter how little I pay those heathen devils who work for me, this mill isn't made of money! No, he had to die."

Libby was beginning to piece together the true nature of the death at the Rose Paperworks. "Matt was blackmailing you . . . because you were carrying his child . . ."

Eva sobbed. "Yes, and like a fool I went to my brother for help. And his idea of help was to kill Matt!"

"Eva, control yourself. Don't get hysterical." Hiram returned his focus to Peter and Libby.

"I don't understand," Libby continued. "Why did you go to all the trouble of making it look like a failed attempt on yourself? Why not just kill Matt and dump him beside the road somewhere?"

Hiram actually smiled. "Now, that wouldn't have been very clever of me. Who would have wanted Matt Karlsson dead? He wasn't rich, he wasn't important. If people had begun asking questions about Matt's past and background, how long do you think it would have taken them to uncover Eva's little secret? This way no one even asked those questions. So long as I was the presumed target, I could hardly have been a suspect." Libby had to concede that made sense, but she wished she could come up with some comeback that would wipe that smug look off Rose's face. "Now, in a minute we're going to take a little walk." Hiram used his gun to wave them toward the outer office. "Out to the stables. I'm afraid that this evening someone is going to set fire to them as a warning to me, and unfortunately some trespassers will have been found to have burned to death by accident."

"Another accident?" Peter's tone was belligerent. If he was at all frightened at having a gun aimed at his head, he didn't show it, and Libby marveled at his bravery and self-control. "Like the accident that took Billy's leg? Just tell me why, Rose. What on earth can that boy have done to deserve what you did to him?"

"If he had been out selling newspapers, he'd have two legs today." His look asked Peter whose fault that was. "He left me no choice . . . I found him outside my sister's window eavesdropping on a . . . disagreement we were having." He glanced in disgust over at Eva. "Seems my sister felt so guilty about that worthless blackmailer she'd been carrying on with, she went and gave money to the family he left behind. I only found out about that later, of course, when Matt's sister-in-law—humorless woman, by the way—came here to beg me to drop the charges against her husband. She said, if I recall it correctly, 'If your sister can see that Matt was an innocent victim, then surely you must see that my Jan has done nothing to try and harm you!' I told her to go to the devil, of course, but naturally I was upset." He seemed to get upset all over again just thinking of it, and turned to Eva.

"What could you have been thinking? Giving money to the family of the man accused of trying to murder me? How did you think we could explain that if it came to light? It would look as though we knew all along Dutch Karlsson was innocent . . ." He controlled his temper and went back to his story. "In any case, those were my feelings that day. So apparently I was too upset to notice your boy following me as I rode over to my sister's house to remonstrate with her. Once there, he hid beneath the window and overheard everything that we said."

"I don't understand," Libby interjected. "How did he come to be lying out by the workers' camp?" She answered her own question, in a tone of horror. "You attacked him outside the Fowler house, carried him out to Harbor Road, and then Eva rolled that enormous rock on top of an unconscious child, in cold blood, like he was nothing but a piece of meat!"

"I didn't like it, but it had to be done." Rose sighed, "Just like I'm going to have to make sure that what you two know doesn't go any farther." He got up from his chair, keeping his gun hand steady. "Enough dawdling, it's time to head out to the stables."

"And if we refuse?" Peter's bravado hadn't failed him yet.

"I'll be forced to shoot you before carrying you out. The job will get done just the same. But if you force me to do this the hard way, believe me it will be less pleasant for you, because I won't kill you outright . . . just incapacitate you so you'll die a lingering death in the flames. If you do as you're told, I promise to dispatch you with a quick bullet to the temple . . . and I'll even let you decide if you want to go first, or watch your lady friend go before you."

Peter didn't answer, and for the first time a look of apprehension crossed Hiram's face. Reaching back into his desk, he pulled out a second gun, this one a small pistol, which he handed to his sister. "Eva, keep this trained on Miss Seale. I believe I'd better do this in two separate trips."

Peter made a last-ditch effort, using the final weapon he had at his disposal. "All this to protect your family name and your precious family paper mill, Rose? Sad . . . for all it's worth you might as well just shoot us right here and burn the mill down around us. At least that way you'd get the insurance money." He gave a cocky grin. "I assume the mill is insured?"

Hiram looked unnerved. "What are you talking about?"

"Why don't you ask your sister? In a short enough time it'll be you who has to go to her to ask for help if you have financial problems. And you most assuredly will have financial problems."

"Eva?" Hiram approached Eva. "Do you understand this lunatic?"

"I . . . I swear I don't know what he means."

"Come, Mrs. Fowler," Peter said silkily, "surely your husband wouldn't plan on opening a wood pulp paper mill with Unsworth Manning without discussing it with you first."

Hiram's face grew bright red, almost like a balloon that was getting ready to pop. "Augustus . . . and Unsworth Manning?"

"Yes, that's about the shape of it." Peter's tone was mocking.

There was a deathly silence in the room, as the other three waited to see what Hiram would do next. All at once the portly mill owner seemed to deflate, and he sank back into his chair with a wheeze like the last air being squeezed from a bellows. "So I'm ruined."

Eva Fowler walked over to her brother and placed a hand on his shoulder. "Hiram . . ."

"Don't start, Eva. You may tell me it was all Augustus's idea, but I can't believe that you didn't know. Women always find out what their husbands are up to."

He gazed up at his sister, and almost unconsciously swung the gun, still grasped tightly in one hand, toward her swelling abdomen. "Perhaps Eberle here was right to warn me against you . . . while you may not have been trying to kill me, you'll have ended up destroying me just the same."

Eva recoiled in horror. "How can you say such things to me? After all the things you made me do—shooting arrows at you, staging the attack on that poor boy, watching Matt's brother languish in prison—and I never said no. I didn't turn you in, even when I found out you killed my lover."

"Ex-lover. Not that it matters." Now his gun was definitely leveled at Eva's midsection and the unborn child within. "You did all I asked because you wanted this baby, and you wanted your good name. I wanted my mill, and I wanted peace under my roof, and now that's all being taken away from me. You've killed my dream, so perhaps I should kill yours, and then we'll call it even." He was standing now, and took a step toward his sister.

"Mr. Rose!" Libby bolted up out of her seat. "You can't be serious. You'd shoot your own niece or nephew, and kill your own sister? What kind of monster are you?"

"What difference does it make now?" Hiram laughed mirthlessly, but he backed into the corner of his office, by the safe, where he could keep all of the three other people in the room covered with his gun. He smiled again, but it was a smile as warm as ice water. "But of course I'm not serious. At least, not about shooting Eva. You, on the other hand . . ."

Hiram addressed his sister. "There's some rope in there." He cocked his head at the small room Eva had emerged from. "I need you to tie Mr. Eberle and Miss Seale to their chairs, since I can't put down my gun." He turned back. "I'm indebted to you, Mr. Eberle. You're quite right again. I might as well burn you up in here as out in the stables. Capital idea. Insurance money, and all that. Shame your cleverness won't do you any good where you're going."

Eva had made no move to get the rope. Instead she raised her own small pistol and aimed it at Hiram. "No. I refuse to help you any more. You are not going to kill Miss Seale. She is a friend of mine. Nor Mr. Eberle. You're going to let them go, and we are going to go home and wait for the police to come for us."

"Don't talk nonsense. I am not going to jail."

"Then leave right now. I will give you two hours head start—run away, leave Portland, go to Timbuktu for all I care—two hours, and then I am letting these people leave here, to do what they must." Eva stood ramrod straight.

"Or what? You will shoot me? You haven't got the guts." Hiram took a step toward Eva. The two of them now had their guns trained on each other, and if it had not been for the massive desk that stood between Libby and Peter and the siblings, Peter would have attempted to tackle Hiram and wrestle the gun out of his hand. As it was, all he could do was watch and see how this scene played itself out.

In sixty seconds it was all over. With a roar of anger, Hiram Rose launched himself at his sister, grabbing her wrist and causing her to drop her gun. At the same moment Peter vaulted over the desk, kicking out as he did so, catching Hiram in the lower back. Rose swung around and, raising his arm above his head, brought his revolver down on Peter's temple, knocking him to the floor. Libby screamed as she saw the hand with the revolver rise back into a shooting position, the barrel aimed directly at Peter's chest. And then there was a shot. But it came from behind Rose, from Eva's gun, which she had retrieved from the floor.

With an anguished cry Hiram Rose sank to the ground, a pool of blood staining his clothes and the floor below him.

SEVENTEEN

DUTCH KARLSSON SMILED DOWN at his sleeping son, occasionally reaching out to stroke his hair, as if he couldn't quite take in that he was truly within reach. Pim had been asleep when his father arrived home that evening, straight from the city jail, with a euphoric Peter Eberle beside him. As soon as he explained to his astonished wife, mother, and sister how he had come to be released, Dutch sought out the boy's bedside, the reporter and the clamoring women of the household behind him. Now the room was quite crowded, with five adults squeezed in around the sleeping child.

"He's going to be so excited to see you when he wakes up tomorrow," Peter whispered.

"You don't need to whisper," Dutch said in a normal voice, not looking up. "I suppose that is one small blessing—noises in the night don't wake him up."

Peter smiled inwardly. Of course, he should have realized that whispering was unnecessary around a deaf child. Anna smoothed over the moment by addressing Peter. "Mr. Eberle, we can't thank you enough for all the help you have given us."

"If it were not for you, we would not have Jan back here with us tonight." Tilda sounded more gentle than Peter had ever heard her. "We won't forget that."

Needless to say, all the charges against Dutch related to Matt's death and the attacks on Hiram Rose had been dropped, but Peter had seen to it that he was not going to be charged as a part of the Cinderella Gang either. Macon had been all for retroactively accepting the testimony of the other robbers that Dutch had helped commit the crimes, but Peter had been adamant that it was too late for the police to change their mind on the matter. And, Peter had none too subtly hinted, if the police chose to proceed with a case against Dutch for robbery, the *Gazette* would help him pursue legal redress for his wrongful imprisonment for murder. The threat of a lawsuit did the trick, and Dutch had been released immediately.

Anna laid her hand softly on Peter's arm. "Mr. Eberle, may I speak to you alone for a moment?"

"Of course," said Peter, "but only on the condition that you stop calling me Mr. Eberle."

She smiled, and her china-blue eyes sparkled with happiness. "Yes, Peter." They made their way to the settee in the parlor, and for a moment there was no sound but the crackling embers of the dying fire. "I wanted to apologize to you. The other day, when you were here, I snapped at you, and . . . you have been nothing but good to us, and you didn't deserve that."

"Please, Anna." He made her name almost a question, and she nodded her permission to the familiarity. "I understand completely.

Tonight, during the unpleasantness out at the mill, Mrs. Fowler admitted to having been your mysterious benefactor. I know she swore you to secrecy, and I can only imagine the strain that put you under—accepting money from the sister of the man responsible for causing your family so much misery."

"She seemed so nice," Anna said wonderingly. "I can hardly believe that she helped her brother do all those terrible things."

"If it is any comfort to you, I believe her when she says she didn't have any idea that her brother was going to kill Matt. It was only after the fact that she helped him cover it up."

"Still . . . I don't know how to feel. If she had not gone to her brother for help, Matt would still be alive. And yet, the baby in side her is a part of Matt, and I want to believe that she will be a good and loving mother to the child." There were tears in her eyes. "Matt's baby. It's as if at least one small part of him survives."

Peter cupped her chin in one hand and wiped a tear away with the other. They stared into each other's eyes, and then they were kissing. Peter couldn't say who had initiated the kiss, but it felt good. It felt easy . . . it was a lovely feeling to kiss a woman and not worry that you could not have her, that she was already married, that she might leave forever and go back across the country. Anna broke the kiss first.

"I've hoped to do that since the day you first came to see us," she said and then blushed. "I shouldn't have said that."

"You should say whatever you want." He gave her a crooked grin. "It's one of the things I like best about you." And then he kissed her again.

———

The door to the Rose house was opened by a smiling Elliot. "Miss Seale! Did you hear? We're moving to New York!"

She was taken aback to see him so happy. It was quite a change from the last time they had spoken. But she was glad to see he had come in from the shed . . . she guessed he must have made his re-appearance when news of his father's arrest had somehow reached his ears. "No, Elliot, I hadn't heard. That's wonderful news."

"Would you like to come in? I'm afraid my mother isn't really feeling up to seeing people, but—"

"No, that's all right. I just came to drop off this last piece of sewing. I trust you to give it to your mother." Elliot took the pack-age, but made no move to shut the door. "I take it you're leaving soon, then?"

"Yes, Celia and the maids are already packing everything up. Celia's coming with us—oh, and Stubbins, of course. Mother says I can study art in New York, and she's promised me that we can go to a different museum every day that first week. She has cousins there, and we are going to stay with them until we find our own house. We're leaving just as soon as . . ." Suddenly he stopped. He tried to affect a more somber, adult tone as he went on. "They've told my mother that Father will be moved out of the hospital in just a few days. And then he will be moved to the jail to await trial, but Mother says she doesn't want to be here for that. So as soon as he leaves the hospital we are going to take a train east."

It was almost indecent how little the boy seemed to care about the fate of his father. Of course, if her father was anything like Hiram Rose, she would surely feel the same way. She pushed the thought of her father out of her mind. "I'm pleased for you, Elliot.

I expect one day to hear you have become an important painter." Elliot beamed at her words. "Tell me, is your aunt at home?"

His smile faded. "Yes, I suppose so. I don't think she has gone out for the last three days. I guess I should see if Mother needs any help getting things packed."

They wished each other goodbye and made empty promises to exchange letters. Then Libby made her way through the gap in the laurel hedge to the Fowler's front door. She knocked once, twice, and then tentatively opened the door a crack, calling out, "Mrs. Fowler? It's Libby Seale. May I come in?"

A drawn, weary-looking Eva Fowler appeared in the arched doorway at the far end of the parlor. She looked as if she had not slept in days. "Yes, I suppose so." She turned and walked back into the dining room, trusting Libby to follow.

"I would offer you something," she said, when they were seated opposite each other at the dining table, "but I am all alone here. My husband has moved into a hotel downtown. He's very busy, what with all the preparations for his new mill." The news of the new papermaking partnership and the coming of wood-pulp processing had been made public the day before. It had been heralded with great bombast by the city's newspapers as the latest sign of Portland's grand march toward modernity.

"Will you stay here then? All by yourself?"

"I . . . don't know. I need to remain in Portland for as long as the trial goes on, of course." Peter had informed Libby that, in exchange for testifying against her brother, no charges were going to be filed against Eva. Nobody on the force had the stomach to prosecute a woman, and a very pregnant woman at that, as an accessory after the fact to the murder of Matt Karlsson and the assault on little Billy. "After that, well, Hiram and—" she seemed to choke on her brother's name and changed course entirely. "I have a school friend in Washington who is a midwife. I may stay with her and her husband for a while, at least until the baby comes."

With the mention of the baby the tears started to flow, and once they started it seemed as if they would never stop. Libby rose and walked around the table to Eva, patting her and trying as best she could to soothe the grief and guilt that were now pouring out of her.

"You can't know what it's like, Miss Seale. To know that Matt died because of me! He was so gentle, so kind . . ."

"But he tried to blackmail you."

"Yes, I suppose, but that wasn't him, not really. That was desperation. You have to understand the way it was. Oh, I never should have taken up with him, I know it. But Augustus had grown so distant, it was as if he didn't see me any more. This all happened last fall, and I know now that Augustus was upset because Hiram was planning to fire all the workers at the mill and hire the Chinese, and he must already have been planning how he might be able to get out from under Hiram's thumb and start his own mill with Mr. Manning. But I didn't know any of that then. All I knew was he was distracted and moody and . . . if only he had confided in me. Trusted me. I might never . . ."

She wiped her nose on her sleeve and tried to collect herself. "Matt was so strong and handsome. And attentive. It didn't go on for very long, but before I knew it, all my prayers were answered. After all those years of hoping, all the despair Augustus and I shared, with Matt it happened so fast. And, God help me, all I could feel was joy. I had given up hope of ever conceiving!"

She grasped Libby's hand in hers. "You don't know. My joy was swiftly followed by despair. After all the time I had spent praying for a baby, to finally become pregnant but have the child not be my husband's. Can you imagine how it feels to know the baby you are carrying is a child of adultery? To want it and be scared of it all at once?"

Libby was at a loss. In truth, she couldn't imagine all the conflicting emotions Eva must have been feeling. Eva had stopped crying, but she went on speaking in a low voice, as if trying to expunge all that she had kept hidden for so long. "I knew that I had to end things with Matt. I couldn't let him know about the baby, or he might tell Augustus and I might lose him. Of course, now it looks like I have lost my husband anyway. But at the time I tried to do what I thought was right, and at first Matt did as I asked. He wasn't happy, I could see that, but I knew that it would be better for him as well in the long run." She took a deep breath before continuing.

"And then came the trouble at the mill. When Matt's father and brother both lost their jobs, and then his father became ill and passed away, something changed in Matt. He became belligerent and surly if he was out driving me on errands, or if we passed each other in the yard. And one day in the stables he asked me for money. He said he would tell Augustus what had happened between us if I didn't pay him. The amount was relatively small, and so I was able to take it from the household cash in my brother's house. That happened twice, and then Hiram started locking up the money box."

"Celia told me. You know Adele blamed the maids?" Libby put in.

"I knew others were being blamed, but I was beyond caring. I didn't know what to do!" She sounded as if she wanted Libby's forgiveness, or at least understanding. "And then it got worse. When Matt heard about my pregnancy he guessed the baby was his. I tried to deny it, but to no avail. And he asked for more money—five thousand dollars. I knew I could never raise that kind of money so I went to my brother. He said he would take care of things, but I never dreamed he meant to harm Matt. Until Hiram walked through that door . . . you were there, that day . . . I believed it was my brother who had been killed in the accident at the mill. But when Hiram showed up alive I knew right away, in the pit of my stomach, that the body must be Matt's."

"Did you confront him? Hiram? You could have gone to the police."

"And turn in my own brother? I railed at him, I wept, but nothing I could do could bring Matt back. And Hiram convinced me that I needed to help him cover up the crime by staging more attacks, and out of guilt and horror I went along with it. Each step along the path seemed so straightforward, but by the time I realized how much wrong I was doing there seemed no way to stop."

Libby said gently, "But you did find your way back in the end. What you did a few days ago in Hiram's office was very brave. I have not thanked you properly, but I suppose I owe my life to you."

"No, please. I don't deserve your gratitude. You rushed to my defense when Hiram threatened to shoot my baby, and when I saw that, I knew I must stop Hiram once and for all, no matter the personal cost." Eva's tears started flowing again, and Libby embraced her, stroking her hair the way she used to do with her little sister Rebecca when she scraped her knee. Gradually, Eva's tears stopped.

"I should go," Libby said, rising.

"Thank you for being so kind. It's not everyone who is willing to forgive." Unconsciously Eva's gaze had strayed out the window to where her sister-in-law resided, as if she was seeing through the laurel hedge directly into the Rose house.

"Time is a great healer." Libby hated to resort to platitudes, but somehow nothing she had experienced before had given her words for a situation like this. Without further conversation she let herself out of the house, leaving Eva as she had found her, sitting alone in an empty house with nothing but her own memories and self-recrimination for company.

———

"Petey, I wouldn't have guessed you could wield a hammer so well!" John Mayhew groaned with exertion as he heaved the last of the lumber into the small room where Peter was already nailing boards together into shelves and a sturdy bed.

"You forget, John, I grew up helping my father with all his duties as groundskeeper at Yale . . . and that included building fences and sheds," Pete paused to strike a heavy cross-brace into the bed frame with a thick mallet, ". . . as much as watering the lawns."

For a few minutes, the men worked together in silence, Peter showing John where to hold wood in place as he fashioned quite a serviceable-looking set of furniture in what had up until that morning been a storeroom for extra printing supplies. "What's that?" John motioned toward what looked like a banister running the length of the wall between bed and doorway.

"I thought that might be handy once he's not using the crutches, to hold on to when he gets up in the mornings, if he wants a little extra support."

Mayhew looked at Peter appreciatively. "I think Half-Cent will have a fine little home here, Petey."

"Bill," corrected Peter. "He says we're to call him Bill from now on, now that he's a man with a real job and a home . . ." Both the men smiled at that.

"He's going to be a fine reporter, Petey. And I can tell already, he's got the touch. He can give an engraving the printer's kiss better than I can!" Mayhew referred to the elusive skill of pressing letterpress to paper so lightly that a finished woodcut illustration had perfectly crisp and even lines of black against white, devoid of any dark patches or heavy gobs of ink. Billy was learning every step in the printing process from start to finish, and was proving himself an apt student, showing heretofore unseen talent for even the most intricate facets of the trade.

As Peter and John finished their carpentry work, talk turned to other business matters. "Did I tell you, I decided to sign a contract with Manning Fowler Fine Papers for our paper supply?"

Peter stopped his hammering and looked at the editor. "I heard they locked up *The Oregonian's* contract as well. Seems like with Rose Paperworks out of the picture, Fowler is going to be a very rich man."

Mayhew chuckled. "Yes, despite having nothing to do with his brother-in-law's crimes, you can't deny that he's certainly making out like a bandit."

The bell on the front office door interrupted them, and both men emerged from the new bedchamber just in time to see a very proud Half-Cent walking with only the slightest limp as he made his way into the *Gazette* office. Libby trailed behind him, shaking the rain off her umbrella as she entered. "Peter, John, they fitted my new leg. Look, I'm walking pretty well, ain't I?" Billy corrected himself sheepishly. "Aren't I? No more crutches!"

"That's great, Half . . . er, Bill." Mayhew grinned with an almost parental pride. "Miss Seale, thank you for taking Bill here over to the hospital."

"It was my pleasure. I enjoy this young ruffian's company." She smiled affectionately. Peter had told her about the surprise he and Mayhew had planned for Half-Cent (as she couldn't help still thinking of him), and she had insisted on being there when the new room was unveiled.

Billy leaned on the front counter. "Also, I have a story. On my way back from the doc's, Miss Seale and I stopped by the police station and Sergeant Branson told me they're sandbagging the riverbanks. They're worried about a flood—and a big one. They say it's likely to happen if these rains don't stop soon. So, I thought I could go to the library and research other big rainstorms and floods—that might help flesh out a story, right, Peter?"

"I don't know how we ever put out a newspaper without you," Peter laughed. "I think that's a grand idea, Bill. I know the river flooded in 1890 and I think several years before that. Maybe you can see what you can find out. But first, come take a look at something. John and I have a surprise for you."

Mayhew ushered the boy through the print room, covering his eyes with a large, work-roughened hand, and into the room they had been busy transforming all morning. Standing in the doorway, he removed his hand and presented the reborn storeroom to the astonished boy. "Welcome home."

The boy was silent as he walked over to the bed, touching the shelves, the banister, the walls. "It's mine, for me?"

"As long as you want it," said Mayhew, clapping him on the shoulder although he looked away, lest either of the others see the tears forming in the corners of his eyes.

Peter, sensing his friend's emotions, distracted Billy by leading him around the perimeter of the room, showing off all its special features. "We wanted to build you a place to stay on the ground floor, so you won't have to use the stairs every day."

Mayhew ducked out for a moment, and then returned brandishing a bottle of brandy (which he kept for purely medicinal purposes, of course) and four tin mugs. "I say this calls for a celebration!" he cried. Bill's face was wide with pleasure as he shared a first grown-up toast in his new home.

"Now, I'm afraid I need to rush," Peter said, rolling down his sleeves and buttoning his cuffs. "I'm meeting Anna—Miss Karlsson—for lunch at the Porter House."

"Enjoy your date." Mayhew gave a broad wink, and even Billy gave Peter a look of shared masculine ribaldry.

Peter caught sight of the stricken look on Libby's face and said, "It's not a date! Miss Karlsson insisted she be allowed to take me to lunch as thanks for my help in getting Dutch out of jail. It's also a celebration of sorts for her, as both she and her brother have been hired at the new Fowler Manning mill." He slipped on his suit coat and turned to Libby, "Would you like to join us? I feel certain Anna won't mind." Unconsciously he slipped back into using Anna's Christian name.

"No, no," Libby demurred. She had no desire to be a third wheel at Peter's lunch date. And it was a date, she felt certain, despite his denial. Which bruised her heart a little, but she reminded herself sternly that Peter was a free man, and it was right and proper that he should seek female companionship. What had happened in her room the night of Billy's accident had been a one-time mistake, with a rare set of extenuating circumstances. "I'm really not hungry," she added, and as she said it, she realized it was the truth.

Peter rushed out, and Libby made her farewells to Mayhew and Billy, then left the building. Slowly she meandered toward the streetcar stop through the heavy rain, thinking about Peter and his rendezvous with Anna Karlsson. Truthfully, the thought of lunch made her feel slightly queasy. In fact, she had been feeling ill for the past few days, from morning until around lunchtime. She hadn't recognized it as a pattern until this moment, but now that the penny had dropped, she couldn't stop her mind from whirring. She had noticed that her monthly bleeding was late, but put that down to the excitement of the last phase of the investigation, and put it out of her mind. But now she realized that she was at least a week past her expected time, and wondered if that could mean what she feared it might.

She couldn't be pregnant, she told herself severely. Don't jump to conclusions. Best to wait and see. Only time will tell. Darn it, she was doing it again, taking refuge in platitudes! That couldn't be a good sign. The memory of Eva Fowler's hollow voice dropped into her head. *Can you imagine how it feels to know the baby you are carrying is a child of adultery? To want it, and be scared of it all at once?* Suddenly Libby didn't have to imagine. She stood stock still, letting the rain drip off her umbrella like a circular cage of droplets around her, scared and excited, queasy and exhilarated, doubtful and certain all at once.

A BRIEF HISTORICAL NOTE ON PAPERMAKING

Although all of the facts outlined in *A Death at the Rose Paperworks* are accurate, slight liberties have been taken regarding the advent of the wood-pulp papermaking process and the timing of its adoption. In truth, by 1894 (the year in which the novel is set) the change over from rag pulp to wood pulp was substantially completed in this country.

The first wood-pulp paper was actually created in 1838 by Charles Fenerty of Halifax. He neglected to patent his invention, and (given that, at that time, wood needed to be pulped by an expensive mechanical process) the innovation was slow to catch on. Still, in 1863, the *Boston Morning Journal* became the first U.S. newspaper to be printed on wood-pulp paper.

The first paper mill in Oregon was established in 1866 in Oregon City, southeast of Portland, on the east side of the Willamette River. It was founded by newspaper owner Henry Pittock (publisher of *The Oregonian* and chief competitor of John Mayhew's fictional *Portland Gazette*) and a partner. This mill's paper was manufactured from rags, ropes, and old sails, but financial difficulties led to its closure only a year later. A second mill, opened two years later on the Clackamas River, had a workforce that was half Chinese, and fared better.

Also in 1866, spurred by ongoing rag shortages around the world, a chemical process for breaking down wood cheaply into the slurry pulp needed for paper production finally became available. This hastened the demise of rag pulp paper. By 1885, *The Paper Trade Journal* boasted that the first pulpwood paper ever manufactured in the Pacific Northwest had been produced at LaCamas (in what was then the Washington Territory), and the American Paper Manufacturers Association added a division specifically for producers of wood-pulp paper in 1887.

While it is true that the switch from rag pulp to wood pulp proceeded at different rates in different parts of the world, it is likely that by the time in which this book is set, the mills of a major metropolitan center like Portland would have already been converted.

WWW.MIDNIGHTINKBOOKS.COM

From the gritty streets of New York City to sacred tombs in the Middle East, it's always midnight somewhere. Join us online at any hour for fresh new voices in mystery fiction, book club questions, author information, mystery resources, and more.

Midnight Ink promises a wild ride filled with cunning villains, conflicted heroes, hilarious hazards, mind-bending puzzles, and enough twists and turns to keep readers on the edge of their seats.

MIDNIGHT INK ORDERING INFORMATION

Order by Phone:
- Call toll-free within the U.S. and Canada at 1-888-NITEINK (1-888-648-3465)
- We accept VISA, MasterCard, and American Express

Order by Mail:
Send the full price of your order (MN residents add 7% sales tax) in U.S. funds, plus postage & handling to:

> Midnight Ink
> 2143 Wooddale Drive
> Woodbury, MN 55125-2989

Postage & Handling:
Standard (U.S., Mexico, & Canada). If your order is:
$49.99 and under, add $3.00
$50.00 and over, FREE STANDARD SHIPPING

AK, HI, PR: $15.00 for one book plus $1.00 for each additional book.

International Orders (airmail only):
$16.00 for one book plus $3.00 for each additional book

Orders are processed within 2 business days. Please allow for normal shipping time.
Postage and handling rates subject to change.